PIONEERS II:
THE VOLUNTEER

Carson,
Keep Chasing your
Dreams!
Live Each Day!

PIONEERS II:
THE VOLUNTEER

Larry Allen Denham

iUniverse®

PIONEERS II: THE VOLUNTEER

iUniverse books may be ordered through booksellers or by contacting:

iUniverse
1663 Liberty Drive
Bloomington, IN 47403
www.iuniverse.com
1-800-Authors (1-800-288-4677)

ISBN: 978-1-5320-6341-1 (sc)
ISBN: 978-1-5320-6342-8 (e)

Print information available on the last page.

iUniverse rev. date: 01/12/2019

THE VOLUNTEER

1

Joey kicked his legs over the bar, bringing him to the rounded-hollow shape he needed to set up the tap-swing for his dismount. As his body swung down toward the bottom, Joey opened from his hollow position to a big arch, bending the horizontal bar and creating the torque he would need to catapult him into the air, high above the bar, for his dismount; a full-twisting, double layout.

As Joey's feet sank into the Royal Blue vinyl of the landing mat, he knew it was one of his best routines, yet that feeling was tempered in the knowledge that it was the last routine he would compete as a Pioneer, and possibly, the last High Bar set he would ever throw.

"Great way to finish, Joe!" said Coach Lowery, patting Joey on the back as they stepped down from the High Bar podium.

"Thanks, Coach. Too bad it wasn't enough to get us back to NTI's."

"Well, you did the best you could." Coach Lowery could see that his comment would bring no comfort, "Look, what your team did last year was a fluke. We had never been to the National Team Invitational before, our little gym club in East Tennessee just doesn't have the pool of athletes to draw from, like the big cities do. The team we had last year was a once in a career group of guys, most of which were very talented. You can't just lose 4 out of 6 guys from a Championship team, and replace them with Freshmen and expect to compete on the same level with programs that churn out tons of good guys, year after year."

"It's not just that," Joey said, "it's just that, well, if you're gonna close the gym after this season, I wanted to make it a little further than State Championships."

"Joey, I've got almost 30 years of memories in that gym, and almost all of my favorites have nothing to do with a National Championship."

"I guess I thought if we could somehow pull it off, maybe you might just change your mind about closing." Joey slumped down into a chair for athlete seating and began stripping off his grips, tape and wristbands.

"Closing the gym has nothing to do with winning meets. It does, however, have everything to do with getting kids in the doors. The big gym that opened last year has just killed us with not only gymnastics, but their other programs are just more attractive than sweating out in my little cracker box."

"But you are a way better coach than any of them! You could move or build even bigger! With your reputation, you'd get all those kids and a bunch more! I know it!"

"You may be right, but you're talking about a HUGE risk, one the banks aren't all that eager to take. Besides, that's something that a thirty-year-old should do. Heck, at my age my reputation isn't the problem, having confidence that I'll live long enough to pay off the note is!"

"Surely there's someone out there that knows you, and what you can do, and has the money to bankroll a new gym?"

"Perhaps, but I would hate to put that kind of risk on someone else. Besides, I'm ready for this. I've worked a long time trying to make that gym a success, and although it has made a decent enough life for me, it's time to turn the reins over to someone else. Most of my friends who coached with me have all retired to the world of gym ownership, hiring young coaches to bring up the next generation, or gotten out of gymnastics altogether, finding out what life outside the gym looks like."

"Yeah, but what about me, and all the guys coming up? We deserve a coach like you!"

"Well, there are plenty out there, many much better than me. Besides, as much as closing is really gonna hurt, I'm really looking forward to spending my time traveling. I've been booked at several programs to mentor their coaches. The other guys will find their way. Either they'll end up at the other gym or find a different sport that fits them. And you, you are headed to my old stomping ground."

"Don't remind me," Joey said, stuffing the rest of his gear into his gym bag and putting on his warm up jacket. They headed for the exit.

"You're not at all excited about moving to Michigan and training with my old teammate?"

"Don't you think if I had been excited about moving up north I would'a done it back when my dad moved up there last year?" Joey hit the metal bar that opened the exit door, flinging it open, almost pulling it off its hinges. Joey stomped off toward his motorcycle.

"Joey, slow down!" Coach Lowery caught up to him just as he finished loading his gear into the pack on his vintage Harley Sportster, "Look, I hate the thought of not coaching anymore, especially athletes like you that make it worthwhile, but you didn't cause this to happen and, quite frankly, there's really nothing that can be done to change it. You are a great athlete and you are going places. I just hate that you came along at the end of my career instead of the beginning. Come by the gym tomorrow and we'll talk about your future."

"You're right Coach, everything will be fine. Sorry I blew up. It just hurts."

"I know, son."

Joey realized that Coach Lowery was hurting just as much as he. And even though he had internalized it, it really wasn't his place to try to change coach's mind, if only for his own benefit. Coach Lowery gave him a smile and a pat on the shoulder as Joey hit the accelerator and sped away.

Joey sped down the back roads of his sleepy little town in the shadow of the Great Smoky Mountains, going over the familiar terrain, thinking about his gym, his coach, and his future. He realized that his frustration was coming from not being in control of his situation. If he had his way, Coach would stay in business and he would spend the last two years of high school representing Pioneers, and like his hero, Patrick Goodman, would form the next team to go on and win the National Team Invitational. But it wasn't his destiny. Pioneers would be closing within a week, his mentor would be out of the mentoring business, and all of the memories created at Pioneer Gymnastics would be lost over time. Sucks

Joey pulled into the drive, parked his bike and went inside.

"Hello, dear, how did it go?" Shirley Johnson called from the kitchen.

"About how you'd expect. I hit, and the others did okay, but we just couldn't keep up with the competition. So, looks like we'll be watching NTI's on TV this year."

"Don't take it so bad," she said, emerging from the kitchen, "you did the best you could and your teammates are all new to this. Remember last year you were the one wet behind the ears and it was Patrick who was hoping you could keep up."

"Not that they needed me, we were already kinda stacked."

"Yes, but with their help you did step up and helped the team win. Now it's your turn to nurture the newbies!"

"Well, not anymore, with Pioneers closing at the end of the week."

"True, but when you move to Michigan I bet there will be plenty of young guys to bring along."

"More likely it'll be them schooling me."

"Now, Joey, you're selling yourself short."

"I don't think so, mom. These guys go to NTI's every year. It's like they breed national qualifiers there!"

"That may be, but they are not the only ones producing great gymnasts. I think Jim has done a fine job at Pioneer. Just look at Patrick, who's still competing up at school in Michigan. Dallas and Mackee are both still competing, and doing well. I'm sure with their reputation that everyone that comes out of their gym is a world beater, but they haven't seen you!"

"Whatever. Anyway, I'm gonna find out soon enough. You got my stuff ready?"

"Ready and packed. I'm taking your things to be shipped tomorrow so they'll be there when you get there. Are you leaving first thing tomorrow?"

"Yeah. I've got one stop to make. Coach Lowery wants to talk to me before I leave."

"Well, fine, get washed up. Supper is about done."

"Roger that." Joey scampered up the stairs to wash and put his things in his room. He stood for a moment to look at his bedroom wall. The banners, the trophies, the awards, all because he was a Pioneer.

"Joey! It's gonna get cold!" Joey shook out of his trance and walked slowly down the steps, thinking about all of the 'last times', the last time in that house, last time driving that path, the last time training in that gym. For the first time the road ahead was a blank slate.

The next morning, Joey rose early. Shirley had prepared his favorite breakfast; a sausage, mushroom, and cheese omelet, whole wheat toast and juice. Her plan was to fill him up so he wouldn't have to stop too many times on the eight-hour trip to Michigan. Joey finished in a hurry and was nearly out the door before his mom could reel him in for a final hug and kiss before he left. "Call me when you get to your dad's."

"I'll shoot you a text when I get there." Joey gave his mom a big hug and she pecked him on the cheek.

"Be careful," she said. Joey looked back over his shoulder as he started up his Harley.

"If you wanted me to be careful," he gunned the engine, "You should've never put me in gymnastics!" Joey spun a half doughnut in the drive and peeled out toward the street.

As he pulled up to the front of the gym, he couldn't help but notice the 'For Sale' sign on the front lawn. The parking lot, which most of the time would've been quite busy for a Saturday morning, was eerily quiet and void of cars (Coach Lowery always parked around back to give the best spots to his customers). Joey strolled in the front door. The gym was quiet and dark, but he could make out the boxes and moving crates that were ready to be moved into storage. The equipment they had trained on up until this past weekend was still set up. He had the urge to go out into the gym and do one more tumbling pass on the floor or one more turn on the High Bar. But before he could set foot in the gym, Coach Lowery called from his office, "Joey, there you are! Come inside my office." Joey turned and walked into Coach's office. The walls were covered with plaques and awards from the years of Jim Lowery being one of the most respected coaches in Tennessee.

"I see you still have most of the equipment set up. Are you having second thoughts?"

"No, I've got some guys coming in on Monday to take it all down and move everything into storage."

"So, you might open up again?" Joey asked, hopefully.

"No, no, it's all going into storage. I've got an ad in an online company that buys equipment. I'm sure I'll sell most of it off right away, the rest as time goes on. You never know when a pal needs an extra High Bar or Pommel Horse."

"Great," Joey said, disappointed.

"So, are you ready to go?" he asked.

"I guess that depends. If you tell me you've changed your mind and are gonna keep Pioneer open, then, no, I'm not ready. I'll call my mom and have her not ship my stuff." Coach Lowery chuckled, "but, short of that, yeah, I guess I'm ready. Not enthusiastically, but I'm ready."

"You'll be fine Joe. I know this is kinda tough, but you'll find your way."

"Are you sure? Are you sure the guys at Dagar's Edge are even gonna like me?"

Coach laughed, "Who cares if they like you? If your goal is to get back to NTI's, Gene Dagar is gonna be your best bet."

"He's that good?" Joey asked.

"Yes," he said, "He doesn't come without quirks. He's a bit of a jerk, and drives hard, and certainly not how I would coach, but there is no questioning his results!"

"Great. I'll get up there and look like a country bumpkin to them," bemoaned Joey.

"Joey, look, you're gonna get up there, show them what you know and you'll see, they put their pants on the same way as everybody else. There's gonna be good guys and not so good guys. There'll be awesome gymnasts, and some rather pedestrian ones. You will definitely find your place."

"How can you be so sure?"

"Well, for one thing, I know your new coach well. He and I were teammates in Taylor back in high school."

"Y'all weren't with a club?"

"Back in the 70's when we were doing gymnastics, there were no clubs, just high school programs. No clubs, no pits, no spring floor, none of the training devices we have now, and certainly not the knowledge and training techniques that are commonplace today. Heck, we had to share the gym with every other sport, so we had to drag the equipment out every day for training and put it back at the end of the workout."

"Wow. I'm surprised y'all got anything done at all." Joey said, shocked.

"Yeah, it was a heck of a time. Quite frankly, I'm surprised we survived!" Coach Lowery switched gears, "Have you contacted Coach Dagar? Let him know when you're coming in?"

"Just once, over the phone, I told him that I would see him for practice Monday morning."

"Well, since I set you up with Gene, I feel I need to warn you."

"Warn me? About what?"

"Well, let's just say that Gene Dagar is just a bit 'intense'."

"Intense is good."

"It can be, but not when it's filtered through a giant ego, and Gene Dagar possesses a HUGE ego!"

"What do you mean?"

"Well, there's tough and then there's Gene. He is not a very compassionate guy and he pushes a lot harder than I would."

"I don't know. You push pretty hard."

"Yeah, but I'm a pussycat compared to Gene. He is serious, old school."

"Example?"

"Well, you know how I never use conditioning as discipline?"

"Of course, you said it's because you want us to love conditioning, and associating it with a bad feeling would make us resent it. Therefore, we would condition less, thus not get strong."

"Exactly, well some programs don't exactly buy into that idea and continue to use the methods of the past."

"And, Coach Dagar is like that?"

"In spades. He takes his gymnastics very seriously, and personally. If you don't jump when he says, it will be a long day. My advice to you is keep your head down, your mouth closed, and focus on your training."

"Are you sure you want me to be coached by this guy?"

"Well, as his friend I can say he can be a bit dick-ish, but he's the best coach in Michigan and he has the only club up there that has produced NTI qualifiers for the past 20 years. He's rough around the edges, but if you don't get on his bad side, he will be the ticket to get you back to that championship and punch your ticket for college gymnastics."

"That sounds great, but what if I get up there and we don't, exactly, hit it off? Maybe college gymnastics is just too big a reach, especially if I have to put up with a coach intent on making my life miserable."

"Just remember, he can't get to you without your permission. 'Life is ten-percent of what happens to you…'"

"…and ninety-percent of how you choose to react to it.' Got it." Joey had heard that phrase thousands of times in his career as a Pioneer. That, and a hundred other clichés regularly used by Coach Lowery, were now stuck in his head.

"Great, not only do I have to deal with my dad, who wasn't that crazy about me doing gymnastics in the first place, but I have to walk on eggshells to keep from upsetting my new coach, who might just be a homicidal maniac, got it!"

"Oh, I'm sure it's not that bad. Besides, didn't your dad give you that Harley before he left?"

"Yeah, as a way to shut me up after all the crying I did when he left us to take that job up North."

"Perhaps, but it was a big move he made, and a hard choice; stay in East Tennessee and carve out a meager existence. Or take the opportunity that would mean being able to provide so much more for his family, at the cost of separation. I'm sure it was much harder for him than he let on."

"I guess you're right, but it certainly has sucked not having him around."

"Well, you will have plenty of opportunities to make up for lost time when you get there, which you are prolonging more and more by the minute wasting time with me." Joey knew it was time to get on the road, but his emotions got the better of him and he began to sob as he hugged his coach, his mentor, his surrogate dad, his pal, one more time. "You'll do fine, Joey. And I'm always just a phone call away."

"I'll text you when I get up there."

"Call me. You know I don't do that text stuff."

"I'll call, coach." The two pushed away from their embrace and Joey looked at the last familiar thing he had known in his whole life, turned and walked away. "Love you, Coach!" he said over his shoulder as he walked out of the office.

"Love you, too, Joe." Coach Lowery sat down at his desk, looking at the photos of past and present athletes, team pictures of teams past, locking in on the picture of his National Team Invitational Team Champions photo from just one year ago. The Cinderella team that came out of a tiny gym in East TN, that had helped him achieve his highest goal, National Champions. He thought of all the years he'd spent giving his all to create great gymnasts, and good people. He laid his face in his hands, and released the tears that he had been holding in all morning.

2

As Joey crossed the State Line into Michigan, he couldn't help noticing how flat everything was. *Yeah, I could really open her up on these roads, but what is the point when everything is straight and flat!* he thought. Taking the Telegraph Road exit off of I-75, Joey soon found himself in the Detroit suburb of Taylor. As he turned into the neighborhood where his dad lived, he noticed rows and rows of houses that all looked the same, on similar little plots of land, and more than half of them with For Sale signs on the front lawn.

If Joey had misplaced the address it wouldn't have mattered much, as his dad Jonas, was waiting out on the front lawn, video camera in hand, to document his son's approach. Joey pulled into the drive and up to his father's outstretched arms. "Hey, son, how was the ride? How's the bike holding up?" Jonas asked as Joey shut off the motor on his Harley.

"It was fine, and my bike is doing just fine. Nice camera."

"Thanks. Being up here for the last year, one of the things I missed most was watching your gymnastics. Well, I'm gonna try to catch as much as I can."

"It's awfully flat here," Joey said.

"Haha, yeah, you'll get used to it."

"I doubt it."

"Well, don't let it bother you. There's a lot of things up here that will take your mind off of the terrain."

"Like what?"

"Well, girls, for one, when you start school there will be tons of new girls to meet."

"Well, it's May and school doesn't start until after Labor Day, so what am I supposed to do until then?"

"Are you kidding? There's just as much to do here as there is back home, only it's all close together and easy to get to."

"Lakes?"

"Are you kidding me? You're in Michigan! We not only have lakes, we have Great Lakes!"

"Very funny." Joey said, not amused.

"Besides, once you make new friends at the gym, I'm sure they'll introduce you to a lot of things you haven't even considered. Which reminds me, when do you go in?"

"Nine a.m.. Just enough time for me to decompress from the ride and get a good night's sleep."

"Great, let's get inside and catch up." Joey and Jonas went into the prefab house and tried to catch up on two years' worth of family news. "So, how's your mom?"

"She's fine. Story is still the same; she hates where she teaches, small town politics and all, but she loves the kids she works with. I guess that's what keeps her there. Any news on teaching positions up here?"

"Not at any school where she would want to teach. The climate is so bad up here with the decline in the auto industry. I'm sure you saw the 'For Sale' signs on all the lawns as you came in. Well, most folks can't wait for the industry to turn around and have moved out, most leaving the state. As a result, schools are closing right and left. In fact, my old high school has been closed for some time. There are a few private schools that are still operating, since most of the people still here are on the high end of the income spectrum, they can afford it. Nothing open for the next term, but you never know when that will change."

"Hopefully soon. It sure will be great to have the whole family together again."

"Speaking of family, have you heard from your sister?"

"Haley? Not really. Since she went off to school and got a job, we rarely see her except holidays. She tries real hard not to come home much. We keep up with texts and social media, but it's not the same."

"Well, maybe when we get your mom up here, Haley will feel more like visiting."

"I hope so. I sure miss her."

"Me, too. Are you hungry?"

"Did you fix supper?"

"No, but there is this great little Chinese place just around the corner."

"Sounds good." Joey and his dad jumped into Jonas' little BMW roadster and headed to the restaurant, just two blocks away.

3

"Joey, it's 8:30! You're gonna be late for your first day! I have to go to work, so I'll see you tonight." Joey was a little disoriented as the cobwebs were swept out of his head, and he remembered he wasn't in his old, comfortable bed back home. "Okay, Dad" he called as he tousled his hair and got his bearings. As he heard the door close, he jumped out of bed and went to the bathroom. His things hadn't arrived from Tennessee yet, so he had to use his dad's soap, shampoo, toothbrush, and deodorant, "Great," he said, "I get to go to the gym smelling just like my dad."

He pulled into the parking lot at Dagar's Edge Gymnastics Academy at 9:05 and hustled into the gym as quickly, but coolly as he could. He stopped in his tracks at the sight of the inside gym. Much larger than it appeared from the outside, the gym had huge ceilings, an elevated running track on the perimeter, and every gadget and gizmo and training device you could think of. One entire wall was covered with banners from every major competition, including nine NTI Championship banners.

Yeah, I got one of those. Joey thought.

"I was beginning to wonder if you were going to make it, Johnson," came the booming voice of Coach Eugene Dagar, standing on the Floor Exercise carpet, watching the other athletes running around him at the start of warm up.

"Sorry, Coach, I just got in yesterday and I'm a little beat. I guess I overslept a little bit. It won't happen again."

"I'm sure it won't. And to be sure, why don't you take 20 laps around the gym as a gentle reminder." Joey could feel that he was already off to a bad start, and had the deep burning feeling that it was likely not going to get much better. He tossed his grip bag off to the side and found a set of stairs that led to the running track. He immediately noticed he was not the only one taking the scenic route around the gym. A guy that reminded him a little of his younger self was also serving penance for some infraction of the gym. Joey increased his pace to catch up with him.

"What are you in for, kid?" Joey asked as he caught up to his new teammate, his long, brown ponytail already dripping with sweat.

"Huh?"

"I was 5 minutes late and got 20 laps. What did you do?"

"I fell off … Pommel Horse … at the end of yesterday's workout."

"That's it? How many laps did you get?"

"Only 20, Not too bad," he said while struggling to breathe.

"That sucks. Does he give laps to everyone that falls off an event?"

"It's not always laps… Sometimes it's push-ups, or dips, … or other not fun stuff."

"Wow, that's strict."

"Yeah, … but you have a lot less falls!"

"I guess." Joey couldn't quite wrap his head around this method. He thought of all the times he had fallen over the past two years and just how many push-ups, pull ups, and various torturous exercises he would had to have done if Coach Lowery had been as strict. "Oh, well, whatever doesn't kill ya makes ya stronger! Hi, I'm Joey Johnson, who are you?"

"Alex. Alex Story. I joined the team a year ago, but haven't competed yet. I'm hoping to make the line-up for next year. Where'd you come from?"

"Tennessee. Just got here yesterday. Do all of Coach Dagar's guys have to do laps when they miss?"

"Not the top guys, that I've noticed, but, then again, I've never seen any of them miss a set."

"Never? Crap, no one is that perfect."

"These guys are. I haven't quite figured out their secret, but I bet it has something to do with fear."

"I guess that would work as a motivator, but sure takes the fun out of it."

"Fun? What is that?"

"Really? Don't y'all ever just cut loose and have some fun once in a while?"

"Don't let Coach hear you say that. He thinks if you are not 100% focused, 100% of the time, then you are slacking and not serious about your commitment!"

"Gee, I don't know if I'll last here," Joey said, supporting the theory he had had for a few weeks.

"But you just got here! You can't leave and leave me with these guys. They're just as out there as Coach Dagar, but you didn't hear me say that."

"Right. No worries Alex. I'm here to train to be the best. I guess I'll just have to beat them out for my spot."

"Good luck with that, but I'll warn you, Coach Dagar has his favorites, and he might just squash you if you mess with them."

"Thanks for the heads up."

"Are you guys slacking? Do you want me to add some more laps?" Coach Dagar yelled from the Floor Exercise carpet where the rest of the team had started stretching.

"I'll catch you later, Alex." Joey picked up his pace and finished his laps just as the team was breaking up from their stretch.

"Where are you going?" asked Coach Dagar.

"To the floor to stretch," he replied.

"You don't have time for that, it's time to condition. C'mon." Joey picked up his grip bag and followed the team to their first conditioning station, Pommel Horse. "Alright guys, give me 40 circles in a row. You drop before 40, you owe me double the number of circles left with laps around the gym."

Forty circles were a no brainer for Joey, but he was surprised to see so many fall short and have to take up laps. Joey jumped up and kicked out 40 circles without breaking form or a sweat.

"That looked easy, Johnson," called his new coach, "next turn, make it 50!"

By the time it came back around to Joey, half the team was up running laps. *How bizarre,* he thought. Joey chalked up, blew off the excess, grabbed the pommels and jumped up into his circles. As he passed thirty circles, he could feel the sting beginning to build in his wrists.

"Tighten up those legs, Johnson!" Joey's form began to falter as the pain in his wrists climbed. Just three shy of the goal, Joey's legs clipped the top of the horse, flipping him over the apparatus and onto the, only slightly padded, area around the horse.

"OWWW!" Joey's head could certainly make out the metal leg, extending from the base, through the old, worn mat. Joey looked up from the blue vinyl mat and cut a glare at his coach, "You ever think about investing in a new mat or two?" The entire gym stopped. No one, not even the seniors, would have ever thought to speak out at Coach like that. Joey rose to his feet, still rubbing his head and was puzzled at the sight of everyone staring at him. Coach Dagar stared as well. His arms folded, lips pursed, he looked at Joey curiously. After a long pause, Coach Dagar spoke in a calm tone.

"Hmm! I guess Jim Lowery doesn't know how to teach manners to his charges. I guess that's why he only has one NTI banner hanging in his gym. Look around you Johnson. We have nine NTI championships! Nine! We have qualified each year for the last twenty!"

"So, you're nine-for-twenty. That's forty-five percent. I've been once, and won it. Guess I'm batting a thousand!" The rest of the team looked on in disbelief.

Another long pause, "Tell you what, Johnson, although that was

17

a foolish thing to do, it did take balls. And that is an invaluable tool, but it must be properly trained. Since this is your first day, I'm gonna cut you a little slack. But I warn you, I will not be so benevolent the next time."

Joey thought about pushing back once more, but a familiar voice in his head said, *choose your battles carefully.* Joey just nodded his head. "Thanks, Coach. It just hurt like crap. It won't happen again."

"Hmm, we'll see." Coach Dagar looked up at the stunned team, "Bring it in, fellas!"

The dozen gymnasts gathered and formed a line on the Floor Exercise border tape. Coach Dagar was flanked on either side by six athletes.

"Gentlemen, the six fellows you see behind me represent one of the best teams I've ever coached. On Wednesday, we leave for NTI's. For our Seniors, Curtis Wikel and Louie Pitts, this is their last competition for Dagar's Edge and they will soon be going off to start their collegiate gymnastics careers. So, Coach Murray will be coaching you guys Thursday through the weekend. And on Monday, after we return with another NTI Championship banner, I'm sure, we will start our tryout to replace Curtis and Louie. It will be competitive routines, and I will have Coach Murray and a judge here to select the replacements."

Joey raised his hand, Coach Dagar glared at him, "What is it, Johnson?"

"A couple questions, Coach. First, are the twelve of us competing for two spots, or are all of us competing for six spots?" The question had never come up before. Although the whole team had competed in the past, it was customary to always reselect the current team.

"Twelve guys, two spots."

"So, the four up there, they have...tenure? I mean, I don't really know any of y'all, but what if, say, three of us are better than one of them, does he get to stay on the team?"

"That's not gonna happen!" Barked Jessie Tyler, a sandy-haired Junior, headed to his third NTI.

18

"Why not?" chimed Alex, "You think it's impossible that the three best of us couldn't possibly be better than the least of you guys?"

"ENOUGH!" shouted Coach Dagar, "I make the rules around here! And I am doing more than just picking a team. I'm DEVELOPING a team, GROWING a team. This is something that goes much further than just a try-out."

"But how is that fair?" Joey added.

"Fair? Did you see a sign somewhere that says anything has to be fair? The day you drop a million dollars and build your own gym, then you can say what's fair! As long as you are inside these walls, I, and I alone, decide what is, and isn't fair! Twelve guys two spots! That's it!" Coach Dagar's face was flush. "Alright, guys, let's get to work. Edges, we start competition on Pommel Horse, so that's where we'll start. The rest of you will be split into two groups of six; one group on Vault with Coach Murray, the other six start on High Bar with Coach Henson. One-hour rotations, Olympic order!"

Coaches Greg Murray and Jeff Henson were young, both students at Wayne State Community College, and barely more than just extra hands in the gym. Armed with only a cursory knowledge of gymnastics and body mechanics, their job was mostly to monitor the workout, record the number of turns each took, and track the value and number of elements each gymnast used.

The real coaching only took place when Coach Dagar was paying attention, which right now was not at all, as his focus was squarely upon the six that would fly to Las Vegas to try to bring home another NTI Championship.

Joey watched the Edges head to Pommel Horse, remembering what it was like getting ready for NTI's just over a year ago. *What a magical time*, he thought.

"JOHNSON!" Joey was startled from his trance by Coach Henson, "You coming to High Bar?"

"Sure thing, uh, Coach!" Joey grabbed his grip bag and jogged back to join his group.

"Glad you could join us, Johnson." Alex said as he strapped on his grips.

"You don't have the bar warmed up yet, Alex?" said Joey, gripping up as quickly as he could.

"Just about." Alex pulled his ponytail tighter, then grabbed a handful of chalk and rubbed it into his grips, clapped, then jumped up onto the Horizontal Bar over a pit; one direction was an in-ground mat, the top flush with the floor, the other direction, a six-foot deep pit, 8' wide pit filled with 8" cubes of foam. He pumped his swing until he was doing back (over-grip) giants. Each one faster than the one before. Then Alex closed his hips and shoulders as he came over the top of the bar, leading to a big arch at the bottom and a huge PING off the bar, doing an effortless double-layout dismount, well above the bar, disappearing into the foam cubes.

"Nice!" said Joey as he jumped up for his turn. Joey piked his hips to bring his feet to the bar and shot them forward, downward, then backward, his body rising up to a handstand. He turned on one arm to do a full spin on the way down, swung through the bottom, then turned the other way, completing the full turn on top of the bar before putting his other hand on the bar. Joey then jammed his legs between his arms, swung around the bar and jammed out to handstand in El-grip. After an inverted giant, Joey hopped to an under-grip handstand and pirouetted into several giants before one-upping Alex by adding a full-twist on the second flip, landing on an 8" mat on the in-ground pit mat.

Alex was still only just emerging from the pit on the other side of the bar, slowed by watching Joey look every bit as good as any of the Edges. "Yeah, that'll work!"

"Dude, I just competed that combo two weeks ago."

"And you didn't get to NTI's?"

"You kinda have to have 3 more scores on each event."

"What about the rest of your team?"

"All Freshmen, with very little experience. We just lacked the depth."

"But you were there last year?"

"Yeah, but when you lose four seniors, it kinda puts a dent in repeating."

"You'll get back."

"I have my doubts. I don't think I'm making much of an impression on Coach Dagar."

"Well, you're certainly making an impression on someone." Alex nodded his head in the direction of Pommel Horse, where the Edges were trying to act like they weren't paying attention. "Their jaws were dropping a second ago."

"Did you see that?" whispered Curtis to Louie as he took a seat after his turn on Pommel Horse.

"Johnson looks pretty good."

"Story's no slouch either. It's gonna be a close competition between them and your brother."

"Keith can hold his own," said Louie, not altogether convincingly.

"Maybe, but do you want to bank on that?"

"What's it to us? We're done after this. Let's leave it to those guys."

"What about legacy and all that?"

"It'll be what it'll be. Keith will have to take care of himself."

"A little help wouldn't hurt," Curtis pondered.

"What do you mean?" asked Louie.

"Nothing, nothing. Just thinking."

"WIKEL!" yelled Coach Dagar, "You're up! Hit this set or I'll give your spot to one of those guys!"

Curtis jumped to his feet, "Yes Coach!" He chalked up and hit another set.

After the workout was over, and the Edges dismissed, Coach Dagar went over the data recorded by coaches Murray and Henson. "Nice, Job Johnson! Your sets are pretty packed! And you're pretty consistent at hitting! I think you might make a pretty good Edge."

"Thanks, sir. I was coached well." Joey smirked.

Coach Dagar glared at Joey over the top of his papers and his 2.0 reader glasses, "Not that there's not room for improvement…" Joey's face changed to deadpan. "Where's Alex Story?"

"Right here Coach!" Alex waved his arm.

"Where are you from, Story?" asked Coach.

"Um, right here, Coach! I've been at Dagar's Edge for a year now."

"Why haven't I noticed you before?" Of all the smart-ass answers Alex ran through in his head, he opted for diplomacy, "Guess I'm a late bloomer, Coach."

"Hmm, not bad. You've got some good basics, good form. We need to beef up your difficulty," Coach Dagar looked back at his papers, "and your stamina, it appears. You only took three to everyone else's four turns."

"But they were choice turns, Coach!" said Alex, defensively.

"You do have a higher hit percentage than everyone but Johnson. But if you had taken as many turns, that may not be the case."

"Work smarter, not harder, I always say."

"Well, I'll need to see the work harder part for you to make this team."

"You bet, Coach!"

""Smarter, not harder", My coach used to say that all the time." Joey whispered to Alex.

Coach Dagar turned his attention to Keith Pitts, "Keith, son, I'd have thought you'd be ready to fill Louie's shoes by this time, but the numbers don't lie. You better come up with something special before next Monday or it may be 'wait until next year' for you. I still have hope for you to make the team, but as it stands right now, you are only third best." Keith dropped his head.

I wonder if anyone would notice if I killed those two, he thought.

Coach Dagar finished with the evaluation and dismissed the gymnasts, "Rest well, boys. One more workout before I leave for

NTI's. If you want to impress me before the try-outs on Monday, tomorrow is your last chance. Give me twenty laps and hit the showers." The group broke up, at least five with the hopes of making the team gone by the wayside. *Seven to make two*, Joey thought.

As the guys finished their laps and headed for the locker room, Keith was pulled aside by Curtis before he reached the door, "Meet me in an hour, Pitts. We have to talk."

4

Joey rose early and got in a mile run before a shower and off to the gym. When he arrived, he tossed his helmet and backpack into an available locker, right next to Alex, who was checking his grip bag before heading out to the gym.

"Where is everybody?" asked Joey.

"Well, Team Edge is already out there, and I guess Coach Dagar scared off most of the other guys."

"Hey, guys! How we doin' this beautiful May morning?" came the unusually, cheerful voice of Keith Pitts. He whistled as he tossed his belongings into his locker and grabbed his grips.

"You feeling OK?" asked Joey.

"Sure! Great! Why do you ask?"

"It's only that you were dragging a bit after workout yesterday," added Alex.

"It was a tough workout. It's not like we didn't bust our asses yesterday."

"Yeah, but Coach Dagar was a bit over the top with you yesterday," said Joey, "it was pretty bizarre how tough he was on you."

"Dude, I have been here for four years. My brother is a hero. Of course Coach Dagar is gonna be tough on me. He expects a lot."

"Maybe unrealistically so," Joey suggested.

"Naw, I'm good. I'm a Legacy. That should count for something."

Alex jumped in, "Well, I'm glad you're good. You looked good yesterday."

"Thanks. We better get out in the gym. We don't want to do laps we don't have to!" Keith jogged out to the gym, leaving Joey and Alex perplexed, but they soon joined the team.

"I guess the thought of competing against you guys scared off a few yesterday!" barked Coach Dagar, noticing that the ranks had dropped by half. "That's just as well. It works perfect for my plan today!" the boys looked at each other, "For our last workout we are going to have a mock meet, Team Edge against Team Plebe." While the rest looked in disbelief, Joey relished the idea.

"How many scores count?" asked Joey.

"Count for what?"

"Team score," replied joey, "there's six of them and six of us. How many scores count for the team total?"

"Haha, this is not a real competition, Johnson, just a test for hitting sets in meet format."

"Well, like my grandpappy used to say, 'You wanna put meat on the bone you gotta have a dog in the fight.' You can't expect us to count all six scores, that wouldn't be close! Let's, at least, make it a challenge."

"Alright, Johnson. Let's say five scores count."

"We only get to drop one score? No way. How about three scores count?"

"Why don't we split the difference? Four scores count, just like NTI's will be. I'll judge."

"Can you be impartial?" asked Alex.

"Do you want to live through this workout, Story?" said Coach Dagar, angrily, "Tell you what, I will count difficulty and Coaches Murray and Henson will do the execution deductions."

"Seems...fair" said Joey, "What are the stakes?"

"Are you crazy?" said Alex, spinning Joey to face him, "we are gonna lose, lose bad. You want to put stakes on this rigged, mock meet, that you know WE are the ones who will have to pay?"

"Double the conditioning set," barked Curtis.

"Pfft!" dismissed Alex, "TRIPLE the set plus one lap for every fall!"

"WHAAT?!?" cried Joey.

"Deal," said Louie.

"Wait a minute," pleaded Joey.

"Nope," Coach jumped in, "That's it!"

Joey stared Alex down, "What are you doing!?"

"I thought that was the plan?"

"Yeah, but I didn't want to commit suicide!"

"Alright then, plebes, we start competition on Pommel Horse, so let's start there. Ten-minute warm up, then compete." The athletes made their way toward Pommel Horse. Coach Murray grabbed a clipboard, a calculator and a score flasher.

Each athlete took his turn warming up until Coach Dagar called, "TIME! Warm ups are over. Team Plebe, you first." Joey and Alex gathered the other four newbies together. It was agreed that the weakest routine should go first, Bill Dombrowski, a 16-year-old Rings specialist with little talent for swinging in circles. The team flinched with each fall of his tragic routine, adding up the laps they would surely have to do if his score counted. Fortunately, with two scores to give, his score was likely to be dropped. They still had a score to give.

"I have 2.1 in difficulty," said Coach Dagar, laughing, "what do you guys have in execution?"

"Still adding!" said Coach Murray, in mid belly-laugh.

"'Execution' is a good word for what he did! He deserved to be executed!" said Coach Henson, chuckling.

"Alright, straighten up, you guys, they're gonna drop that score anyway."

Team Edge led off with the weakest set as well. Two falls later his routine was complete. Next up for Team Plebe, Logan Merwin, a 16-year-old from nearby Inkster, hit a respectable routine, matched by a similar routine by the Edge counterpart.

"Dude, you can swing!" said Joey, "I gotta admit, that was a pretty set."

"Thanks, man," replied Logan, a caramel-skin Columbian, "Pig is my favorite!"

"I could tell! If I knew you had that set I'd have put you after Keith." a comment that was not entirely lost on Keith.

"Keith, come here," Joey took Keith aside, "the only way we stay close is to put up a big number here. You gotta add some beef!"

"Now? I'm up next. What do you expect me to do?"

"You've got a couple skills in there that you could add a circle and make it more difficult."

"Maybe, yeah, but just by, like a tenth."

"Not if you ADD it to what you're already doing. It'll be at least a half a point higher!"

"But that's a long routine!"

"If you're not in shape to add two skills, maybe you could use the extra laps. C'mon, man! It's us versus them. Show them that you're just as good!" Joey shook his shoulders and lightly smacked his face, "You GOT this!"

Keith slowly paced to the chalk bucket and studied the horse as he bathed his hands in the white powder. He stepped up and saluted his coach, exhaled, and jumped up to begin his set. Knowing he had a lot ahead of him, he decided to do the hardest changes first. Swinging counter-clockwise, Keith posted and turned on his left arm, bringing his right hand to the same pommel. Then, where he would normally turn to the end of the horse, Keith turned on his left arm twice more to end up back in the center! Surprised at the result, Keith continued with the other additions to the routine, but as he got the end of the set fatigue got the best of him and instead of swinging to a handstand for his dismount, his momentum stopped, forcing him to bend his arms and press up to his handstand, and falling to one knee on the landing.

"That was, um, different, Mr. Pitts," demeaned Coach Dagar.

"Yessir. I guess I thought if were gonna keep up with Edge, we'd have to add, you know, more difficulty."

"Difficulty that you, obviously, are not ready to handle! You added about a point, but gave it all away with the fall and sloppy dismount. And your team is counting on you to do your job, which is to hit the set you trained for! I'm deducting another full point for not doing your routine!"

"How is that fair?!" yelled Joey.

"No, he's right," said Keith, "I should've done my set. Thanks for nothing." Keith took a seat and dug out his Ring grips.

"Way to go, Joe!" said Alex, "You're not very good at this making friends thing, are you?"

"He should be grateful! He added almost a full point to his set in one try!"

"Maybe this is not the place and time to take that risk?"

"Is there a better time?"

"I think Keith would say so." Keith was still in a daze.

"He'll come around." Joey turned his attention to Alex, "Alright, it's your turn, Killer, attack!"

"Story!"

"Yes, Coach!" answered Alex.

"You planning on cutting that mop and those sideburns before Monday?"

"I hadn't thought about it, Coach, but now that you ask, I guess my answer is, 'No'"

"That's the wrong answer!"

"No, ...thank you...?"

"Listen, Story, you have until Monday to get a decent haircut and those sideburns trimmed, or you can forget making this team!"

"I will consider it, Coach. But, I'm generally a hairy guy. Cut it off today, it's back tomorrow. I get a 5-O'clock shadow for breakfast!

Not shaving so much really saves my folks enough money to make a car payment!"

"Shut up, Story! Just deal with it! Now let's see if you've got gym to back up that hair!"

Alex snugged up his ponytail, and mounted the horse. He put on an impressive display, moving from end to end on the leather, and multiple skills on one pommel, dismounting to handstand and pirouetting to the other end before sticking his feet into the landing mat.

"WHOA!" screamed Joey, giving a high five to his new pal. Both looked at Coach Dagar for some reaction. Nothing.

"I've got 4.6 in difficulty," said Coach, without much reaction, "what do you boys have in execution?"

"One-point-five, Coach." Replied coach Murray.

"That's still a 13.1, Alex!" exclaimed Joey.

"Yeah, but Louie is next and he beats me by over a point in start value. He just has to stay on to build on their lead."

"But, he has to stay on. Look," Joey motioned toward Curtis, "he's sweating and he hasn't done anything, yet."

The senior mounted the horse, and in his first complex skill, Louie missed the pommel and put his hand on the other hand, causing him to fly off of the horse.

"No credit," exclaimed Coach Dagar, meaning he received no credit for the skill he fell on, and would have to repeat the sequence to get the combination to count for his difficulty score. Louie walked over to the chalk bucket. More to collect his senses than to reapply chalk. He cleared his head and saluted his coach to signify he was ready to resume. He made it through the combination, with some bent knees and leg separations, but before long he missed another hand placement, and found himself standing on the mat in disbelief. Louie finished his routine and sat down dumbfounded. He hadn't missed a routine all season, and it had been over two years since he had two falls in a routine.

"I sure hope you got those falls out of your system, Pitts! That will not help us on Saturday," barked Coach Dagar.

"I can't explain it, Coach, but it sure as heck not gonna happen Saturday. I guarantee it!"

"It had better not! I'm sure Coach Ross at State would hate to see that before you sign."

After five events, the teams were only 1.5 apart. As they prepared for their final event, Floor Exercise, Joey approached the corner of the carpet, and was joined by Curtis.

"Nice move getting' Pitts to do a harder set. This is gonna be a walk," said Curtis

"Hey, he almost hit that set! If he had, we would be in front."

"Right. Losers do tend to use the word 'almost' a lot."

"Yeah, like, 'I *almost* took a pop at you when you came up to the dish', but I opted for, "I'm *almost* gonna feel bad about the drubbing you're about to take."

"Big talk for a skinny red-headed Hillbilly." Joey bit his lip at the attempt to rile him.

"Well, this hillbilly is about to wipe that smile off your smug, Yankee face." Joey grabbed a chuck of chalk to dry his palms, and clapped off the access, and coughed into his fist, sending a cloud of chalk dust directly into Curtis' face. "Awright, Yankee, how's about this, regardless how this mock meet turns out, I beat you here on Floor, right now, and you do my conditioning?"

"I don't think so, Johnson. I have an NTI to prepare for, and after that I doubt I'll set foot in here again." Joey couldn't comprehend not wanting to come back after graduation and share time with his coach. "Well, as long as you have an excuse…" Joey was four inches shorter than the senior, but that didn't stop him from standing eye-to-eye with Curtis.

"Ok, ok, you're on, Hillbilly!" Joey smiled and blinked.

Joey shrugged his shoulders a couple times and pitched his head side to side to loosen his neck muscles. One more breath and Joey opened his eyes, looked to his coach and saluted.

Joey stepped up to the corner, took a breath and sprinted across the diagonal for his first tumbling pass, a double back with a full twist, stuck. After puffing a breath, Joey darted back from where he came, front-handspring, whip, whip with a full-twist, to layout with one-and-a-half twists, stuck. He dropped to the floor and began doing Pommel Horse circles that became flairs, he popped up to a pirouetting handstand, back to flairs, finishing in a middle split. As Joey pressed from his split to another handstand, the team caught their breath. Joey continued his set along the side of the area with some combination tumbling, and finished his routine with a double back in piked position, stuck!

Everyone's attention turned to Coach Dagar as he finished his computation.

"5.3," said Coach.

"Only .8 in execution, Coach," added Coach Henson.

"Crap, Johnson!" cried Alex, "that's a 14.5! That's huge!"

Curtis tried not to show his nerves, but regardless of the value of his routine, it was quickly cancelled out by two falls.

"5.5 in difficulty," exclaimed Coach, looking at his assistant coaches for what he already knew, "We got over three points in deductions, Coach."

The Plebes jumped and high-fived. This win was a big victory for a group that, until now, never thought they could compete with their, more accomplished, teammates.

"Hey, that doesn't count! It was a fluke. You ready to do this again, Johnson?" cried Curtis.

"Of course, Wikel. We'll do the same thing on each event!" countered Joey.

"Nope!" interrupted Coach Dagar, "I'm putting an end to this. My goal was to get you guys ready for the biggest meet of the season. And instead, you let yourselves get psyched out by a bunch of dorks that can't even make your team!" Coach Dagar was beside himself,

"Edge Team head to Rings. I need five hit sets from each of you in the next forty-five minutes, or I'll throw you into conditioning with these guys!"

"Hey, we won the contest!" pleaded Alex.

"Nope, there was no contest!" countered Coach.

"We smoked your guys!" said Joey.

"What just happened was a fluke!" joined Curtis, "when we get back we are gonna finish this!"

"I thought you weren't setting foot in here after this weekend?"

"Dude, I will make a special trip just for you!"

"I'll be right here waitin' for you!" Joey barked.

Curtis just laughed, "We'll see, Hillbilly!"

"ENOUGH," Coach broke in, "get back to Rings, Wikel! Johnson, I think you have some conditioning to get to."

Joey continued to stare down the senior. Then broke into a smile, "Have a good trip, Curtis! Hit six!" Joey extended his hand, but Curtis turned and walked back toward Rings.

"That thing about you and making friends, Joe?" asked Alex, "you aren't getting any better at it."

Joey and Alex joined Team Plebe back at the weight stack. Each of the Plebes began their conditioning with, likely, the best attitude they had ever had. Except Keith, who wasn't really crazy about having to condition. Keith stole a glance toward Curtis, who inconspicuously threw a wink at the younger Pitts.

Two hours later, the Edges finished their last workout before NTI's, while the Plebes were down to just the laps they had to run for the six falls they had on Pommel Horse.

"Hey, you guys!" shouted Coach Dagar, from the center of the gym, "you almost done? There's a Tiger game on in an hour, and I'd sure hate to miss the opening pitch!"

"Just… a couple laps left, Coach!" shouted Joey, nearly out of breath.

"So, … your idea… WAS…. to kill us …before tryouts!" gasped Alex.

"No… my idea… was to put… heat on the… other guys. YOUR idea… was to put us down like dogs!"

"So…" Alex and Joey pulled up to a walk to cool down after the run, "why… put heat… on them?"

Joey walked to a wall, turned at a post, and slid down against his back until he was seated, "Didn't you see it? …We were being played… like Guinea Pigs, …ego food for the big boys… I just wanted them… to feel it was more than just a walk-over."

"Well… "Alex put one hand on a wall and stretched his quads with the other, "you managed to piss off the whole Edge team… Curtis wants to strangle you, … I'm sure Louie would like to punch you in the nose, …In fact, there's a whole bunch coming up behind us… that wished you'd never walked in the gym, especially Keith Pi…"

"What about me?" Keith interrupted as he approached.

"Oh, nothing, I was just telling Joseph, here, what a great job he was doing, alienating everyone on the team in less than forty-eight hours!"

"On the contrary!" Alex and Joey looked at each other, puzzled, "I wanted to … apologize for being mad… after Pommel Horse."

"Oh, forget about it." replied Joey.

"No really… I thought about it… It wouldn't take …long to be … strong enough… to hit that set."

"That's what I said," said Alex, who had said no such thing.

"Hey man, don't sweat it… I mean… we're all in this together… right?"

"Exactly, … That's why I want to … invite you guys to a party."

"A party?" Alex's eyes lit up.

"Yeah, Louie's buddy, Sal is having a get together Friday night. Louie is mad he has to miss it."

"I don't know," said Joey, "I mean, I don't know anyone around here. I'll feel real out of place."

33

"All the more reason to go! There's gonna be tons of kids there. And a ton of girls."

"We're there!" demanded Alex, "come on, Joe, this will be your chance to show that you are not totally devoid of any personality!"

"You sure this is legit?" Joey asked.

"What're you, a cop? Of course it's cool. Sal Kemp was captain of the swim team, for cryin' out loud. He's cool."

Joey thought about what his father had said about reaching out to find new friends, "OK. Sure."

"Great, Logan and I will be by to pick up you guys at nine."

"Um, I'm a big boy, I'll take my bike."

"Negatory, Maverick. Very limited parking there, and since we can't all ride in on your Harley, we'll have to pool."

"Ok. I hate that I'm not in control of when I come and go."

"No worries, you tell me when and we'll book."

"What if I instantly find it's a drag?" asked Joey.

"No prob," Keith reassured, "I'll bring you back. Of course it'll have to be quick, cuz I will definitely want to get back!"

"Ok, cool. I guess we'll see you Friday night, then."

"Capitol!" Keith slapped Joey on his shoulder and jogged off to the locker room.

"I stand corrected," said Alex, "apparently you haven't pissed off everyone. Although I wouldn't have guessed Pitts to be a fan."

"I guess that goes to show that some people aren't as hardheaded as they appear at first glance."

"Either that ... or..."

"Or what?" asked Joey.

"Nothing. I just had a stupid thought."

"And?"

"You don't think it could be a set-up, do you?"

"Don't think so. I don't think he's that conniving. Besides, I'll have you to keep me from doing anything stupid."

"Yeah, I guess you're right, it was a silly thought."

"He did seem sincere."

"Or…"

"Quit it with your conspiracy theories. They're almost always wrong."

"Just because I'm paranoid, doesn't mean they're not really after me!"

"Fair enough." Joey held the locker room door open for Alex to pass, and he caught a glimpse of Curtis in the doorway across the gym. He smiled as he disappeared through the exit. Joey had an uneasy feeling about the weekend and the try-outs on Monday. As Coach Dagar cut off the lights, Joey disappeared into the locker room.

5

"I don't know son," questioned Jonas, "a party? So soon who's hosting this?"

"A good friend of Louie's."

"And who is Louie?"

"He's one of the seniors, his brother Keith is trying out on Monday, too!"

"But isn't Louie going to be in Las Vegas with the team?"

"Yeah, he hates that he can't be there, but, like, everyone I'm gonna meet in school is gonna be there. You said it yourself, 'I need to get out there, meet some girls', and here's my first chance to get to know everyone!"

"I guess I did say that," he conceded, "but no drugs or alcohol!"

"Dad, I know you haven't known much about me over the past year and a half, but I can tell you this, you have absolutely nothing to worry about. I am an athlete, and I'm trying to get somewhere, and I can't get there with that crap!"

"So, no beer!"

"Dad, juice and pretzels, that's it!"

"What about your friends?"

"Well, I can't vouch for whatever they might do, but nothing they do will influence me. If it gets out of hand, I'll walk."

"If it comes to that, call me and I'll come get you."

"Deal!" Joey's cell phone rang, "Yeah… yeah, I'm in … ok, see you in a bit." Joey closed his phone, "They're about ten minutes out."

"Ok, son. Have fun. Be safe."

"Roger that, dad." Joey darted out the door just as Keith and Logan pulled up to the curb. Joey jumped in the back and scooted over to the center of the seat.

"You good to go, Joey?" asked Keith from the passenger side of the front seat.

"Good to go!"

"Ok we have to pick up Alex. He lives across the tracks from you." said Logan from behind the steering wheel of his Camaro.

"Dude, they call this a back seat?" cried Joey, as he folded his legs to fit, "they should just call it a back shelf."

"Sorry man," answered Logan, "we're not going that far."

Logan's Camaro pulled up to the curb in front of Alex's house just as Joey's legs had lost their feeling. Logan jumped out and Joey pushed the bucket seat forward, unfolding his legs, and wobbly got to his feet. "I'll be right back." Joey jogged up the path to Alex's door.

Logan got back in his car, "Dude, just let me say again, that I think this is a stupid idea. Are you sure it's even gonna work?"

"Of course, it will," replied Keith, "Curtis set it all up. Even an anonymous call to the police."

"Still, it seems awful risky."

"At this point, I'll do anything to get rid.... LOOK!" Keith noticed that, in the cramped space in the back seat, Joey had dropped his cell phone, "I have an idea!" Keith pulled the phone from the back seat and dialed a number on a piece of paper in his pocket. "Yeah, it's Keith... Louie's brother... Yeah, just checking to make sure we're set ..... Ok, great we'll be there in about twenty minutes." Keith closed the phone and returned it to the back seat and crumpled the note and threw it in the floor board in front of him.

"Hey, pick that up!" screamed Logan.

"Dude, your ride is a mess. Just clean it out when you clean out your car, which should be soon, right?"

"Yeah, Ok, I'll clean it out tomorrow."

"What's taking those guys?" Keith looked at his watch, then up the drive, where Joey and Alex were talking on the porch.

"Is that, seriously what you're gonna wear?" Joey was shocked to see Alex dressed in a suede leather jacket, striped, flaired-bottom pants, platform boots, and a beaded headband around his forehead.

"Dude, this is me. What can I say? I'm the product of hippies."

"Are those Bell-Bottoms?"

"Flairs."

"What's the difference?"

"Flairs just, kinda flair out at the bottom. Bell-Bottoms are much bigger. Very gaudy!"

"I don't know if I can trust your fashion sense."

"Can we just go?"

"Sure you don't want to reconsider your ensemble?"

"NO!" Alex stuck his head back inside the door, "CARMEN, TELL MOM I'LL BE HOME LATE! Ok, let's go."

"Then I guess we're going." The two made their way to the black Camaro.

"I think we might've been more comfortable with the four of us on your Harley!" said Alex as Keith opened the door and pulled his seat back forward. He started to climb in.

"Nice get up, Story!" said Keith, "was nothing else clean?"

"Bite me, Pitts! With you and Merwin and this car you guys look straight out of a 70's cop show, 'one black, one white, one Camaro…'"

"I'm Columbian," Logan replied.

Alex continued, "…fighting crime on the mean streets of Taylor, Michigan. It's "Spastic and Crutch!'" Alex aimed his foot in the tiny floor board of the tiny back seat.

"Al-eeex, is that any way to treat your host?" asked Keith. Alex had just ducked his head, but pulled it out to stare at Keith, "Is that what you are?" After a few seconds, Alex smiled and returned to conforming his wiry frame within the limited confines behind the passenger seat. Joey was already sitting with his knees in his chest, "Everything good?"

"I don't know. I got a funny feeling…" The Camaro peeled out, compressing the backseat passengers even more.

"You guys ready to PAR-TAY!" shouted Keith over the sound of the motor, the radio, and the wind whipping through the open windows.

"Maybe when we can stand!" replied Alex.

After being cramped up for twenty-five minutes, Joey spoke up, "Much further?"

"Just off the next exit," replied Keith.

"And if this is a total bust?"

"You say the word and we'll bug out."

"Great."

The Camaro pulled into a long driveway, "The party is here?" asked Alex, noticing that the neighborhood was very upper middle class. As the four poured out of the Camaro, Joey noticed his phone had fallen out of his jacket. Thinking nothing of it, he reached back into the car, grabbed his phone, closed the car door, and joined the others.

Keith knocked on the door, and it was soon answered by a tall, thin fellow with a mustache.

"Sal?" asked Keith.

"Yes, you must be Louie's little brother! C'mon in!" Sal opened the door to allow the four inside.

"Thanks!" Keith led the way. Once inside, it was wall-to-wall people.

"Perfect!" said Alex, "I'll catch you guys later!" In a moment, Alex was lost in the crowd.

"Let me get you a drink," offered Keith, "Beer?"

"Seriously? I'll take a soda."

"Soda?"

"Um, 'pop', I guess?"

"Aw, sure. You go mingle, I'll get you a 'soda'" Keith disappeared before Joey could tell him what kind of 'pop' he wanted. Joey peered out over the sea of people, looking for a nook where he could hole up until he could build up the courage to approach someone. Finding his new perch, Joey excused himself a dozen times as he weaved his way through the crowd. He could hear the sound of music coming from down a hallway. The view in the next room was a considerable improvement. The dining room had been cleared of furniture, replaced by a state-of-the-art sound system, lights, smoke and mirrors, and a bunch of folks dancing, mostly female.

Joey cozied up to a gap between conversations, and began one of his favorite hobbies, people watching. Not just the girls, but certainly the girls, looked so interesting to Joey. He imagined being in any of their shoes. Before he could scan the entire room, his eyes locked on a red-head, dancing with a group of girls. Her hair was the color of sunset that cascaded down across her shoulders. The electric blue dress, that looked sprayed on, hugged her slender, but ample 5'6" frame. She moved much more gracefully than the other girls, drawing the line at any type of grinding, but certainly the possessor of such moves!

As the song ended, and the dancing stopped, Joey dug up the courage to ask her to for the next dance. As he approached, she turned to see him. Once Joey's blue eyes met hers, he was hit with panic. Her dark brown eyes made his heart stop. She gave him a smile, and Joey exhaled and proceeded forward.

"Would you…"

"Would I like to dance? Of course. I've been dancing here for ten minutes trying to get your attention."

"You looked busy."

"You looked scared."

"Touché."

The music blared as Joey, for the first time, thought moving to Michigan was the right move. And, right now, there was nowhere he'd rather be. After the song ended, Joey offered to go get another drink. "Something fruity!" she called, as Joey disappeared into the swarm.

"There you are!" called Keith, a drink in his hands, "I've been looking all over for you to bring you your pop, I mean 'soda'. I'm afraid all the ice has melted."

"Great, uh, thanks." Joey took the beverage.

"Thanks for coming, Joe," Keith gave Joey a bear hug, almost spilling Joey's room temperature, diluted Pepsi.

"Sure?" said Joey, confused.

"Hey, pal, I've just got an offer I can't turn down, if you know what I mean, so I'm gonna bug out. Think you can find a ride home?" Joey thought about how well it was going, and it was still early, "Sure, no problem. This party isn't as lame as I imagined."

"Glad you're having a great time. Have fun. And be safe!" said Keith as he darted out.

Joey looked at the lukewarm cola and carried it to the bar where he set it aside and ordered drinks. As he turned with his cola and fruity drink, Alex was in his face. Alex took the cola and downed it.

"What's up with you?" Joey asked.

"Did you not see the cops come in?" he said in a panic.

"What? It's a party. Cops are gonna drop by to make sure that all is good. All is good, isn't it?"

"Well, I just saw them hassle this guy and take him outside."

"Maybe he was being unruly..."

RIIING! Joey's cell phone was ringing. He looked at the number he didn't recognize. He answered.

"Hello?"

"Who is this?"

"You called me, pal. You first."

"This is detective Brewer, with the Detroit Police Department. Who is this?"

"Joey Johnson."

"Are you at the party at 1853 Highland Street in Dearborn Heights?"

"Yeah, I think that's the address."

"Would you please step outside."

"Sure?" Joey walked out the front door to see two undercover police officers, and another man in handcuffs.

"Joey Johnson?" Asked one of the gentlemen, tall, hair slicked back, thin moustache.

"Detective Brewer?" Joey asked.

"Yes, and this is Detective Cox. Do you know this man?" Det. Brewer asked as he pointed to the man in cuffs.

"No sir, never seen him before."

"Are you sure? After all, you were both at this party."

"There's a lot of people at this party. Heck, I don't know, hardly anyone here. I just moved here from Tennessee, like, a week ago!" Joey pleaded.

"Can you tell me why your number came up as last number dialed on his phone?"

"Again, there must be some mistake! I have no idea who this guy is or why he has my number!"

A crowd was beginning to gather at the front door to see who was being questioned.

"Can you empty your pockets, please?" Det. Brewer asked.

"Sure!" Joey complied. As his hand hit the bottom of his right jacket pocket, Joey's heart dropped. There was something in his pocket he didn't at all recognize. He pulled it out of his pocket to reveal a baggie with at least two dozen tablets.

"WHAT THE HELL?!!!" Joey screamed, "I have no idea where this came from!"

"Drop the bag and put your hands against the car!" ordered Det. Brewer.

Alex had just gotten to the door as Joey was read his rights and placed in the police car. He watched as the police cruisers pulled away.

"Call my dad, Alex!"

All of the onlookers turned their attention to Alex. Considering his options, Alex chose to bolt from the house and hitch a ride back to Taylor.

Joey and his dad emerged from the police station at one-o'clock in the morning. Jonas walked just ahead of Joey, his face twisted from a combination of rage and embarrassment.

"Dad!" Joey called as he picked up his pace to match his father's, "Don't you want to hear my side of the story?"

Jonas stopped in his tracks, "Your side! You have a side that explains how drugs ended up in your pocket and your phone number in a drug dealer's phone? A DRUG DEALER!"

Joey could not think of a story that explained the night's events. "Well, no, but dad, I'm innocent! I was just minding my own business, dancing with a girl…! Oh crap!"

"What? Did you finally think of some detail that sheds light on this debacle?"

"No, I mean, I never got her name!"

"Who?"

"The girl I was dancing with."

"YOU EXPECT ME TO BELIEVE YOU, WHEN YOUR BIGGEST CONCERN IS SOME GIRL'S NAME?"

"No, it just occurred to me. It has nothing to do with it, but dad, I swear when this is all straightened out, you'll see, I'm innocent!"

"Well, it's obvious that the guys at your gym can't be trusted. So, until this is resolved, I'm not paying for any more gymnastics!"

"WHAT?! You can't do that! What about innocent until proven guilty? Due Process? Don't I get a fair trial?" Jonas thought for a moment.

"Ok, sport, since this is an ongoing investigation, I am placing you on probation."

"Probation?"

"Yes, until this is resolved, I am not paying for any more

gymnastics. If you make the team Monday, you will have to figure out how to pay for tuition. If, after all this is over, and you are exonerated, I'll start paying again."

"Deal."

"However, if it goes bad, you have much more to worry about than gymnastics!"

"I know."

Jonas put his arm around Joey's shoulder and walked him to the car, and put him in. Joey was asleep before they got out of the parking lot.

6

Joey woke Saturday to the sound of his cell phone. "Hello?" Joey said as he got his bearings.

"Joey, man, you up?"

"I am now. Alex? What time is it?"

"12:30" Joey looked at the bright sunshine pouring in through his window.

"Oh. What's up?"

"You ok, man?"

"You mean am I grounded for life? No, but I am on probation."

"Probation?" asked Alex.

"Yeah. Until this gets cleared up, dad refuses to pay for gymnastics."

"That sucks. What are you gonna do."

"Well, I plan to go through try-outs Monday, if I make it, I guess I'll get a job."

"Yikes. So, what were you doin' with drugs in your pocket?"

"For the millionth time, I didn't have any drugs, I mean, I did, but I have no idea where they came from."

"There were tons of people there. Anybody could've planted them, but why?"

"That's what I was wondering, who would want to frame me? Nobody knows me."

"Maybe someone saw the cops and just picked you because you were handy."

"Maybe, but how does that explain my cell number being on his phone?"

"What!?"

"Yeah, the call I got when you showed up? It came from the dealer, himself."

"Dude, that sucks. What are you gonna do?"

"Well, I'm cooperating with the police, so they aren't breathing down my neck. So, I figured I would just keep a low profile and not panic. It's bound to work itself out."

"Well, I've got something to cheer you up," teased Alex.

"Oh yeah? What's that?"

"Edge guys fell on their faces last night! They didn't make it out of the first round! They had to count six falls! Epic collapse!"

"Anybody get hurt?"

"Don't think so. I think they just folded!"

"Coach Dagar is NOT going to be happy when they get back."

"No joke, he's probably gonna take it out on all of us."

"Right! We don't get much consideration, usually, but if the Edge guys screw up, it's us that has to do the conditioning!" Joey concluded, "I think we should go in Monday and demand an open try-out. It's not fair that only two of us can take those spots. Heck, Logan and Keith are every bit as good as the other four, and we're better than them."

"I think you're right," agreed Alex.

Monday morning Joey pulled his Harley up to the gym with fifteen minutes to spare. He walked into the locker room as if there was nothing special going on.

"How was your weekend, Plebe," chided Curtis.

"Judging from the NTI results, better than you, Wikel. What are you doing here? I thought you were never setting foot in here again?"

"Louie and I are overseeing tryouts. We're kinda the reality show judges. We don't get a vote, but we get to critique the routines."

"Great. Now not only do we have to beat out the other guys, we have to endure hecklers, too!"

"I don't think you have much to worry about."

"Thanks, I think…" Curtis left the locker room just as Alex was coming in.

"What's he doing here?" asked Alex.

"He and Louie have been asked to be the peanut gallery for try-outs."

"Wonderful. So, when do you plan to push Coach on the try-out?"

"Well, let's do the try out first. Let's see the results. It should be the top six in rank order. So, it may work out anyway."

"If you say so. You ready?"

"Always."

Joey and Alex were the last into the gym and joined the team on the floor exercise carpet.

"Glad you guys could make it," started Coach Dagar, "I'm sure you guys have heard by now, we didn't fare so well this weekend."

"That's an understatement." Alex whispered to Joey. Joey shushed him.

"And as a result, I've decided this will be an open try-out. No guaranteed spots." Joey looked at the incumbent team members, each with their heads down, like a puppy that just wet on the living room floor.

"So, let's get at it, men. Ten-minute warm up on floor and we'll get started."

"Joey looked at Curtis, Keith, Logan, and Louie to see if they would give away any clues as to who might have been involved in framing him. Nothing.

Joey walked to the corner for his first pass and lined up behind Keith. "What happened Friday?" asked Keith over his shoulder.

"It's a long story, but it's working itself out.'

"Sorry I left so early, I would've vouched for you." Keith took off on the floor for his tumbling pass, a double back. Joey watched Alex cross the other diagonal before sprinting across the floor to do a round-off, back handspring, to a layout ten feet in the air, to a stuck landing.

"Dude, that was high!" said Keith as Joey jogged to line up behind him for his next turn.

"Where did you end up?" asked Joey.

"A girl I know, Brenda, she was coming on to me at the party, and she wanted to leave, you know?"

"Sounds like you had a much better time than me."

"From what I hear, everybody else did, too!"

"Thanks, why don't you tumble?" Keith crossed the diagonal and did his front tumbling, front handspring, whip, full, full-and-a-half. Joey watched to make sure the diagonal was clear, blew out a breath and darted across the floor to round-off, back handspring, double-layout.

"Wow!" exclaimed Keith, "that was HUGE!"

"Thanks." Joey walked off the floor shaking out his wrists. Having finished his warm up, Joey watched as the others finshed. Each of the athletes shook hands and wished each other good luck.

"Good luck, Joey!" Keith smiled as he shook his hand. *Clammy?* Joey thought.

"Same to you, Bubba, hopefully neither of us need it."

"Some of us, yeah." Joey walked away puzzled and sat in a chair to wait for his turn.

Unlike the other day, where the team score mattered, today would be every man for himself. No scores would be posted, no results announced, just who's in and who's out. Although the graduates got to add their two-cents, all that really mattered was who Coach Dagar wanted on his team.

With each routine, Joey was on his feet, cheering on each gymnast. The other athletes looked on, wondering why someone would be cheering for the guys that were trying to take his spot. Each routine completed was followed by a critique by Coach Dagar. Oddly, the current Edges, as well as Keith, received complimentary comments, and Coach Dagar freely increased scores if combinations that the Edges would usually make, were less than perfect, and at the same time, devalued elements and lowered scores of those trying to break through. It was apparent that the results would not reveal the true abilities or accurate standings of the recruits.

After three hours of warming up and competing routines, enduring the barbs thrown by Louie and Curtis, it came down to High Bar. Each athlete put on a respectable performance. Keith finished with the last routine on High Bar.

"C'mon. Keith!" Joey yelled, whipping a towel. Keith compressed his pike to set up for his dismount, a double-layout.

"YEAH!" shouted Joey. He had gotten what he wanted, *everyone hits their sets and let the chips fall where they may!* He could hear Coach Lowery in his head.

"OUCH, DAMMIT!" exclaimed Keith as he approached Joey.

"What's up, Keith?" Joey asked.

"I tore a callous off," he replied, looking at the nickel sized tear in his left palm, "all I got left is a flap."

"Here," Joey said as he pulled a finger nail clipper from his grip bag, "I hate rips," he said as he handed the clippers to Keith.

"Wow, you are just like a Boy Scout, Hillbilly," said Keith as he took the clippers and cut off the flap of skin, "always prepared." Keith handed the clippers back to Joey.

"I try to be," replied Joey, "You Yankees must have tender skin."

As the athletes gathered on the floor for the announcement of the new Team Edge, Joey noticed Louie, Curtis, and Coach Dagar talking. Coach Dagar had a newspaper in his hand and Louie seemed more than a little upset. The trio rejoin the team.

"Well that was a great job, fellas," Coach Dagar announced, "First I'll give the All Around results, then I will name the new

Team Edge. First, the All Around. The winner, with a score of 79.45, rising senior and three-time NTI competitor, Tom Shultz!" the team cheered. Tom was easily the best Edge gymnast after Curtis and Louie, "Second place All Around, with a score of 78.85, junior and two-time NTI competitor, Billy Hopkins!" more cheering and high fives.

The first two places were already locked, Joey thought, *from here on will be the interesting.*

"Third place, with a score of 78.15, Junior from Knoxville, Joey Johnson." Not as much cheering as the others, but Alex offered a high five, "Forth place, with a score of 78.00, junior from Inkster, Alex Story!" Even less cheering than for Joey, but he returned the high five to his bud.

"Fifth place, with a score of 73.75, Junior from Taylor, James White. And sixth Place with a score of 73.40, Sophomore from Taylor, Danny Dukes!" Joey looked at Keith and Logan. Their names weren't called, yet they didn't look upset.

"And now the announcement of the new Team Edge," called Coach Dagar, "now the All Around scores here are only part of the determining factor for selecting the team. It took it all into consideration, I've selected the following athletes: Tom Schultz, Billy Hopkins, James White, Danny Dukes, Keith Pitts, and Logan Merwin."

Joey and Alex were stunned. Joey looked at Logan and Keith, they were shaking hands, "Hey, Coach," shouted Joey, "What gives?"

Coach Dagar pulled out the morning paper from under his arm, "Well, we can't have a junkie on Team Edge."

"I'm not a junkie!" cried Joey, "it was a set-up!"

"I'd like to believe you, son, but it's here in the paper, in the arrest reports," he opened the paper and read, "'possession of a controlled substance, with intent to sell', that's pretty damning!"

"But it's still under investigation! I'm innocent!" Joey pounded on the floor.

"Look, Johnson, we know nothing about you, other than what

your coach told us, which said nothing about your apparent drug habit."

"I DON'T HAVE A DRUG HABIT! THE DRUGS WEREN'T MINE! I WAS SET UP!" Joey rose to his feet and had to be held back by Alex.

"If you can somehow clear your name, I'll reconsider it, but until then, you are not allowed in this gym. And with this kind of publicity, you might not want to try to get into any other clubs. For sure they will have seen this." Joey eased up and only seethed. "I'm sure he'll see to that," Alex whispered. It then occurred to Alex that his name wasn't called.

"What about me, Coach? I'm not the drug dealer!" Alex pleaded.

"I'M NOT A DRUG DEALER EITHER!" screamed Joey.

"I just don't like you, Story!" said Coach, casually, "I've demanded that you cut that hair and sideburns, and I see that you are still hairy. Besides, from what I've heard, you were with Johnson, Friday looking very much the hippie. For all I know, you're the one who framed Johnson!"

"WHAT?!" Alex was astonished at the accusation, but the suggestion got Joey thinking about that night and his contact with Alex.

"Joe, don't even think it! No way I would set you up, dude! Heck, you're the only guy I don't hate at this joint!"

"Then you'll be glad that you never have to come back," barked Coach Dagar, "now if you gentlemen don't mind, we have future plans to make with my new team. And if you weren't called, you can go as well."

Joey slowly headed toward the exit in a fog.

"And, Johnson," Coach Dagar called. Joey turned to face him. "Maybe you should go back to Tennessee. They probably haven't heard about it down there, yet."

Joey turned and exited the gym to an awaiting Alex.

"Dude, that totally blows!" Alex exclaimed.

"All I ever want to do is train. This sucks so much. What the heck am I gonna do now?"

"Have you thought about going back south?"

"There's no point. My coach closed his gym."

"Have you considered retirement? Another sport?" Joey stared a hole in Alex's skull, "Ok, I get it. You want to keep training, but no club is gonna take you."

"…and my dad wouldn't pay even if we could find anyone who'd take us."

"Us? Whatchu mean 'Us'? *You're* the drug dealer."

"I'M NOT A…" Joey yelled.

"… a drug dealer! I get it, but me? What am I?"

"My hippie side-kick, I guess."

"Right. I'm Easy Rider and you're Captain America!"

"What?"

"Easy Rider? Dennis Hopper and Peter Fonda? Forget it, dude."

"So, what are we gonna do?" asked Joey.

"Well, if retirement is not your bag,"

"It's not."

"Then I may have a temporary solution for you." Joey's ears perked up.

"What?"

"Well, have you ever been camping?" asked Alex.

"I'm from Tennessee, of course I camp! What does that have to do with anything?"

"Well, be prepared for as 'primitive' a set up as you can imagine."

Joey couldn't imagine what he could have in mind.

"We're about to jump back in time about 30 years. Follow me." Joey got on his bike and followed Alex in his '69 Chevy Nova.

7

Joey watched Alex turn his Nova off of Wick Road, and he followed him up the circle drive of what apparently used to be a high school.

"Hey, I know this place," Joey said as he took off his helmet and read what was left of the letters that welcomed students every school day, some time ago, "Taylor Center High School."

"It used to be, at least," said Alex catching up to Joey.

"So, this is where Coach Dagar and Coach Lowery went to school?"

"One in the same. They were one of the last classes before Detroit caved, and everybody left. So many of the families that enrolled kids here were all tied to the auto industry. When Taylor was at its peak, they had, like twenty, some odd, sports, full drama department, choir, orchestra and band. Then, when things started to go bad, people started moving out. First, the extra-curricular stuff got dropped, then most of the sports. Football was the last sport to go. Then it became necessary to condense from three high schools, to two. And with TC being the oldest, it was the first to go."

"And so it's become, what?" asked Joey.

"A Rec Center run by the city. Soon after the school was closed, the two, two-story classroom wings were torn down because of asbestos, but the city was able to save the gym, the pool and locker rooms, and the cafeteria with stage, for public use."

"Cool beans." Joey and Alex climbed the cracked, concrete steps to the front doors, and went inside. Laid out in block tile, covering the entire floor of the lobby, formed interlocking 'T' 'C'. Trophy cabinets still had photos, trophies, and medals of successful Taylor Center athletes. Sandwiched between two of the athletes that would later become teachers at TC, is a photograph of a gymnastics team. Joey searched for a familiar face.

"Hey, there's Coach Lowery!" Joey shouted.

"Yeah, I know, and there's Coach Dagar right next to him, C'mon!" Alex grabbed Joey by the sleeve and pulled him in the direction of the gym. As they entered the gym, there was a basketball game going on. Joey looked at the walls, still adorned with school records and championships, for all their sports. Joey spotted their gymnastics State Championship banner, still hanging in the rafters. 'Home of the Rams' stretched the entire length of wall, above the wooden collapsible bleachers. Joey thought for a minute what it would've been like to be a part of a school team. Quite different from club gymnastics, where you toil in relative obscurity, Joey could imagine training in this gym. Doors open, girls walking by and watching a bit of workout. He would be a part of the 'in' crowd, well-known and respected by teachers and students alike. *Yeah, it must've been great!* He thought.

"Hey, Joe, over here!" Alex called from the other end of the gym, at the locker room entrance. Joey made his way around the basketball game, making sure not to interfere. However, by the time he got to half court, the ball escaped from the game and rolled his way. Rather than dodge it, Joey picked up the ball and looked for someone to pass to.

"Hit me, I'm open!" came the plea from the shortest guy on the court. Joey threw him the ball, and the diminutive baller re-joined the game, and resumed his trash-talking the much bigger, and better players. *What a goof!* Joey thought.

"The stuff is in here!" Alex opened a large double-door to reveal a storage closet that couldn't possibly have a gym's worth of equipment.

"This is it?" asked Joey, "the High Bar is full of rust, the pommels are round, the Rings are hanging from a rafter, for cryin' out loud!"

"I told you it was primitive, boss."

"I bet there's not even a spring floor!"

"Would you believe wrestling mats?"

"Wrestling mats?!! Are you nuts?!"

"I do have a spring strip in the back." Joey whirled around to see a man in a flannel shirt and jeans. His salt-and-pepper, shoulder-length hair and perpetual 5-O'clock shadow, suggested mid-fifties.

"How long?"

"Sixty-feet. They use it for exhibitions," said the stranger.

"Yeah, ya said that. What are the odds of draggin' all this old equipment out and see if any of it is salvageable?" Joey asked.

"Why would you want to do that?"

"Cause, I need to train."

"Why don't you just go to one of the gym clubs around here? There's a bunch of fine ones…"

"Look, old dude, it's a real long boring story, so what do you say? Can we drag this stuff out, or what?" asked Alex.

"Do you know what you're doing? I mean, I'd hate to get sued because I let some daredevil get himself kilt on a High Bar he had no business using."

"For your information, I've been to the National Team Invitational. My team won. Maybe you've heard of us, Pioneers?"

The stranger raised his eyebrows, then relaxed, "No, no, I never heard about no Pioneers. But then, I don't know anything about gymnastics today."

"Like, was there ever a time when you did know something?" barbed Alex. The stranger look Alex in the eye, "You'd be surprised at what I know. Now, let's go do the paperwork, so you can drag this stuff out."

The pair followed the stranger through the locker room to his office. The plaque on his desk read 'Don Wheatley'. "Are you Don?" asked Alex.

"Yes, indeed. Don Wheatley, custodian and facilities manager for the Taylor Parks System, specifically, the Taylor Center Recreation Facility. At your service."

Joey looked at Don's office, cramped and crammed with books on physics and motion mechanics. "You like Biomechanics?" Joey asked, "You have a lot of books on the subject."

"I guess it's more of a hobby," Don presented a clipboard with a release form, "Ok, sport, you sign this, you agree to take care of any equipment you pull out, and you'll be responsible for any damages. And if you go and get yourself hurt, you'll man up, take the blame for being stupid, and not sue the city!"

"Like this stuff could be any more damaged?" said Alex.

"Any more damage than was there when you check it out," replied Don.

Joey signed the form and included his contact information. Alex followed suit.

"Alright, boys, you can now get what equipment out that you need, but keep it to only one or two events at a time. We have other folks that use this space as well."

"Fair enough," said Joey, "since we've already trained for today, how about we come in in the morning and do inventory?"

"Sounds good. What time do you guys want to get started?"

"Fairly early," replied Joey.

"Six?" asked Don.

"He said 'fairly' early, not the *definition* of early!" cried Alex.

"Ok, you tell me."

"How about nine?" asked Joey.

"Nine works. It's not real busy. I'll have everything laid out for you."

"That'll be awesome," said Joey as he shook Don's hand, "Thanks!"

"No problem. Just promise me you won't get hurt."

"I wish I could promise that, but I will try."

Joey and Alex emerged from the locker room. The basketball

game had ended but the little loudmouth from earlier was trying to get someone, anyone to give him a game.

"Hey, man, you look like you can shoot hoops. You want a game?" asked the kid, dribbling the ball between his legs.

"You run out of tall guys to taunt?" asked Alex.

"No, man, they just all had stuff to do. I got nothing going on at home, so I hang here."

"Every day?" asked Joey.

"Every day."

"Great. You got a name kid?"

"Rodney. Rodney Joiner."

"How old are you, Rodney?"

"Call me Rod. I'm fifteen. You playin' or what?"

Alex took off his shirt, "This won't take long, Joe." Alex took the bounce pass from Rod, "by one's to ten?"

"Make it, take it," replied Rod.

Joey left Alex to do one-on-one battle with Rod, and walked toward the other end of the gym. As he approached the doors, Joey could hear music coming from just down the hall, toward the cafeteria. He walked in through the open double-doors to find a massive, but empty cafeteria. On the far end of the auditorium stood the stage, where, years ago, dramatic productions, and choir and band concerts had taken place. At center stage was a single frame, rehearsing a dance combination.

Joey walked slowly across the auditorium toward the stage. Her movements were so fluid, like an angel! As he got closer he realized who she was, the red hair was a dead give-away.

It was her!

Joey slowed his pace, partly because he didn't want to be a distraction, but mostly because he wanted to savor the moment as long as possible. By the time she noticed him, he was almost to the stage. She glanced at the voyeur, only slightly, as she rose from contraction to extension, until her back was fully arched, her red hair following the track of her movement, until it touched the floor. She paused.

"Can I help you?" she said, eyes still focused on the floor, extending one leg until it pointed skyward.

"You already have!" replied the star-struck Joey, "I thought I'd never see you again."

"THAT sounds a bit melodramatic!" she said, slowly rising from arched position to fully erect, on toe, making sure not to make eye contact.

"Sorry I never came back with your fruity drink."

"Hmm, fruity drink? Nope, doesn't ring a bell," she dismissed.

"Party? Last Friday. We danced. We laughed. I left to get you a fruity drink…?" Joey walked to the edge of the stage.

"Oh, yes, I do recall someone of whom you describe, but the memory was so fleeting, it's all a blur. I remember, vaguely, someone offering to refresh my thirst after trying to keep up with his prehistoric gyrations on the dance floor, before disappearing without even telling me his name."

"Sounds like a nice guy," he said as she rotated her extended leg from front to back, then bending over at the hip, holding a final position, now looking at Joey eye-to-eye.

"Yeah, right up until the part where he ditched me!" She broke character and moved downstage to the footlights and stare down the stranger. Joey couldn't take his eyes off hers.

"He did .., I mean, I didn't ditch you." He pleaded.

"I've been ditched before, and that was a text-book case of ditching!"

"I didn't ditch you." She stared more intently into Joey's eyes, her arms folded.

"So… where'd you go?"

"I kinda got… arrested?"

"Arrested?! That was you?" Her demeanor immediately changed from curious to repulsed, "Look, pal, this was fun and all, but I'm not remotely interested in getting involved with a drug dealer!" she hopped back up on the stage floor and hurriedly started gathering up her things.

"I'm not a drug dealer! I was set up!" Joey pleaded. It was enough to cause her to pause.

"Explain. You have thirty seconds."

"Someone planted drugs on me at the party, and somehow the drug dealer that, evidently the detectives were waiting for at that party to bust him, had my number in his phone!"

She thought for a moment. There were only three possibilities. One, he's lying through his teeth and he's a lying drug dealer. In which case she should have nothing to do with him. *But he's so darn cute* she thought, *and he seems sincere.* Two, it's all a terrible coincidence, and he's just a patsy in a Chevy Chase romantic comedy. *Do I really want to get involved with a dupe?* Or third, he is the victim of a conspiracy. *Although it's the least likely, it's at least the most interesting of the possibilities!*

"Alright, I believe you," she concluded, "this time! You're starting with a very short leash, mister."

"So, this is a start?"

"Of something. We'll see what," she sat down on the edge of the stage next to Joey, "but first things first. What's your name?"

Joey smacked himself in the forehead, "Of course! I was so bummed that I didn't get your name, I hadn't even considered that I didn't tell you mine!" Joey chuckled. "It's…"

"JOEY JOHNSON I'M LEAVING! CARMEN, DO YOU NEED A RIDE!?" Yelled Alex from the other end of the cafeteria.

"CARMEN?!" he said.

"JOEY?" she said.

"You're Alex's Sister?"

"You're the guy Alex hasn't stopped talking about? The one that got my brother kicked out of Dagar's Edge?"

"I don't think I had anything to do with that," he said, "I think that was just Dagar's way of killing two birds with one stone."

"But Alex said you guys beat the other two. What happened?"

"I guess Dagar believed what his minions told him about this weekend and Alex was just unlucky to be there with me."

"Right, YOU got him kicked off!"

"I would'a walked anyway," said Alex as he approached the pair, "After how they shafted Joey."

"I'm pretty sure there was a fix in place," suspected Joey.

"Really?" said Alex, "You come up with that on your own or did you have help."

"You know, for being my only friend in this town, you sure don't give me much slack."

"What can I say," said Alex, "You're in Michigan. This how we treat our friends."

"And your enemies?"

Both paused.

"So, have you gotten to meet anyone besides your teammates? And me, of course," asked Carmen.

"Not really. Haven't had much time to get to know anyone, I've been pretty busy in the short time I've been here."

"Like getting arrested, and all."

"You know, gotta build my street cred. It's like when you go to prison, you gotta take out the big guy first so no one messes with you."

"So, you've been to prison, then?"

"NO! No, like in the movies."

"So, how's that working out for ya?"

"I don't think I've earned anyone's respect just yet."

"Well, Mr. Joey Johnson, you've only been here two weeks. Maybe you've got time to knock over a liquor store before the 'back-to-school rush'!" concluded Alex.

"Thanks for the tip," they chuckled.

"I truly believe Coach Dagar to be a warmongering capitalist, who cannot fully embrace the free-spirit, peace-loving, pacifist agenda." said Alex

"He kicked you out because you're a hippie?" asked Carmen.

"Yeah, he's pretty sure I'm a drug dealer, too!'

"I'M NOT A DRUG DEALER!" cried Joey once again.

"Sure, you're not," Alex said, condescendingly, "anyway, since Joseph, here, and I are sans training gym, we have decided to train… here."

"Seriously?" said Carmen, "is any of that old equipment usable?"

"Yeah, most," said Joey, "we're gonna go through it all tomorrow and see where we're short."

"Hmm. You guys seem serious. So, what's the goal?" she asked. Neither of them had stopped to think of an end game, they just knew they had to keep training.

"To keep training," said Joey.

"For what," Carmen pushed.

"I don't' know. This is all I know to do; figure out how to keep training."

"For what? For competition? For college?"

"Both, and neither. I don't know. I have no idea if I have what it takes to take gymnastics to the next level, but rather than ponder, I'm just gonna do whatever I have to keep it up as long as my body holds out."

"And what about you, little brother?"

"I'm just following him," Alex deflected, "I wanna keep training, and since we got the boot, this looks like a viable option."

"Why not go to a different club?" prodded Carmen.

"Well, none of the other gyms will take a drug dealer," said Alex.

"I'M GONNA PUNCH YOU!"

Alex turned to Carmen, "Drug dealers are so emotional." Joey dropped his head in defeat.

"So, back to my question, Carmen, do you need a ride home?"

"No, of course not. You know I have my bike here. Thanks."

"Hey, Alex, why not toss Carmen's bike on the bike rack on the back of your Nova, and I'll give her a ride home." Alex doubled over in laughter.

"What's got into him?" asked Joey.

"I think it's the thought of throwing my bike on his bike rack."

"Why?"

"C'mere." Joey followed her to a nearby window. He looked to see parked outside, a Honda Shadow. Joey chuckled at the image of skinny hippie, Alex, trying to mount her Honda on his car.

"Maybe you should throw his Nova on the back of your Honda!" both laughed.

"Alright, you guys," said Alex, rubbing laugh-tear from his eye, "I'm out. Can I tell mom when to expect you home?"

"No," she barked, "you may not. I'll be home early."

"Right, just don't make it TOO early! Bye, sis. Later, Joe!"

"Bright and early, Alex." Joey called as Alex reached the exit doors, "What did he mean 'TOO early'?"

"Our code. Early is before midnight. Late is after twelve, and too early is 'too early to get up'!" they both laughed, "So, you ready to get out of here, Mr. Johnson? Would you like to toss your bike on the back of my Shadow?"

"Think it can hold a Harley?" more laughter. Then another voice came from the front of the café.

"You guys gonna be much longer? I sure would like to get home at a decent hour!" called Don.

"Headed out now, Don!" said Carmen.

"I've got the rest locked up, just let that door close behind you. And I'll see you in the morning Mr. Johnson!"

"Yessir!" Don withdrew from the doorway, letting the door lock. Joey stared into Carmen's eyes, *Yeah, this is worth sticking around for,* he thought.

"So, yeah," Joey said, "since I've only been here for a couple weeks, I haven't found a decent place to ride. Everything is so flat!"

"There's a couple of good places. Just follow me, we'll hit a couple before I have to be home."

"At your command. I'm out front. I'll meet you there."

"Nonsense. It's a long walk. I'll give you a ride to your bike."

8

It was a quick fifty-minute ride to Irish Hills, half on interstate, half on fairly straight backroads. By the time they reached Brooklyn, the roads were a little more to Joey's liking, but could, in no way compare to the Tennessee hills back home. *Carmen would love the winding roads in the Smokies*, he thought.

After thirty minutes chasing Carmen (now he knew why racing dogs ran!), the two pulled up the Irish Hills Tower. They found two parking spaces and parked their bikes.

"Wow, this place is neat. I'm glad not all of Michigan is flat!" Joey exclaimed.

"This is about as close as hills get, but there's quite a diverse topography the further north you go."

"What are you, a tour guide?"

"Maybe in another life, but I just think this is a cool place." They had arrived just before sunset. Joey jumped up to sit on a stone wall. Carmen took his hand and turned into the space between his knees, her back to the wall, his arm across her shoulder. Joey settled his chin on Carmen's head and looked out as the setting sun cast longer and longer shadows across the rolling Michigan hills.

"So, this tower," he said.

"Yes?" she replied.

"It looks so, majestic. Does it have any historical significance?"

"None." She replied.

"None?"

"Nope. They built it in 1924. Purely to draw tourists."

"Hmmm. I guess it would be more significant if it were stone instead of wood."

"Shut up and watch the sunset." Joey obeyed.

As the sun disappeared on the horizon, Joey felt Carmen shiver.

"You want to head back?" he asked.

"Not just yet."

"Cool."

"Can I ask you a personal question?" she asked Joey.

"Um, sure, I guess."

"So … what happened?"

"I told you, the first thing I know is, my phone rings…"

"No, tell me all of it."

"All of it?"

"Yeah, the only way you're ever going to be able to compete again is if you clear your name."

"Yeah, there's a nice couple of detectives looking into it."

"Seriously? Do you think this case has any priority in their day-to-day? There's, like, real crime going on out there. I don't think they are ready to bring out the bloodhounds for your little inconvenience."

"Hadn't thought about that."

"*Hello?* Maybe in Mayberry, Tennessee the local Barney Fife has time to look into misdemeanor drug possession, follow clues, put a guy on the street, call in favors, just to clear your skinny ass, not when there's murder, crime and restroom gender identity violators to bust."

Joey pondered his situation.

"So, we'll do some bad ass CSI stuff and clear your name."

"Ok, where do we start?"

"By you telling me everything that happened Friday."

"At the party? I told you, I got a call…"

"No, dummy, everything, like from when you woke up Friday

morning until you got the phone call. And don't leave out any details."

"Ok, well …"

"Wait!" Carmen interrupted. She reached over Joey's leg and grabbed a voice recorder out of her bag.

"You carry a voice recorder with you?" joked Joey.

"Well, you never know when someone is going to confess to capital murder, or misdemeanor drug possession. So, I like to be prepared?"

"Seriously?"

"No stupid. It's for recording ideas, lecture notes, my personal philosophy, you know, me stuff," she hit the record button, "This is Carmen Story and Joey Johnson, these are the events of last Friday. Okay, start with when you first heard about a party…"

Joey recalled everything he could remember from that day, and the day before; from what he ate, to every conversation. It wouldn't be an early evening, but not too early.

9

Joey pulled into the circle drive of Taylor Center as 8:45. No sign of Alex's Nova, no sign of anything really, except the rows and rows of school busses enclosed in chain link fence. Not even activity in the row of houses that lined Wick Road across from the former school. Joey tried to imagine what it looked like, years ago, when thousands of students got off those buses daily, loyal to the Black-and-Gold.

On the third try, Joey found a door that was open and walked through the foyer to the gym. All of the gymnastics equipment the school had was laid out for inspection. Folded panel mats were stacked against one wall. Next to them were the several 'big' mats, 8"ers, 12"ers, old and battle tested. Back toward the locker room entrance, Don was on a scissor-lift, working on the Rings attachments.

"Oh, good. You're here. Wasn't quite sure you'd be in this early," said Don.

"Hey, I said I'd be here, and I'm here, early, I might add."

"But I saw you leave with young Carmen last night. I figured you might've made the smart move and go with the better option."

"Listen, dude, what happened after we left last night is none of your concern. Anyway, you didn't think I would show, yet you went to the trouble of pulling out the entire gym, for…what?"

"Well, I did hope…"

"Well, here I am. Let's get at it," Joey clapped and rubbed his hands back and forth, "what have we got here?"

"Ok, first, as you saw, I was tightening the beam clamps up there, wouldn't want you guys falling when it ain't your fault. Then I added a new spring mechanism so you boys don't rip your shoulders out. I've checked the cables, the straps, and the rings themselves, and they appear to be in working order, but there's no guarantee you won't break one of those old rings."

"Great, so we have that to look forward to," sighed Joey.

"So, Rings are good to go," concluded Don, although Joey had his doubts. Don walked over to the Pommel Horse, "Now, this here is a shame," the leather body sliced crisscrossed, with strips of leather hanging off the length and both ends.

"Well that is a total loss."

"You were gonna replace the pommels anyway. Shame though, this one has a chip out of it and still has Tony Mann's blood in it."

"But they're round!" exclaimed Joey.

"I know, I'm just nostalgic, that's all."

"Were you around here back then?"

"Oh, yeah, I was a Ram. I watched those boys workout. They were pretty good."

"Pretty good? The only State championship team Taylor Center ever produced!"

"Wow, your coach really gave you a history lesson. What all did he tell you?"

"Just that this where he was from and that they won State one year. Oddly, he only brought any of it up since we've known I was moving up here. So really that's about it."

"Hmm, well, yeah, it was a magical kinda time, and those boys had everybody talking about gymnastics."

"So, you knew Coach Lowery?"

"And Gene Dagar. Quite the team. Only time the team had the whole school behind them. Quite the run."

"Has Coach Dagar always been so, um, *intense*?"

"You mean, *a dick*? Yeah, he ain't changed much."

"Okay, what have I missed?" announced Alex as he arrived at the gym at 9:05.

"Doing inventory," said Joey, "so far, rings are good, but it might be wise to replace the set if we ever have the extra cash. The pig looks more like a piñata than a pommel horse."

"That's what I was sayin'," interrupted Don, "you're gonna replace the pommels anyway, so I'll strip it down, put some new padding on it and recover with something that may not be leather, but should work. I'll have it ready before your pommels get here."

"What about Vault?" asked Alex.

"As you know, back in the day, Vault was done over a horse with no pommels. The women vaulted with the horse sideways, the guys, turned long ways."

"Man, that sounds dangerous!" said Alex.

"Why do you think we vault over a table now, Alex?" said Joey.

"You mean that thing that looks like a tongue?" asked Don.

Joey had not thought about the table looking like a tongue, "Yeah, I guess so?"

"We ain't got no vault table! If you want to vault, it'll have to be over a horse!"

"I imagine it'll be a quick transfer to a table," reasoned Joey.

"If we survive training!" exclaimed Alex, "This should definitely be high on the list of replacement stuff!"

"It's all about priority," said Joey, "let's see what we've got, see what we can fix, build, or replace based on our budget."

"Which is?" asked Don.

"Actually, we don't have a budget."

"Meaning you have no ceiling? Well, heck that auditorium stays empty most all the time. If money is no option, why don't you just build a gym there? Throw this stuff out, buy all new?" Don ranted.

"Actually, no budget means, no funds. I have no Idea how we can make this work. My dad won't even pay for my gymnastics until this is all worked out. He was never thrilled with me being a gymnast, so I doubt he would buy any equipment."

"At least now you don't have to worry about paying to train!" encouraged Don.

"You get what you pay for," said Joey, "let's see what were gonna have to pay for here." The three continued to evaluate the apparatus, the mats, and looked at the tally.

"If all you need, in the short run, is a set of rings, new pommels, a springboard and some new mats, you're looking at about $2,000.00, on the used market. It's not much but it's a start."

"That's a chunk," sighed Joey.

"What about chalk?" asked Alex.

"I've got a case ordered, but here's a couple blocks I bought at the Sporting Goods store last night after I left."

"But I thought you thought we weren't coming?"

Don paused and smiled, "But if you want to get new rails for our warped P-Bars, Vault table, you're looking at, at least, five grand."

"Where the heck are we gonna come up with any of that? Especially the big stuff?" asked Joey.

"Dude, we're gonna have to walk up and down Telegraph Road and find a job!" cried Alex, "A JOB!"

"Alex, we knew this going in."

"Yeah, that sounded great when we were talking about it. But, now, it seems … so … definite!"

"Hahaha!" Don laughed, "I can't help you with the big stuff, but I would be willing to advance you two enough to get the little things."

"Advance?" asked Joey, "as in, a loan?"

"As in a job! I have certain privileges as the Facility Manager; hire, fire, stuff like that."

"And you'd hire us to do what?" asked Alex.

"General maintenance, mopping floors, whatever else I tell you to do."

"What's our pay grade?" asked Alex.

"Alex?" cried Joey, "Are you mental?"

"NO, man, I just want to know if we are employees or indentured servants?"

"Haha," Don chuckled, "I don't have a pay grade, junior. In fact, I don't have a payroll. I'm paying for it out of pocket, and you jokers and going to pay me back with sweat."

"Deal," said Alex.

"So, when do we start?" asked Joey.

"Right now," answered Don, "you can start by putting all this equipment back in storage, except whatever you were gonna work out on today."

"I was thinking of swinging some pipe and doing some strength on Rings," said Joey.

"Well, there's still a ton of rust on that High Bar. You guys put this stuff away and I'll get to work on that bar. You better get on it; the basketball players will be here in thirty minutes. Why don't you guys do your Rings strength first, after you put everything away, that is."

"Roger that," replied Joey and the two started packing the equipment back to the closet, now affectionately called, 'the dungeon'.

"What'chu guys doing?" said Rodney, bouncing a basketball as the other two finished putting away all but the mats they would use under the Rings and High Bar.

"Calculus, genius, we're putting equipment away," snapped Alex.

"You're just in time to be too late to help, Rod," said Joey as he and Alex jammed the last mat into the tiny closet.

"It's all about timing, my man," answered Rod, "what was the gymnastics stuff doing out?"

"Because it's much easier to use out in the gym, than in the closet," quipped Alex.

"You guys do gymnastics?"

"Another incredibly obvious observation, Rodney."

"Let me see some!"

"We're not trained monkeys, Rod," added Joey, "we have a set workout. Right now, we're about to do some strength conditioning on Rings!"

"Awesome! Let's do it!" said Rod, eager to join in.

"Let's?" asked Alex, "I don't think you're an active participant in this."

"Don't sell him so short, Al, let's see what he's got."

"Yeah, teach me sumthin'! Can you guys do one of them, Iron Crosses?"

"One thing at a time, Rod, we'll get to crosses soon enough," said Joey, "show him a muscle-up, Alex." Alex chalked his hands, jumped up to the Rings and pulled himself up to a support on top of the rings.

"That looks easy enough." Rodney stuck his hands in the pail holding chalk and rubbed it all over his hands."

"Are you gonna grip the rings with the back of your hands?" asked Joey.

"Um, no?"

"Then why are you looking like you're scrubbing in for surgery? Just use what chalk you need to grip." Rodney tried to rub the excess off his hands and arms, which proved difficult to do with your hands full of chalk.

"Alright, Rodney," called Alex, "I'm not standin' here forever." Alex was in position to lift the diminutive Rodney to the Rings, nine feet above the mats. Rodney stood in front of Alex, waiting for his assist.

"Rule number one, Rod, don't kick me in the balls when you jump."

"No balls, check." Rodney stood for a long time.

"Are you gonna jump?" asked Alex.

"Oh, I thought you were gonna lift me?"

"NO, dummy, it's a cooperative effort; you jump and I help."

"What if I miss the Rings?"

"Then, of course, it proves how uncoordinated you are. Just make sure you get one, and you can hang until you grab the other."

71

"Grab one, got it!" Rodney jumped just fine. Both rings at once, "Ha-HA!" Rodney thought he had, actually, done something cool.

"Alright, Rod," coached Joey, "you got a good grip?"

"I think so." Alex stepped back. Rodney pulled up to his chin, but could go no further. Thinking it would help, he started kicking his legs, which only made it harder to hang on. Exhausted, Rodney dropped to the mat. "How do you guys do that?" he asked, staring up at the Rings, swaying back and forth, as if they were laughing at him, "Shut up!" he yelled at the inanimate apparatus.

"Haha. There is a trick to it, Rod," said Joey, "you have to learn a false grip."

"False grip? What's that?"

Joey pulled over a big mat and stood on it, bringing his head to the height of the rings, "You hold the rings with your thumb and forefinger, but instead of holding the ring with the ring and pinkie fingers, you position the heel of your hand over the ring so your wrist touches the ring." Joey kicked the mat out of the way and hung on the rings, doing several slow motion muscle-ups to show Rodney the detail of the movement. Joey hopped down, "Your turn!" Joey helped Rodney to the rings and helped him pull a little higher so he could get his false grip. Joey eased him down to a hang and Rodney tried his muscle up. This time he was able to pull up until the rings were at his upper chest, but could go no further.

"Roll, Rodney!" shouted Joey while he motioned his fists from his mid-chest to his sides to simulate the action Rodney still couldn't do. Joey stepped up under the rings and gave Rodney just enough help to get to a bent arm support. Rodney pushed down on the rings, and kicked his legs, until he arrived at a straight arm support on top of the rings.

"I DID IT!" he said, still kicking his legs.

"Technically, 'We' did it," added Joey.

"Ok, WE did it. Now, how do I get down?"

"You drop," said Alex

"Just drop? Can I just go down the way I came up?"

"You can try, but that's a lot of energy," said Joey. Rodney couldn't bring himself to unlock his elbows for fear of falling, so he stayed there until he could no longer control his arms. It didn't take much for him to lose his support, and awkwardly land on his face as Joey jumped out of the way.

"Nice spot, Johnson. Remind me to have you spot my double-backs, NEVER!" said Alex.

"Whoever expects they have to spot a muscle up?"

"Ow, my face," said Rodney as he pulled his face out of the mat.

"Not bad for your first try," said Joey, "Look, we're gonna be here every day, so just come back and we'll get that muscle up." Joey helped Rodney to his feet and shook his hand.

"A'aight, check you dudes later!" Rodney slapped the chalk off his hands on his shorts, grabbed his basketball and headed to the other side of the gym, where his other players had started to arrive.

"Think he'll be back?" asked Joey.

"If only to annoy us," answered Alex.

"Here ya go, boys. I think I knocked most of the rust off. At least in the middle where you swing most anyway."

"Thanks, Don," replied Joey, "Where do we put this rascal up?"

"Right over here. We even have floor plates to hook into!" Don, Joey and Alex carried the High Bar, the uprights, and the associated cables over to the very same spot where Coach Lowery and his team trained to be the best team the school had ever produced.

"This is the same bar my coach swung on?" Joey asked. He and Don held the uprights in place, as Alex went around attaching the four cable anchors into the floor.

"One and the same. Of course, they had a different brand of rust back then!" Once the four anchors were attached, Joey and Don adjusted the chains and turnbuckles until the uprights were plumb and the cables tight.

"There ya go," said Don "that ought to hold you fellers!" Joey and Alex pulled the mats over from Rings and spaced them under the bar. Don retrieved the plastic pail that held the chalk, while the guys put on their grips. Joey grabbed some chalk and stood under the bar. He thought of what it must've been like to be standing in the same spot, thirty-some years ago; screaming fans, competition coming down to the wire, the whole school counting on you and that last High Bar routine to win it all!

"You gonna swing?" asked Alex.

"Yeah, sure!" Joey jumped up to the bar and pumped two swings to get his giants going.

"How does she feel?" asked Don.

"Like every other bar I've swung on! Feels good!" Joey stretched his giants, turned inward on his left arm into front giants, "Yeah, feels pretty good!" Joey pirouetted and cranked a few giants before tapping in a layout flyaway, well above the bar, and came to a, harder than expected, landing.

"Ow!" Joey grabbed his ankles, "the bar feels great! These mats, on the other hand…"

"I guess we may need to double up some mats until we can get some new ones!" Don said casually.

Alex and Joey continued their workout, as Don looked on. The basketball game was stopped several times to watch the two do skills none of them had ever seen before, outside of television.

"Those are my boys!" claimed Rodney to the other players, "I'm gonna be one of them!" The other guys dismissed him, like they always did.

As the boys finished their workout, Rodney was still hanging around.

"Don't you have some place to be, Rod?" asked Joey.

"Not really. Nobody really lookin' for me at home. Besides, I dig watchin' what you guys do. I wanna do that."

"Dude, we've been at this since we were kids. You're just too old to start!" said Alex.

"Too old? Just watch this!" Rodney took off across the gym floor and did a round-off and several back handsprings, before punching a huge, ugly flip.

"You should try that when you dunk!" yelled Alex, as he started loosening the cables to take down the High Bar, "You'd get a lot higher!" Rodney jogged back to the boys.

"So, can I train with you guys?" Joey and Alex looked at each other.

"No," said Alex, at the same time Joey said, "Yes! You may be rough around the edges, but you've got tools. And, since I don't see anyone busting down the doors to train with us, it'll be good to have some comic relief."

"Thanks, guys! I ain't never been a part of nothin'. You'll see, I'll work hard!"

"Well," added Alex, "in order for you to be on the team, you gotta help us put the equipment away!" Alex was trying to lift the bar, with the uprights attached, and having some difficulty. Rodney got the clue and jumped in to help.

"You boys about done?" asked Don.

"Yep," responded Joey, "we're gonna head down to Greektown, get some chow, listen to music, watch people act silly. You wanna come?"

"Thanks for the invite, but I've got to lock up. Bullet, don't you get in their way."

"Naw, Mr. Don. These guys are gonna teach me gymnastics!"

"I'm sure that will be a sight. You boys be careful."

"You bet, sir. Oh, and, thanks for all you've done for us. I don't know where we would be if you hadn't come along."

"Well, the pleasure's mine. It's a nice change of pace for the place and I get a front row seat to watch Bullet bounce around."

"I can't wait for the chance to prove you wrong, Mr. Don."

"I think he might be a diamond in the rough," said Joey, "I've seen more done with less."

"It's all a matter of momentum and trajectory, boys."

"Are we talking physics?" asked Joey.

"Of a sort. You think about it. You boys stay safe and have fun." Don headed to his office as the guys locked the storage closet. Alex and Rodney headed toward the front door, Joey turned toward the café, "I'll catch up, you guys go ahead."

"You ready to go?" he called to Carmen from the hall.

"Yeah, just wrapped up. I'll see you out front!"

Joey headed for the front door and caught up to the others.

"You mind if I come wich you?" Rodney said.

"I don't mind," said Alex, "but he's riding with you."

"Seriously? You have a perfectly, well, near perfectly, running car, seats and all, and you want me to carry him on the back of my Harley?"

"I'll ride on the back of your Harley!" said Rodney, excitedly.

"Stay out of it. You're lucky to be going at all. You'll ride in the back of Alex's Nova, and like it!"

"What if I don't want to ride in the back?"

"I LEAVE THAT ENTIRELY UP TO ALEX! Now let's go!"

"You're riding in the back, Jack!" said Alex.

"What if I don't wanna…"

"One more word and you're riding in the trunk!"

Rodney adopted his interior designer voice, "You know, I just love what you've done with the back of your, lovely, vintage Chevy Nova, a perfect blend of dry-rotting leather and locker room aroma!"

"Ok, up front."

"Yes!"

With Alex and Rodney out front, and Joey and Carmen close behind, they headed toward downtown Detroit.

"I don't think I've ever eaten so much," said Rodney as the foursome walked Monroe Street.

"We could tell," said Carmen, "you kept ordering and they kept bringing!"

"Don't worry about it, Rod," said Joey, "glad you got to come out with us."

"So, Joey," asked Carmen as she grabbed his hand, "what are you gonna do about the investigation, thing?"

"That again? Heck, I don't know, leave it to the police I guess."

"Taking the fall, I guess! This could really hurt any chance of you competing in college!" said Alex.

"I know, but what am I supposed to do, y'all? All I know to do is keep training. I'm innocent, and I don't see this making a difference when the truth comes to light."

"You really don't know how the justice system works, do you? Well, I hope you don't mind if I snoop around a bit, do you?" demanded Carmen.

"I'd rather you didn't."

"Don't worry. I'll be careful. We are talking about high-school, how deep can this conspiracy be?"

"Well, watch your back," said Alex.

Alex jumped in, "So, back to gymnastics. Do you have a master plan, or are you flying by the seat of your pants? Or do we just train until that antique equipment gets one of us killed?"

"One of us... killed?" pleaded Rodney.

"Nobody is getting killed. The equipment will do fine, for now. Let me think." Joey's eyes were drawn to a kid on the sidewalk, breakdancing. Joey walked through the crowd that had gathered. The others followed and watched the street dancer tear it up. At one point, he popped onto his hands, hopping and turning in the air. When he finished, he swung from his, near handstand, to flaired circles, his legs straddled and corkscrewing with each turn.

"I think I have a plan, Alex." Joey jumped down on the ground and began imitating the dancer, flaring and hopping in sync with the music coming from the dancer's boom box. Joey dropped into windmills, corkscrewing on his shoulders, and the dancer followed suit. Joey popped back up into counter-turning flairs, and the dancer was only one step behind. Joey turned backward and thrust his hips over his head and continued to pirouette while in a straddled handstand. The dancer copied, and when the music hit the final beat, both pulled their legs together and stopped in a motionless handstand. The crowd erupted and tossed money into the dancer's hat.

"Can't you find your own street corner?" barked the dancer as he gathered his night's earnings.

"Dude, I didn't mean to dis you, I was payin' respect!" The dancer paused for a moment, "My name is Joey Johnson. I'm from Tennessee, but I live here now. And I wanted to tell you that was some cool stuff."

"Man, that was amazing!" said Carmen, "You look like a National level gymnast!"

"Where did you learn gym?" asked Alex.

"I taught myself... at home."

"Dude, I taught myself at home and I don't look nothin' like that!" added Rodney.

"Yeah, but you suck, in general, Rod," said Alex.

"That hurt." Rodney grabbed his chest.

"What are you guys? A traveling theater troupe?"

"No, man," said Alex, "we're gymnasts! Well, I'm a gymnast. And Johnson is a gymnast. The other two aren't."

"So you've never trained formally?" asked Joey.

"Naw, just me and a few of my buds started tricking together a while back. We get together now and then and cut loose."

"And you learned that? Can all your friends do that?" added Alex.

"Well, we can all do some stuff, but I guess each of us has our own thing we do best."

"Are you the best in the group?" asked Carmen.

"No, no, not by a long shot! Some of my boys are straight out, bad-ass!"

"When are you guys getting together again?" asked Joey.

"Tomorrow night."

"No kidding? Can anyone come?"

"Of course not anyone, but you're cool. I'll sponsor ya."

"And my pal, Alex?"

"Can he do what you do?"

"Even better!"

"Hell yeah! But no one else, we keep these parties small."

"Roger that," said Joey.

"What is your name?"

"Bobby Hamman." He replied.

Joey exchanged contact info with Bobby and got the address for the gig tomorrow night, and Bobby made his way back up to earn a little more.

"So, what is your big plan, boss?" asked Alex.

"We are gonna stop Dagar's Edge from qualifying to NTI's!"

"How are we gonna do that? Break someone's leg?"

"NO. We are gonna beat them at State. They don't win State, they can't qualify to NTI's."

"Beat them with what? Just you and me?"

"And Bobby, and Rodney, and whoever else we can find."

"*ARE YOU NUTS*?? I mean, you and I can hang with those guys, but these guys have never seen the inside of a gym before. How you gonna pull this off?"

"I'm only piecing it together but I think it can work. State meet format is six guys up, three scores count, right?"

"Right, but we don't have six guys."

"Not yet, but we don't need six guys. I mean we will, but they don't have to be a good as us everywhere. We really only need to count one extra score on each event. We just need four guys to fill in those six routines!"

"Fabulous," exclaimed Alex, "you're gonna take on the best gymnastics team in Michigan history with a bunch of misfits. Sounds like a tragic comedy." The quartet had made it back to where they had parked.

"Only if we lose. Let's get home, we've got strategy to figure out. Can you take Rodney home, Alex?"

"Sure, where do you live?"

"Right by you!"

"Really?"

The four headed back downriver toward Taylor, Joey and Carmen took the long way.

10

Carmen pulled her bike into the parking of the Post Office across the street from Dagar's Edge. There on the end, she saw Logan's classic, 1969 Camaro parked out front. She looked at her watch. It was still ten minutes until the morning workout wrapped up, so she went inside and bought a book of stamps. Carmen pulled a sucker out of her bag and stuck it in her mouth as she crossed the street. She walked over to the jet-black, muscle-car, and leaned against the door and waited. Soon Logan showed up.

"What are you doing here, Story?"

"I was at the Post Office to get some stamps for my mom, and when I came out my bike wouldn't start. I was wondering if you could give me a ride home." She looked at him with puppy dog eyes, while working on her sucker.

"Why don't you get a ride from your brother?"

"Are you kidding? How long do you think I'll have to listen to him rag me for breakin' my bike. Besides, ... it's not the same as riding with a guy like you." She touched his arm.

"Haven't I seen you with Johnson?"

"... and Dukes, and Schultz, but who's counting. I'd just like to, you know, get to know you."

Logan cracked, "Ok, get in." Carmen got in the passenger side and, just as she had thought, he hadn't cleaned out his car any time recently. Logan peeled out of the gym parking lot.

"So, how do you like being an Edge gymnast?"

"It's Ok," he said, guarded, "It's a lot of hard work, but it's worth it, you know? I mean, Dagar is a…"

"Yes, I just love what gymnastics does for your bodies," Carmen interrupted. She moved as close as she could without climbing over the console, and put her hand on Logan's leg. He immediately accelerated to ten miles over the speed limit. "Hey, Logan," she said, "I'm thirsty. Would it be possible for you to stop at the convenience store and get me a pop? It's on the way."

"Sure!" Logan whipped into the first convenience store he saw, and parked.

"Just a pop?" Logan leaned back in the window.

"Nope. Just any Diet Cherry Cola. Oh, and a pretzel. Warm please?"

"Ok." Logan disappeared into the store.

There's got to be something in here! She thought.

She started digging around the trash in the floor board in front of her. After eliminating the pop cans, cups, and French Fry cartons, she found a crumpled piece of paper. She unfolded it.

'Chad (313) 555-1212'

She studied it for a moment, then folded it and put it in her shoe just as Logan arrived.

"They didn't have Diet Cherry Coke, so I got you…"

"NO DIET CHERRY COKE!!!? I only drink Diet Cherry Coke! How dare you offer me a substitute!"

"I'm sorry, I just thought…"

"You just thought! Well, that was your first mistake, mister! Never assume you can replace a lady's beverage!"

"I said I was sorry, Carmen!"

"Sorry?! Sorry doesn't begin to describe you! How can you expect me to be seen with a guy who keeps his car an absolute pig sty, and thinks he has the wherewithal to assume he can replace a lady's drink of choice? I'm sorry, Logan, I had so much hope for you!" Carmen got out of the Camaro, and took the beverage and the pretzel with her, "I hope you study about women a little bit before you approach a lady. AND CLEAN YOUR CAR! I'M WALKING HOME!"

Carmen politely closed the passenger side door with her hip, leaned down to look in his window, and put on a big smile, "I hope you don't take this personal, I think you have the potential to be a great guy."

"Thank you? Can I … call you sometime?"

"Clean up your car, study what a girl likes, and I'll consider it."

"Deal, Carmen. Sorry for the mix up. Check you later." Logan backed out of the parking space and gunned the engine to jump into the highway traffic. Carmen pulled her cell phone out of her purse, and dialed Joey.

"Come get me, you Ritchie Cunningham looking thing … I'm at the Seven-11 on Telegraph … no, I don't have my bike … never mind why I'm here, just get your ass over here, pronto!" Carmen stashed her phone, took a bite from her pretzel and a big swig of whatever it was that Logan had bought for her.

Hmm, pretty good! she thought. She took another slurp.

11

When Joey arrived at the gym for practice, Alex was already stretching out on the Spring Floor Don had put together earlier that day, and Rodney was up on the Rings, doing muscle ups.

"How long has he been here?" Joey asked Alex.

"He was here when I got here."

"Did I just see him make a muscle up?"

"Yep, he's done six, and he won't shut up about it."

"Don't you know how to shut him up? Do what he can't do."

"Hey, man!" Rodney said as he approached, "did you see? I made my muscle up!"

"I did see that. Good job, Rod. You ready for the next lesson?"

"Yeah, yeah! Gimme somethin' else!"

Joey dropped his things, grabbed a little chalk, and jumped up to the Rings. With a straight body, Joey rolled backward and popped up to a Maltese, or Horizontal, Cross, his body level with the Rings. After a three second hold, Joey rotated down to an iron cross. He then pressed up to an 'L' sit and continued to press up to a handstand. From the handstand, Joey separated his arms and slowly lowered until his shoulders were level with the wooden Rings. Pushing back up to a simple support, Joey dropped to his feet on the mat with a thud.

Alex pushed Rodney's chin back up to close his mouth.

"That's your next combination, Rod." Joey blew the excess chalk off his hands.

"Yeah, right!" doubted Rodney.

"You picked up a muscle up pretty quick, it shouldn't take long, just break it down and work the parts. Start with the press to handstand and the cross. With a cross and a press, you just add a little swing and you've got a routine!"

"Really? I'll get on it!" Rodney went back to the Rings, using his newly discovered muscle-up to get to a support, and started working on the 'L' sit and pressing up to handstand.

"You think he'll be able to put a competitive set together by State?"

"Who knows? I mean, he did learn a muscle up pretty quick. If he applies himself, he could do some damage in eight months."

"What do you think of the floor?" Don said from behind Joey.

"Haven't had a chance to look at it, Don."

"Well, I had to replace some springs. And since we don't have any extras, I had to condense the number of boards." Don held up an end panel to show the placement of the springs.

"So, we don't have sixty feet? how long do we have?" asked Alex.

"48"

"Forty-eight?" cried Alex, "That's not even enough to represent a Floor Ex diagonal!"

"You don't use the whole diagonal, Alex," replied Joey, "If we use a 12"er to land on, forty-eight feet is plenty of room to set up everything except the landing. Look at it this way, landing all our passes on a mat will save our ankles!"

"Speaking of ankles," Don chimed in, "I doubled the number of mats on top of the deck to add a little hop and be a little more forgiving on the wheels. And I got some birch panels and Velcro to hold the whole thing together. Should be pretty tight. Better for the bounce!"

"Awesome," said Joey, "I guess it's a Floor day. I'll be ready to tumble as soon as I warm up."

"That junk you just did on Rings wasn't a warm up?" asked

Rodney in disbelief that anyone would need to warm up after that display.

"I wouldn't normally do that without warming up, but I wanted to see your jaw drop."

"It did, brother, it did!"

"Great. So, it's very important to start each workout with an efficient, but effective, warm up."

Joey lead Alex and Rodney through the warm up he learned as a Pioneer. '*The desire to be is pointless without the desire to PREPARE to be*', Coach Lowery would say.

Don, his job done, took a seat in a row of bleachers he had pulled out, and read today's Detroit News.

After warm up, it was time to tumble. Rodney was chomping at the bit to show off.

"Alright, Rodney, let's see what you've got!" said Joey.

"What do I do?" he asked.

"See that line, about fifteen feet from the end of the strip?" said Alex.

"Yeah."

"That's to gauge your round-off. Just put one hand on either side of the line when you round-off, and your back handspring should fit. Then you punch a layout."

"A 'layout'?"

"Back flip with a straight body," explained Alex.

"A big Back No?"

"What?"

"A 'Back No', a back flip with no hands. A 'Big Back No', same thing with a big body."

"Yeah, Ok, first rule; you have to learn our language."

"English?"

"Gymnastics," Alex fumed, "How's anybody gonna take you seriously if you say (imitating Rodney), 'I just did my flip, back hand, back no, wickle-wickle, big back no'?"

"I thought the first rule was not to kick you in the balls?"

"OK! THERE'S A LOT OF FIRST RULES! Now tumble!"

"Ok." Rodney sprinted three steps and jumped into his round-off, back handspring. Like many self-taught street tumblers, he used strength over form; bending his arms, Throwing his head to create rotation, which, in turn, made all his shapes loose, requiring more strength. When he got to the end of the strip, he punched as hard as he could, and launched a huge, arched flip that had to be piked 90 degrees to get to his feet. Don looked over his glasses as he lowered his paper to see Rodney's pass. He chuckled and went back to his reading.

"Like that?" Rodney asked Joey as he walked off the 12" landing mat.

"Not bad, for a start. Plenty of room for improvement," Joey thought for a moment, 'Kick up to a handstand," he asked. Rodney raised his arms, stepped forward, and kicked up to something resembling a handstand.

"Straighten your arms!" Joey yelled while trying to corral his legs.

"How do I do that?" asked the inverted Rodney.

"PUSH UP!" Rodney pushed against the gym floor and attained some level of control of his body.

"Now, push taller." Rodney pushed until his body was completely straight. Joey placed the palm of his hand on Rodney's pointed toes and released the other hand.

"I'm going to slowly raise my hand, the only thing holding you up, and your job is to try to reach my hand." As Joey raised his hand, Rodney pushed harder for his toes to reach it, until he could reach it no longer.

"Where's yo' hand?" Asked Rodney, continuing to push.

"Over here with the rest of me." Rodney took his eyes off of the floor and looked between his arms to see Joey's inverted frame, standing five feet away, waving.

"You're doing a handstand, Rodney," said Joey, "and a pretty good one! Step down." Rodney complied. "Is that good?" he asked.

"Well, if you can tumble with that shape instead of that weak, arched, God-awful shape you've been using, you'll get a lot more out of your tumbling. The key is using your shape, not your noggin to create the power you need." Joey walked Rodney back to the start of the strip.

"This time I want you to slow down just a bit and think about that handstand shape. When you get to the end of the strip, I'm going to hold up a number of fingers. If you can tell me, in flight, how many digits you see, you will go higher and straighter."

"Ok," Rodney said as he turned around to face the length of the eight-foot wide strip.

"Remember, slow down a little and get some control." Joey pat him on the back. Rodney jogged down the strip and tried to stretch his shape through the round-off and hit the handstand shape on the back handspring. He punched the floor and raised his arms straight up. "FOUR!" he shouted, then looked back for his landing, sticking completely upright.

"Wow!" said Rodney.

"Wow!" said Alex.

"Wow!" said Don, over his newspaper.

"Not bad," said Joey, walking to meet him back at the end of the strip, "that was a big leap, but you've got to do it, like that, a thousand times before it's the only way you know how to do it." Don watched as Joey explained to Rodney not just what to do, but why and how it works.

His paper became less interesting.

"Are we done with Gymnastics 101?" cried Alex, "can we get a workout in?"

"Who's stopping you?" replied Joey.

Alex, Joey, and Rodney took turns tumbling into the mat, easy first, then stepping up the difficulty. Rodney resisted the urge to show off what he could already do, knowing it would be child's play for the other two. So, he stayed with basics. Don had put his paper away and had grabbed a cup of coffee from his office, coming back in the gym just as the big skills were coming up for Alex and Joey. He had a seat on a bleacher row as close as he could get to the landing, for the best view of the show. Rodney, reaching the limit of his tumbling several turns ago, took a seat next to Don.

"This should be good!" Rodney said to Don.

"It should be, at least, entertaining," he returned, and took a sip of coffee.

"Alright, Joe, what shall we start with? Front tumbling? Back? Combos?"

"Let's start backward," Joey replied.

Alex sprinted across the floor and tumbled into a sweet double-tuck, stuck.

"Whoa!" shouted Rodney.

"I think they're just getting started," assured Don.

Joey followed with the same pass, with the addition of a full twist in the first flip. Alex countered with the same skill, but the twist coming on the second flip. Joey doubled down on his next pass, doing a full twist in each flip! Don and Rodney cheered each pass and cheered each on as the difficulty got harder.

The two walked to the water fountain for a drink and went right back at it. Joey tumbled a double-layout, Alex countered with Arabian double-front.

"What'd he do just then?" asked Rodney.

"Arabian double-front," explained Don, "out of the back handspring, instead of flipping backward, Alex turn his body on the way up so the rotation would be forward. It's a bit tough, it's a blind landing, which can be dangerous." Don raised his cup to his lips.

"Not bad, Alex," said Joey upon Alex's return to the start.

"Thanks," Alex was breathing hard, "What's next?"

"I've got one more pass left in me. I'm gonna try to twist my double-lay."

"Cool. I got enough gas for a couple passes, but I'm gonna save my breathe for one more, my Thomas."

"Sweet. I'll see you at the end." Joey grabbed a couple gulps of air, then puffed out hard. He exploded out of his jump and turned over a lightning-fast round-off back handspring, and launched a HUGE double-layout! As he finished the first flip, Joey turned his shoulders and twisted a full on the second flip. Stuck!

"WOOOHOO!" shouted Rodney as he jumped to his feet and high-fived Joey, "Dude! That was COLD, bruh!"

"Nice job, son," added Don, "that is a gigantic double-lay!"

"You know," Joey said, "for a guy without a gymnastics background, you sure know your lingo!"

"Well, when you follow a sport for as long as I have, you pick it up." Alex had recovered enough to do his last pass. He took a breath and jumped into his run.

"What is Alex doing for his last pass?" asked Don.

"Hopefully, a good Thomas," answered Joey, just as Alex hit the round-off.

"A THOMAS?!" Don panicked, "NOOOOO!!" Don dropped his coffee cup and darted toward the strip, too late to stop Alex.

Alex punched the floor hard out of his back handspring, reached over his head, and turned his shoulders. Alex drew his arms in to execute a full-twist on the first flip, and continued to twist another half before reaching for the mat to roll out of the one-and-a-half twisting, one-and-3/4 flip to roll out, flawless.

"WHAT THE HELL IS WRONG WITH YOU, JOHNNY?! ARE YOU TRYING TO KILL YOURSELF?!" Don was uncharacteristically screaming at Alex.

"Who the crap is Johnny...?" asked Alex.

"DON'T YOU CARE ABOUT YOUR OWN NECK?! DON'T YOU EVER TRY A STUNT LIKE THAT OR YOU WILL FIND YOUR ASS ON THE STREET, BUCKO!" Don stormed off to his office, leaving the boys dazed, as well as confused.

"What the crap was that about!" Alex shouted, "I was perfectly fine on that Thomas! I've done thousands! And who the heck is Johnny?"

"I don't think it's you, Alex, it's Don! He just flipped when I told him you were doing a Thomas!" "Who the heck is Johnny?" asked Alex.

"I have no idea," Joey replied, "Whoever he was, he had a huge impact on Don, and it must have something to do with the Thomas."

"They weren't doing Thomas' back in his day!" answered Alex, "Heck, THOMAS wasn't doing Thomas' back then."

"No, they weren't, but they were doing one-and-three's." added Joey.

"What's a one-and-three?" asked Rodney.

"It refers to the head-first exit of a skill." Joey continued, "If it ends with a dive-roll, it's considered a three-quarter flip. So, if you do a double-front flip that ends with a roll-out, that's a 'one-and-three'."

"And what makes it a Thomas?" asked Rod.

"Kurt Thomas was the first guy to do a full-twisting, Arabian roll-out," added Alex.

"I see," said Rodney, "why do you think coached flipped out like that?"

"It's a pretty risky skill," said Joey, "Guys have died doing it wrong! He must've seen it first hand and it traumatized him." Joey got an idea and ran toward the lobby.

"Where's he going?" asked Rodney.

"No idea," answered Alex.

Joey, with no traction in his stocking feet, ran to the lobby, and slid to a stop right in front of the trophy case he noticed when he first walked into Taylor Center. He searched out the team photo of the State Championship team. There, next to Coaches Lowery and Dagar, was a big smiling, sandy haired, muscular teammate. Joey look at the legend, 'Front row, from left: James Lowery, Eugene Dagar, and Don Wheatley'.

Holy Crap! He was a gymnast! Joey looked around the photo for more info. Nothing. He crossed the lobby to the other trophy cabinet. On a glass shelf was a picture of a former student who had passed away. The note attached read, 'In loving memory of Johnny Banister, he passed doing what he loved.' Joey dashed back to the other cabinet to look at the team picture again. Back Row, third from the left. A much younger Johnny.

Joey dashed back to the gym. Don was sipping on a glass of water and finally got his wits about him.

"YOU WERE ON THE TEAM!" shouted Joey.

"What?" barked Alex.

"He wasn't a fan; he was a GYMNAST! He was on the State Championship team with Coach Lowery and Coach Dagar! *Why didn't you tell us?*"

Don paused for a moment, staring at the wooden gym floor.

"I thought I had put it all behind me," he started, "I haven't coached in years. I had a kid I loved very much get hurt, and it was my fault. I couldn't bear being in a gym. I couldn't get a job, so when the position opened to run this rec facility, I figured I'd never have to watch that level of gymnastics again. I was happy. Then you guys came along. I thought I might have gotten past it all, but I guess I still carry it a little. I'm so sorry. You boys have worked so hard! Don't let me stop you."

"Well, I'm pretty sure we're done for the day."

"Don't you boys worry about the strip, I'll put it away," exclaimed Don.

"No way dude," exclaimed Alex, "you're not getting me in trouble with the union steward, I EARN my keep. C'mon Rod." Rodney and Alex started breaking down the mats and spring panels, and storing them away.

"You Ok, Don?" asked Joey.

"Yeah, I'm fine. I'll see you boys tomorrow." Don stood and made his way to his office. Joey, seeing that Alex and Rodney had everything in hand, decided to look in on Carmen. There was no music coming from the café as Joey approached, which disappointed him. She had finished up, and was headed toward the gym when they collided in the doorway.

"Ow! Oh, sorry! You OK?" asked Joey.

"I'm fine, we need to put a friggin' mirror in the hall so this doesn't happen," said Carmen as she rubbed her head, "I stopped a little early so I could watch you train, but I see you're done. You guys break early?"

"Yeah, Don had a, uh, a meltdown?!"

"A meltdown? What happened?"

"Alex did a tumbling pass, and he went mental!"

"Wow, that's weird."

"You think that's weird, turns out, Don was on the gymnastics team that won State with my old coach and Coach Dagar!"

"Wow again. So, what now."

"I'm really curious about that team."

"Well, it's a good thing you're at Taylor Center."

"Why is that?"

"Part of the agreement to keep TC open as a rec center was to keep the Library intact."

"And where is that?"

"Right over your head!" Joey knew there was a second floor, but until now, he had no desire to explore beyond the gym and the café. The two dashed up the stairs to the Library. Carmen went directly to the outdated, micro-fiche magnifier. She turned on the unit and spun in her chair to open a cabinet with the files of every Detroit News printed before the school closed. Carmen rifled through the files to find the Sports Page from when Taylor won State. She grabbed the file and lined it up in the reader.

"Here it is! I found it!" she called.

"Taylor Trio Headed to Nationals," Joey read aloud, "Michigan State All Around Champion, Taylor Center Senior Don Wheatley, All Around runner-up, Senior, James Lowery, and State Pommel Horse Champion, Senior Eugene Dagar are headed to the Big

Apple for high school gymnastics' greatest prize, the U.S. National Championships in New York City in June."

"Don was All Around State Champion?" questioned Carmen, "I never imagined."

"And Dagar wasn't even the best guy on the team! Does it say anything about a Johnny Banister?" Carmen scoured down the page where it listed the members of the State Championship team.

"Here he is, Freshman, Johnny Banister!"

"Freshman," Joey thought, "can we dig up anything from around the same date, three years later? Johnny would've been a senior." Carmen turned back to the file cabinet and dug through more fiches.

"Here we go." Carmen spun back and loaded the film, then scrolled through.

"There! Stop!" Carmen centered the page and the two read the results. Taylor appeared nowhere in the State Championships that year.

"Hmm," Joey thought, "Do they have records of the school paper?"

"The 'Ramcharger', yes, I think they do!" Carmen spun from her chair and walked over to another cabinet, "Here's a file with all the papers from that school year!"

"Alright, let's start with the first paper and move forward." Carmen inserted the file and maneuvered to the beginning of the year.

"Rams Start Back to School on Somber Note"

"What the ...?" asked Joey as he read on,

What should've been a joyous return to school at our Alma Mater, instead will be marked as a sad day as students remember the life and mourn the passing, of one of their own. Ram senior Johnny Banister, favored to lead TC to another State Championship, was killed in a training accident over the summer at a training camp where he was preparing to repeat as the Michigan All Around Gymnastics Champion..."

"Oh, my God!" gasped Carmen.

"This is too much!" Joey said and looked away, "I need to find out what happened at that camp."

"Joey!" Carmen shouted, "It says here that he was attending a camp where former Rams, Wheatley, Dagar and Lowery were coaching!"

"Well, talking to Don would be a waste right now, but I know who I need to talk to."

"Oh, I forgot!" Carmen turned to Joey, "I got something for you!"

"What?" he replied, only half paying attention.

Carmen pulled the folded note from her shoe.

"What's that?" he asked.

"I'm not sure, but I think this will help you with your drug problem."

"I DON'T HAVE A DRUG PROBLEM!"

"Whatever. Didn't you say the drug dealer that got busted at the party was named 'Chad'?"

"Yeah, I think that's what the cops said."

"Take a look, but be careful, the police may be able to pull a print. Joey carefully opened the note,

'Chad – (313)555-1212'

"Where did you find this?" asked Joey.

"I'd rather not say."

"The cops are gonna ask, and they won't be so nice."

"OK, promise you won't get mad."

"I won't get mad."

"OK ... I found it in the floor board of Logan's car."

"You were in Logan's car?!"

"You said you wouldn't get mad!"

"I'm not mad!" barked Joey, obviously mad, "I'm … intensely curious! Why were you in his car?"

"To see if there were any clues. And there was! Aren't you happy?" Carmen tried to deflect the conversation.

"If it clears my name, yes, but I'd still like to know how you ended up in Logan's car."

"Well, you said that was how you guys got to the party, so I thought I'd have a look around. My guess is that Logan was only the wheel man, while Keith was the brain. If there was any evidence, it would be where he sat."

"That still doesn't explain how you ended up in Logan's car!"

"I asked him for a ride home."

"Just like that? Hey, Logan, can I have a ride, even thou my bike is Bad Ass, and could probably beat your Camaro. And while we're driving, I can search for clues to exonerate my REAL boyfriend?"

"Something like that."

"Did he know why you were in there?"

"I don't think so. He was a bit … distracted!"

"That's it!" Joey screamed as he covered his ears, "I don't want to hear anymore!"

"You wanted to know!"

"I know! Now, I don't want to know! Just tell me you didn't have to do anything deplorable to get this."

"Not at all. He was a pussy cat. He had no clue."

"Hmm. I need to go to Tennessee," Joey pulled the detective's card from his wallet, "here, take care of this note and call Detective Brewer and get this to him. Tell him what you know. I'll be back in a day or two." Joey gave Carmen a kiss, "Good work, girl, I might compete in college after all."

Joey ran down the stairs, brought Alex up to speed, and told him he was leaving.

"Dude, we're supposed to go to the tricking event with Rodney tonight!" Alex said.

"You'll have to go in my place. See if you can recruit a few more guys."

"How am I supposed to do that?"

"Use your charm. If that doesn't work, you gotta out-trick them."

"And if I can't?"

"Just be the Alpha Male, and if that doesn't get you killed, you might get some respect, at least. That should be enough." Joey dashed out to his bike and raced back to his house to put some things together before the trip South.

12

Alex drove and Rodney directed, "Are you sure we are safe here?" asked Alex as they made the turn into a row of warehouses along the waterfront. Not the best side of town, if Detroit had a better side beyond downtown.

"Of course, you're safe, you're with me!"

"That doesn't do much to inspire confidence, Rod."

"We're here!" Alex looked around at the cars parked outside, a mixed lot of tricked out sports cars and basic transportation. *If the guys owning the nice cars trust this place, maybe my Nova will be here when I get back*, he thought. Alex followed Rodney through the rusty, creaky door into a huge empty warehouse. In the center there were several mats, as well as some rigging that included several bars to swing on. The high-bay metal-halide lights were augmented with several spot lights on the areas of activity.

"Glad you could make it guys," said Bobby as he approached.

"Thanks for inviting us. When does this get rockin'?" asked Alex.

"In a bit. Where's your partner?"

"He had an emergency to deal with. Do you think we can find some recruits?"

"I don't know, man, these guys come from different backgrounds, most kinda look down on organized sport. Rebels, you know."

"Gotcha, Bobby. Just let me know who I should watch. They

need to be eighteen or younger, otherwise they'll be too old to compete."

"Got it."

An announcer's voice called the participants together to explain the rules. There were, maybe twenty guys, half of them too old to recruit, Alex thought, but at least it'll be fun watching.

Carmen followed the address on the detective's card and pulled in to the precinct. She got off her bike and went in. After taking everything out of her pockets and the metal spike that held her hair in a bun, Carmen breezed through the metal detector, gathered her things and made her way to room 2007. 'Detective Andrew Brewer' said the lettering on the opaque glass pane in the door. Carmen knocked as she opened the door.

"May I help you?" said the thin detective as he spun in his chair.

"Are you Detective Brewer?"

"Until they change the name on the door. What can I do for you?"

"My name is Carmen Story, I brought evidence I found to clear my boyfriend."

"I guess it would help if I knew who your boyfriend was."

"Joey Johnson. You arrested him about a month ago at a party on Highland in Dearborn Heights."

"Oh yeah, I remember. He was caught with the dealer's number in his phone and the goods on his person. Kept saying he had no idea how the drugs got there. I remember," recalled Detective Brewer.

"Have you made any progress on the case?"

"Ma'am, I've got a case backlog a mile thick. How much of that time do you think I've spent worrying about your boyfriend?"

"That's what I thought. What if I gave you some solid evidence to go on? Could you see your way to following up?"

"I guess that depends on the evidence." He concluded.

"You tell me." Carmen produced the note from her pocket. She handled it gingerly, making sure not to add her fingerprints to the paper.

"What's that?" asked Det. Brewer.

"A note I found in the front seat of the car Joey rode to the party in. I'm pretty sure it's the number of the dealer."

Brewer examined the note, "How do I know this is the real McCoy? You and your boyfriend may have concocted this scheme."

"I guess that's possible. I guess fingerprints would be the best way. I'll bet if you can lift prints, you'll find no more than four people; myself and Joey, we both read the note, Keith Pitts, who was in the passenger seat where I found the note, and whoever wrote the note for Keith."

"I think you've been watching too many cop shows."

"Are you saying you can't lift prints from paper?"

"We can, but it's not as easy as that. We have to request a forensic to look it over and decide which method may work best to lift them."

"So, it CAN be done!" exclaimed Carmen.

"Yes, but his back log is bigger than mine. I don't know when he can get to it."

"So, you make a request, turn in the evidence and sit on your hands until they get to it?"

"I can expedite the process if I feel it warrants it."

"This does! Joey Johnson is the most honest, genuine, thoughtful person I've ever met. He is hoping to do gymnastics in college, and this will certainly prevent it, unless we can clear him!"

"I can't give you any guarantees, but I'll try."

"I am going to call you every day to keep you on it!"

"Well, I've got …"

"I know, a back log out your butt. I get that, but I'm much more concerned with clearing Joey than your work load. I mean, all you do is drop off the evidence, grease your buddy's palm with some Tiger's tickets, and I'm sure you'll just have to call him every time I call to remind you!"

"Great incentive to get to the end of this."

"Yes, it is, and I will call every day," Carmen handled the note gingerly, as Det. Brewer retrieved an evidence bag for the scrap of paper.

"Oh, I'll be looking forward to it," he said, sarcastically as he zipped and tagged the note.

"Great, thanks! Joey said you were a nice guy."

"He did?"

"Well, not in so many words, but that's what I got out of it!" Carmen closed the door on her way out and motored home.

"These guys are GOOD!" said Alex.

"I told you, man," replied Bobby, "Still don't know who would work out."

Next up in the circle were two brothers. With each trick one did, the other added on.

"Who are these guys?" asked Alex.

"The Baker Boys? Yeah, Timmy and Tommy. They're twin brothers from Allen Park," answered Bobby.

"Are they good?" asked Rodney.

"Just watch."

Alex and Rodney watched as one of the twins moved to the middle of the floor and kicked his leg into a layout, step out, landing on one foot, and kicking the free leg into another layout. Over and over he kicked and flipped. After several flips, he began adding a twist to the flip. Kick, flip, twist, land on one foot, kick, flip, twist, again and again, finishing with a kick double-full!

"Wow! That was awesome."

"That was Timmy. They are identical, man," said Bobby, "the only way to tell them apart is the tricks they do. Watch, Tommy is up next!"

Tommy jumped up on a bar at the end of the bar rig. He kicked into giants around the bar, then did a flyaway over one bar, catching another and continuing to giant without a change in his pace. After several swings, switching from bar to bar, changing grip and direction, until he finished with a double-back, on concrete. Without mats or a spotter. Alex's jaw was agape.

"I told you, man," said Bobby, "These boys are BA buddy! Hey, where you goin'?" Alex stood up, kicked off his shoes and took off his shirt.

"Time for these boys to see something new." Alex made his way out until he was in the corner of the floor, drawing the attention of the whole crowd, who thought the Bakers were the main event.

Alex turned his back to the open floor and started with a couple back handsprings, that became whips, ending with a full twisting double-back, to the cheers of the crowd who had no idea who he was. Alex then walked over to the bar rig. He studied the rig while he put on some chalk. He jumped to the first bar and, easily pumped into giants. Then he launched a flyaway over the middle bar, and caught the far bar with his hands crossed, which turned his body. Swinging back first through the bottom of the swing, Alex kicked his legs up over his head and released into a huge front flip, catching the bar and swinging up to release, turn, and land in a handstand on the middle bar. After a pause, Alex did two more giants, then released a flyaway higher than before, so he only traveled to the end bar. He caught the bar and tapped his swing into a full-twisting double-back onto the concrete floor. "OW", he said, but no one heard that over the deafening cheer of the crowd. Alex grabbed his shirt and shoes and went back to his seat.

The announcer called out the winners, except Alex, which drew 'Boos' from the crowd, unaware Alex wasn't entered!

"Dude," cheered Bobby, "I think you *are* better than your chum!"

"Thanks, Bobby!" said Alex as the Baker Boys approached.

"Dude, that was righteous!" said one of them.

"Yeah, righteous!" said the other.

"Thanks, guys," said Alex, "You guys are certainly no slouches. So, you guys are the famous Baker Boys?"

"Yep, I'm Timmy, he's Tommy. We've been tricking here for years. Never seen you before. Where you from?"

"Inkster," he replied.

"Dude we could learn a bit from you," said Timmy.

"Glad you brought that up, Timmy. I'm here on a mission."

"Oh, yeah? What's that?"

"Looking for gymnasts."

"Any luck?" asked Timmy.

"Not until I saw you two."

"Been there, done that," answered Tommy, "we both started out doing gymnastics at Dagar's Edge."

"You don't say?" said Alex.

"Yeah, up until we were thirteen. Then we quit and started tricking."

"Why did you quit?"

"Mainly because Dagar was a dick!" said Timmy.

"Yeah, way too militant for us. Life has been sweet since."

"If your goal is to be the stars of the backlot tricker's circuit," prodded Alex.

"What's that supposed to mean?" asked Timmy.

"How would you guys like a crack at getting back at Coach Dagar." Alex teased.

"Do we have to do anything illegal?" asked Tommy.

"Nope, just be yourselves." Alex explained the details of the plan, and Bobby and the Baker Boys were on board for just about anything to bring pain to the guy that chased them out of the sport.

13

Joey rode all night to get to Maryville. He pulled his Harley into the parking lot of Pioneer Gymnastics to find it deserted. The 'For Sale' sign was still there, but with a banner that said 'SOLD' placed over it.

He tried the door, but it was locked. He walked around to a window to look in. All of the equipment was gone, the pits were filled and the floors clean. Joey jumped on his bike and headed for Coach Lowery's house.

"Good, he's home," Joey said as he saw the familiar Jetta of his former coach. Joey pulled up into the drive and parked. Placing his helmet on his bike, Joey walked up to the front door and rang the bell.

"As I live!" said Coach Lowery as he opened the door to his last Pioneer, "What are you doing here, Joey?"

"We have to talk."

"Well then, c'mon in." Alex walked in the door and followed Coach Lowery to the kitchen, where he produced a hot cup of coffee for Joey.

"I rode by the gym. Scary to see it so still and empty. I see you've sold it. What about the equipment?"

"I sold a bit of it, the rest is in storage," Jim Lowery knew Joey didn't ride all the way down here to talk about his former home, "So, what's so important that you rode all night to get here?"

"I have to know about what happened to Johnny Banister"

Joey's statement caused Coach Lowery to lose his smile and take a seat at the kitchen table.

"That's a tragic story."

"I know, I know the gist of it, but I wanted to get the straight dope from you."

"You rode all the way down here to rehash a 30-year-old story?"

"It's kinda important. It has to do with Don Wheatley."

"Don Wheatley? I haven't heard that name in years. How do you know him?"

"Well, your bud, Gene, booted me out of his gym, and I started training with a guy who had access to Taylor Center. Don is the facility manager. I didn't know if you knew it had become a rec center."

"I remember when TC closed, and I remember reading that it was saved from total demolition to be a rec center, but I had no idea Don was working there."

"I need to know the story, Coach, what happened at that camp?"

"Well, it goes back much further than that. The four of us were on the State Championship team. Gene, Don and I were seniors, Johnny was only a Freshman. After we won State, the three of us seniors made a pact to stay together, so we went to MSU together. The summer after our Sophomore year, the three of us were hired to work camp together up in Pennsylvania. Don had been working with the guys at TC since graduation, and he talked several of the TC team to come up to camp, including the reigning High School National All Around Champ, Johnny Banister. Don had been working with Johnny since they were in school together, Johnny was a champion because of Don."

"So, what happened?"

"Well, when they got to camp, the boys all pretty much, hung out with Don. It was amazing what he could get out of kids. Anyway, Gene never gave Don the credit he deserved, and started recruiting the other guys. Don didn't really care who they learned from, and Gene was pretty knowledgeable, so Don thought nothing of it."

"Until?"

"Johnny confided in Don that Gene was trying to get him to do an Arabian one-and-three. Johnny was worried and Don advised him against it. The next day, I was on High Bar, Don was coaching on P-Bars and Gene was on floor. Evidently, Gene pushed Johnny to try the Arabian. The gym cheered as Johnny got ready, and Don looked over just as Johnny was already sprinting across the diagonal, but he was too late to do anything about what happened. Johnny looked good in the air, but got disoriented in the middle of the twist, and got lost. He stuck his head out to find the floor, but landed squarely on his head, forehead first. He never had a chance. The trainer tried to revive him, but it was obvious that the impact had snapped his neck. He breathed his last breath in Don's arms. After that, Don completely withdrew, while Gene doubled down on his arrogance, blaming Don for being a weak coach. Me? I left school and came to Tennessee and took over the Pioneers program. I don't think I've been back to Michigan, other than for meets, since that camp."

Joey had no idea what to say. It was much more than he was ready for, "And you sent me up there to train with that dick?"

"Well, in the years that passed, Gene had mellowed out, so I thought it would be a good fit."

"I've learned more in the last two months with Don just watching, than anything I learned from Dagar."

"If you've got Don working with you, you are in good hands."

"But he's not really coaching, just watching us and tossing out random, home-spun, corrections."

"So, what is your plan?"

"I want to beat Dagar's Edge at State."

"How many gymnasts do you have?"

"Right now, just two."

"He'll kill you just with numbers!"

"I know, that's why we've decided to recruit non-gymnasts to build a team."

"Joey, you trained for years to get where you are. How are you expecting to train a team of guys to compete with Gene's guys, especially if they have no experience?"

"The guys we're getting aren't devoid of any training, they just haven't been in a gymnastics gym before."

"What facility are you training in?"

"Taylor Center's gym."

"What? You can't develop competitive gymnasts, in this day and age, in a high school gym!"

"I know. We're making do, and we've got the whole school year to get these guys ready."

"Your only chance will be if you can talk Don out of retirement. He's a great coach. HE's the reason we won State that year. Our coach then was really just an adviser, we coached ourselves, for the most part, and Don was awesome. He had been studying physics and motion mechanics since junior high and was great at getting us to understand the mechanics of what we were doing. I mean, you guys still won't get far without a real facility, but if anyone can overcome that shortcoming, it's Don!"

"Thanks, Coach. I have no idea where this is headed, but you've been a big help. I better get back up to Michigan."

"Do you have to leave so soon? You just got here!"

"Well, I'm probably breaking probation by being out of state, so I better get back."

"Probation?"

"It's a long story, Coach. I'll have to save that until my next visit." Joey grabbed his helmet and headed for the door.

"How is Don?"

"He was fine until one of my teammates, Alex Story, did a Thomas the other day and he went catatonic!"

"I imagine he is still damaged from the experience."

"Up until then, he was cool, calm, funny."

"It will be up to you to bring him back."

"I'll give it my best."

"Good luck, Joey!" Coach Lowery watched as Joey got on his Harley and rode away. As soon as he was out of sight, Jim closed the door and went right to his phone.

14

Joey pulled up to the TC parking lot just before workout was scheduled to start. As he walked in the gym he saw Alex stretching on the floor and Rodney over on Rings, working on strength.

"How'd it go?" Alex asked Joey.

"Good. Found out a lot about Don, Dagar, and Coach Lowery and their run for State Championship. Turns out Don wasn't just a gymnast and a state champion, my coach said he was the one responsible for coaching the guys that won that championship. Don, Gene and Coach Lowery were college students, coaching summer camp, and one of Don's gymnasts, Johnny Banister, was conned by Dagar to do a one-and-three, and it killed him!"

"Wholly crap! That explains a lot!"

"So, how did you make out, Alex?" asked Joey.

"We'll see in a bit." As the words escaped Alex's lips, the door to the gym opened and in walked Bobby, the Baker Boys, and a few others from the tricking event."

"I guess you *did* do well!" exclaimed Joey, "Bobby, you really came through!"

"After hearing what Dagar has put you guys through, we couldn't wait to get here. I'm Timmy Baker, and this is my twin brother, Tommy. You must be Joey." Timmy extended his hand to shake Joey's.

"I must," he replied.

"Tommy and I were gymnasts for Gene until we left when

we were pretty young. He was a dick then, and a bigger dick now. Tommy and I can't wait to get a little payback. My other friends here want to help out."

"Well, there's a lot to do. We have to have at least three good scores on each event by March, when State Championships comes around."

"We should be able to do that with this crew," said Bobby.

"It won't be easy. You and your friends have been brought up just working the trick. We have to start at the beginning and try to incorporate what they know with what will get high scores. At State, we will be able to only compete six total with three scores on each event counting. It will be a process to get the best, and I'm only so knowledgeable about training guys like these to become gymnasts."

"Then we better get to work!" said Timmy. He turned to address the troupes, "Guys, this is gonna be a haul. I'll say it now, some of you won't make it. It's harder work than you've ever done before, but over the next few months, you guys are gonna give everything you've got. These two guys here?" Timmy added as he pointed to Joey and Alex, "these guys are God. Whatever they say do, you do without question. You may know somethin', but these two know more. I am appointing myself as Sargent at Arms. Any of you guys get out of line or slack your training, I'll be the one booting your ass out! Got me?" Timmy looked out over the mass of nodding heads, "Joey, they're yours!"

"Alright, y'all," said Joey, "it's time for your first lesson in competitive gymnastics!" Joey barked, "We, here, do the same thing; defy gravity. Difference is, you guys see it as a fight against gravity, gymnasts look at it as, kind of, a *collaboration* with gravity..."

As Joey went on, Don emerged from his office and watched Joey work with these new guys, and he reminded him of his younger self.

15

For the next several weeks, Alex and Joey taught the new guys about the basics in routine construction; what the requirements were for each, the relationship between a skill's difficulty and its value, what skills will score well, and how to use each athlete's gifts, to maximize score. Although the new guys were making progress, Alex and Joey were barely able to maintain what they had coming in, much less develop anything new. A month into their experiment, the ranks of the newcomers had shrunk by half and the wear and tear of working on the old equipment, without the luxury of newer training amenities, that were standard in most every gymnastics club, was beginning to show. Not only were the new recruits nowhere near ready to compete at all, let alone confront Dagar's Edge, it was becoming obvious that Joey and Alex were slowly losing ground, as well.

"I'm a little worried, Joe," said Alex, as he and Joey starting pulling out the High Bar and Parallel Bars to set up the gym before workout, "I know we still have a while before season starts, but it's fall and I don't see these guys getting anywhere near the level they are gonna have to be to compete against Dagar's guys."

"We just need two extra scores on each event," answered the Tennessean, while maneuvering the Parallel Bars through the opening, "we've almost got that."

"Not if we lose any more guys," stressed Alex.

"Did you think we would keep them all, Al? For some the work

111

was too hard, or slow to come, or it just wasn't their bag. We still have a great group that, together will make up for that third score!"

"Which brings me to our other, pressing problem."

"What's that?" Joey and Alex disengaged the transporters that rolled the heavy P-Bars to their destination.

"Dude, you know the guys at Dagar's are improving. They're gonna be a lot better than back at tryouts, and since we've been so caught up trying to bring these guys along, we haven't been improving our own gym," he concluded, "and it's not just the time we spend with them, it's the crap we have to train on!" Alex emphasized his point as the mat he lifted folded over his arm, "these mats are not gonna protect us much longer."

"What do you wanna do, Alex, quit?" Joey barked as he took the mat from Alex and spread it to cover the P-Bars' base.

"Of course not! But if we are gonna make any progress toward being ready for State in the Spring, we gotta do something about our situation. We need a new facility and a coach."

"We're doing a good job."

"But we gotta do a GREAT job to change these tricksters into gymnasts, and, *WE* need to be making more progress ourselves! When does that happen?"

Joey considered that he may have bitten off more than he could chew. The group, which began at a dozen, was now down to Timmy and Tommy, Bobby and Rodney, and a few guys that were in and out, mostly out. It was only September, but Joey's body felt like it was the end of season, when all the aches and wear hit their peak. As Joey closed the door to the 'dungeon', he gave Alex a look, then turned and beat a path to Don's office. Alex was only a step behind.

Don was seated at his desk, feet propped on an open drawer, having a cup of coffee.

"Don, I know we've made some progress with these guys," Joey pleaded, "but I'm really limited as a coach and Alex and I are spending so much time with them, we haven't been able to maintain our difficulty, much less, add more."

"Joey, we've been through this," Don dropped his feet, closed the drawer with his foot, and placed his coffee on the calendar blotter on his desk, "You saw what happened. I'm sure that if I jumped in and started coaching, it wouldn't be long before I hurt somebody, and I can't deal with that prospect!"

"But these guys deserve a better coach than I can be, and time is running short! The season is just around the corner and I don't know if we are gonna have three good scores on each event!"

"Who cares?" Don blew him off, evoking screwed up faces from Joey and Alex, "Why is this so important? You seem to be a little more worried about what the final result looks like, than appreciative of the progress you've made."

"But if we continue at this pace…"

"Then change your pace, Johnson! Demand more of your charges and yourself. You think it's productive you and the others with your Chicken Little, 'The sky is falling!' attitude? What do you think good coaches do? They find a way. They figure it out, and they keep moving forward. None of us can predict where we finish, we just keep pushing, harder, in the present." Don rose to his feet, "You keep your eye on the prize and keep pushing, right to the end. You run into a roadblock, you don't complain about the obstacle, you figure out how to get around it, over it, or through it. Only in the moment of truth will you know if you did enough." Joey was stunned. Don was right. While he was complaining about his station, he was taking his eye off of his goals. And he hadn't heard Don sound so stern and forceful before. Joey imagined what he would be like if Don were coaching, and what he could do in a state-of-the-art training facility.

"We know we can't do anything about the gym, but we could get so much further with a good coach," added Alex.

"I'm sorry guys. I just can't. I can't be responsible for another … mishap. Sorry." Don sat down and picked up his coffee.

"Fine!" Joey snorted, "you just park it in here and stay safe! But while you're hiding in here, remember something, Don."

"What's that, Mr. Johnson?" Don rose to his feet to go eye-to-eye with Joey.

"While you sit here, content and safe, there are guys out there we are telling to do the exact opposite. 'take risks', 'trust your instincts' 'reach beyond your limits.' These are the things we are pushing in the gym, the gym where you did the very same thing thirty years ago! YOU are the example of pushing the envelope! And, besides, don't you think it might be a bit selfish for you to wallow in regret for something you had nothing to do with? And while you dodge what you love, out of fear, there are some hungry guys out there that could be so much more if they had just a bit of what you have to give!" The two stared for a moment, then Don slowly sat down.

"Fine," said Joey, "we have a workout to run." The two marched out of Don's office and out to the gym where the guys were just starting to show up for workout.

"That was kinda harsh, Joe," said Alex, "Look at all he's done for us."

"I know. I'm just very frustrated knowing the best coach in the country is sitting in there, drinking coffee, while we're out here reinventing the wheel!"

"Maybe something will come around in him."

"Maybe. Hope it comes soon. The clock is ticking."

"So, what's on tap for today, Joey?" asked Timmy as the guys finished their warm up.

"Funny you put it that way, Tim," Joey said, "today we are gonna learn more about tap swings on Rings, High Bar, and P-Bars." Joey and Alex began explaining and showing how to create power from the different swing positions on the Parallel Bars, and then showed how that swing leads to bigger skills.

Having some gymnastics experience, Timmy and Tommy were quick to take what they knew from before and build on that foundation. Bobby and Rodney had a tougher time, learning from scratch, but it made for an entertaining workout as both found ways to peel off the bars that could've earned big money on the 'Craziest Home Videos' program.

"Ok, Bobby," coaxed Alex, as Bobby was in a handstand on the bars, "It's not much different from a giant swing on High Bar, just push out in your shoulders and stretch the downswing, then as you pass through the bottom, you have to push your hips through and turn your body over so you can push up to the dismount!"

"That's all it is to you! I'm dropping face down, here. It's kinda scary watching the ground rush up to your face."

"Just hang on!" said Joey, "You better go soon or you'll be too tired from doing such a long handstand!" Bobby took a breath, pushed out in his shoulders, and started the prone drop.

"AIIIIIIIGH!" Bobby screamed as he dropped. As he passed through the bottom of the swing, he pulled his head back, and caused him to roll down the bars until he came to a stop, straddled on one rail! He rotated slowly around the rail and dropped, pinballing between the two posts before coming to rest on his knees on a mat at the end of the bars. Bobby laid on the mat, taking inventory of body parts, and generally, letting the pain subside.

"I guess I should 'a kept my head neutral?" asked Bobby, as he rubbed new bruises.

"That would've helped," said Alex, "but this result was much more entertaining!" All had a pretty good laugh as Alex helped Bobby to his feet. Joey glanced over toward the window at Don's office just as Don closed the blinds.

"Does he get bonus for distance?" asked Carmen as she walked in just in time to see the comedy.

"Carmen!" Joey said, jogging over to her.

"Have you heard anything?" She said in a voice low enough for only his ears, "It's been, like, a month, and no news?"

"Like he said, those guys have a lot of work to do. We still have a couple months before the season starts. As long as I'm cleared by then, I'll be fine."

"THERE THEY ARE!"

Joey and Carmen looked toward the entrance on the other side of the gym to see Gene Dagar charging toward them. The commotion was enough to get Don's attention as he swiveled in his chair and looked between the blinds to see what was happening.

"You've got a lot to answer for, Johnson!" shouted Dagar as they approached. Don raced from his office and got to Joey just in time to get between Gene and his target.

"Hello, *Eugene*," Don said calmly, "what's it been? Twenty-five, six years? What brings you back?"

"These kids have ruined me! Especially that little bitch!" he pointed angrily at Carmen.

"Now, what could this lovely lady have done to 'ruin' you, *Eugene*?"

"She's got some cop convinced that my boys are, somehow, involved in drug dealing! She found some note that, supposedly, implicates two of my guys, and one of my graduates, in a drug deal where YOUR kid got caught with the drugs AND the dealer's number in his phone. IN HIS PHONE! It's obvious this false accusation is a cover up for what YOUR kid did!"

"First of all, *Eugene*, he's not my kid. I quit coaching that day twenty-seven years ago, and haven't coached since. You know that! I've just opened up a city owned, rec center to some hard working kids, working on their own. Second, the story that I got sounds a whole lot more convincing, but let me see if I follow your version. You contend that this youngster, brand spankin' new from Tennessee, somehow gets himself invited to a party, where he knows no one, mind you, but decides that before he goes, he needs to hook up with a drug dealer he has never met, just a number on a piece of paper that ends up in the front seat of the car of one of his new teammates, even though he's in the back. Then, after getting the goods IN THE MIDDLE OF A PARTY FULL OF STRANGERS, doesn't leave, but stays at the party, even after the dealer is dragged out by police, until he's called by the cops, on the dealers phone, and walks out the front door to get arrested, without even bothering to get rid of the drugs or run. Is that about right?"

"Him and that hippie friend of his knew they couldn't beat out Keith and Logan for a spot on the Edge team, so that hippie called one of his drug buddies and arranged this to get Logan and Keith in trouble, so they couldn't compete for the team spots. Simple jealousy."

"Even though this happened BEFORE the try out?" asked Joey.

"And we kicked their ASSES at tryout?" added Alex.

"Either way, this little shit has cost me plenty!"

"But there hasn't even been a trial, yet. How have they cost you?"

"Well, there won't be a trial, not involving you guys."

"WHAT?" screamed Joey, "I'm cleared?"

Dagar continued, "Once they found Keith's finger print on that note, they brought him in for questioning."

"How did that go?" asked Alex.

"Once they told him what he was up against, he spilled his guts! Ratted out Curtis, admitted to the whole thing. Evidently it was all Curtis' idea, plus he knew the drug dealer. Since there was no evidence that directly connect Keith to the drugs, and Logan only drove, they have only been placed on probation."

"That's great!" screamed Joey.

"I sense a 'but'," said Don.

"Once they looked a little deeper, it seems that there has been a few of my boys involved with drugs in the past."

"That's a little more than embarrassing, Gene," said Don, condescendingly, "has the Federation heard about this?"

"Yes, that's the kicker. The Federation is not waiting for a finding in the matter they just called me."

"And...?" asked Joey.

"They are stripping us of every championship that involved any of the accused athletes."

"How many is that?" asked Alex.

"Six." He said as his head dropped.

"Well, that really sucks, Gene," said Don, "maybe you should 'a kept a better eye on your boys over the years!"

"Maybe, but at least I haven't killed anyone! And I still have my streak of 20 NTI appearances in a row, and THIS year will make 21. I don't know why you picked now to come out of your cave and coach these brats!"

"I'm not coaching anybody. I just have the keys to the gym. They've done everything on their own."

"I find that hard to believe."

"Not that I care, but believe it. I walked away from this sport because I couldn't stand the thought of another kid getting hurt."

"Well, I doubt you, or whoever, could do much with these losers on this shoddy equipment."

"Yet, you thought it was a good idea to come all the way over here to tell me that. Hmm. Methinks you are just a bit scared of these boys, Eugene."

"We'll see, then." Gene turned and walked out. Don stared as he left.

"See what I mean, Don? We need a coach!" pleaded Joey.

"Then be one," replied Don as he withdrew to his office.

"So, what now, Joe?" asked Alex, as Joey stared down Don's exit.

"I guess we get back to work," he replied.

Joey only took a moment, then shook his head as if to reset, "Alright, where was I?" as if nothing had even happened, "Bobby, you OK?"

"Fine, Joe." Bobby hopped to his feet. Joey faced the crew.

"So, this is what we're dealing with guys. Dagar wants our heads, Don is not likely to be much help, our equipment is out of the 70's, and your coach is about as clueless at helping you get where y'all need to go, that any learning you do is gonna be the result of your investment. Y'all down with that?" Joey looked over the group, as they assessed their fate.

"We gonna work out or what?" asked Timmy, or Tommy.

"We are training," replied Joey, "OK, Bobby, that turn was

powerful, but if you start to flip at the bottom of the swing, bad things happen."

"Like going straddle on one rail?" Bobby said.

"Like that. Now let's try it again. This time keep those elbows straight and try to swing up a bunch more before you flip!" Bobby jumped up on the Parallel Bars and swung up to another handstand. This time he kept his body tighter through the bottom of the swing, resulting in a nice reflex from the rails, driving his body up off the bars, over-rotating the flip that followed.

"LIKE THAT! LIKE THAT! Nice, Bobby!" cheered Joey at the junction of correction and application.

Soon everyone was wrapped up in the trying and learning and the outburst by Dagar was just a memory, but fueled each successive turn. They had become so engaged in the process that none of them noticed Don emerging from his office, fresh coffee in hand, to watch the guys train. Just as the team was starting to get to something interesting, Don's entertainment was interrupted by his office phone.

"Don Wheatley.... Hey, Jim, Thanks for calling me back.... Yeah, it has been a long time…"

16

As the team wrapped up Friday practice, and packed the last of the equipment away in the dungeon, Joey slapped the lock on the door, while the rest awaited being dismissed. They learned, the hard way, that there are some things that are exempt from the 'we're not using conditioning for discipline' rule, and sneaking out of the gym before everything was put away topped the list.

"What else we got, Joe?" asked Alex.

"Nada! That's it. I'll see y'all in the morning."

"Hold on there, sport," exclaimed Don, approaching the team, "You guys can't train tomorrow. We're resurfacing the gym floor. It won't be available all weekend."

"All weekend!" Joey exclaimed, "What are we supposed to do?"

"The city still pays to resurface the gym floor?" asked Alex, to which Don ignored.

"I don't know, you might try resting," replied Don, "Why don't you take Carmen down to meet your mother?"

Alex added his two cents, "Dude, we've been bustin' it lately, and I think I speak for the whole team when I say we could use a day off." The rest silently nodded.

"The Baker's and I have a battle Sunday. A rest day tomorrow wouldn't suck."

"Alright, alright. We'll take the weekend off. I guess I'll see y'all back here Monday." Joey conceded.

"Better make it Tuesday. It takes a bit for the lacquer to set up," added Don.

"Tuesday?! We'll be fat by then!" Joey exclaimed.

"Sorry, sport, better now than down the road. Besides, it's the only time, and I'm sure you're gonna love the result.

"I'm gonna love a resurfaced basketball court floor? Did you hit your head? You're confusing me for Rodney."

"Will you guys just get out of here? Some of us have plans." Don shooed the team toward the exits and killed the lights.

"Hey, cuteness, what are your weekend plans?" Joey said as he watched Carmen going through her barre routine.

"I have a feeling whatever I have planned, it's about to change. What's on your mind?" she said without losing focus.

"A road trip. Don says the gym is off limits until Tuesday, So I thought a trip South would be fun."

"How far South?"

"Knoxville. Or thereabouts." Carmen broke character and approached Joey, who was straddling a folding chair in the wings of the stage.

"Are you serious? I mean, of course. Meet your mom? Meet your coach? See where you grew up? Yes, please. Can we leave now."

"I'm just waiting on you."

"Give me a sec," Carmen dashed to the dressing room. Joey thought it would be a harder sell.

17

For late September, the colors were changing early, and made for a beautiful ride through Eastern Kentucky and into East Tennessee. By the time they got to West Knoxville, the sun was setting, but the temperatures were still in the mid 70's. Out of habit, Joey exited the interstate one exit early to go by the Pioneers gym. Joey pulled up to the door and got off his bike. Carmen followed suit. Joey rubbed the dirt off of the pane of safety glass in the entry door, and cupped his hands to see into the building. It was too dark to see anything.

"So, this is 'Pioneers'?" said Carmen.

"Was 'Pioneers'," replied Joey as he turned toward a flower bed next to the sidewalk and Carmen took his spot, straining to see anything inside the dark, metal shell. Joey fished around in a cement urn, and produced a key, "AHAH!" exclaimed Joey, "I wondered if this would be here!" Joey returned to the door and stuck the key into the lock.

"What are you doing?" said Carmen, "do you want to go to jail?"

"Are you mental? I know this place back and forth."

"What about an alarm?" she said just as the door opened and the steady beep of a security system signaled an approaching siren. Joey quickly typed in a code on the keypad until the chirping stopped and a beep signaled the disarming of the alarm. "I'd hoped that coach hadn't changed the code."

Carmen slapped his shoulder as he escorted her inside and hit a few lights. Joey watched as the metal-halide lights warmed up and cast a surreal blue hue over the, now empty, space.

"This is where the pits used to be," Joey said as he pointed out the areas, now filled with concrete, that used to be six-foot deep pits filled with loose foam. Joey led Carmen on a tour of the 15,000-square foot facility that used to be 'Pioneers'. Joey walked out where all of the equipment used to be, remembering every piece of apparatus, and at least one funny story from each location within the gym.

After the tour, Joey killed the lights, set the alarm, locked the door, and slid the key into the mail slot in the door. They mounted their bikes and headed to Maryville.

Joey's mom met the pair in the driveway.

"So glad y'all got in before it got too dark!" said Shirley, as she took Joey's helmet.

"Hi, mom! This is Carmen. Carmen, my mom, Shirley."

"So nice to meet you. I'd like to say I've heard so much about you, but I really haven't heard much from Joey since he left for Michigan."

"Mom, you know that's not true. I've told her tons about you." The trio went inside, where Shirley already had the table set at dinner ready to be served.

"We went by 'Pioneers'. Pretty empty."

"Yes, I know. I saw Coach Lowery just last week. He said he had sold the last of the equipment and he was delivering it personally."

"Who did he sell to?"

"Well, the building sold a couple weeks ago. Something in marine sales. Boats and things, I guess. There was a splash in the paper about the sale and the new owners looked pretty excited to be expanding their business."

"They will have no idea what all went on in that building," lamented Joey.

"Oh, I don't know. They are local. It wouldn't surprise me that they had some connection to Jim before they bought the gym. I think I read that they wanted to recognize what all Jim had done and were going to do some kind of mural, or plaque, or something to remember 'Pioneers'."

"Wow, that's really cool," said Carmen. Joey wasn't so sure.

"So, Coach Lowery is out of town?"

"I believe so. When I drove by yesterday there was a big truck backed up to the gym, I assumed he was packing the last."

"Well, it's pretty bare. They've filled the pit and the rest is cleared, like we were never there! I sure hope they enjoy that place half as much as I did." Joey sighed.

"We all move on, Joey. I think it's time for you to do the same." Shirley shifted subjects, "so, what did you have planned for this weekend, son?"

"To be honest, I hadn't got much further than seeing the gym, and Coach Lowery, and seeing you!"

"Well, if we don't get to go up into the mountains this weekend, you will be going back to Michigan alone!" threatened Carmen, "So, get your head out of your butt and start figuring how you are going to entertain me."

"I think I like her, Joe," said Shirley. Joey wasn't so sure at the moment.

"Alright. What's the forecast for tomorrow, mom?"

"Typical for East Tennessee in September, sunny and low to mid-80's."

"Perfect. I have just the plan."

"Care to share?" asked Carmen.

"Na, I'll let it be a surprise. But, we better rest up, there's a big day ahead of us. You're gonna want to dress to hike and there's a good chance you might get wet." Joey gave her a peck on the cheek, then Shirley led Carmen to the guest bedroom and supplied her with linens.

The next morning, Carmen awoke to the sound of Joey banging on her door, "Are you awake in there?" he shouted.

"I am now." Carmen scratched her head and looked at her phone. 7:45

Shouldn't I be hearing roosters or something? she thought.

"Mom's got breakfast made. I'll see you downstairs."

Carmen heaved a heavy sigh and walked to the guest bathroom, splashed her face, brushed her teeth and threw her hair into a quick, tight bun. In seconds she was dressed, read to roll. She entered the dining room to a full spread; bacon, eggs, sausage, home fries, pancakes, and several juices to choose from, all in buffet fashion on the counter. Joey was at the high-top table, waiting like one dog for another, and was already well into a full plate. "Thanks for waiting."

"Sorry, I was hungry!"

Carmen grabbed a plate and picked her favorites. By the time she sat down, Joey was already through one plate, and up for seconds.

"So, where are you headed this morning dear?" asked Shirley.

"I thought we'd head up into the mountains, check out some scenery, see the colors change, look at some waterfalls and stuff."

"That sounds like fun. You kids have fun."

"Thanks, mom! You ready?" Joey was stuffing a rolled-up pancake, dunked in syrup, into his mouth, trying not to get syrup everywhere. Carmen was only halfway into her course. "Of course not. Sit down and take a breather." Joey sat down and shoveled a huge portion of home fries, and didn't bother to wait until he swallowed it all to answer, "Sorry, I'm just psyched about this morning and anxious to get going!"

"Well, I don't think the mountains are going anywhere, so we have time, don't we?"

"Sure, take your time." Joey stared as Carmen finished her plate. He waited to see if she was going to go for seconds, but she saved him from having to watch anymore, "OK, I'm ready."

"You sure? Don't want to 'rush you?'."

"Let's go." She pushed him toward the door, where his mom

had their helmets and a pack of goodies for the day, "Thanks, mom, you're the best!"

"Thank you, Mrs. Johnson."

"You're welcome dear. Now, you kids be careful. When do you expect to be back?"

"This evening. It'll be too chilly to camp out, but we may stay out long enough for a campfire before coming back."

"Sounds like a full day. So, I shouldn't plan on you for supper?"

"I think that's a good call. We'll see you tonight."

Joey and Carmen started their bikes and headed toward the mountains.

Shirley shook her head as they pulled away, pretty sure she knew what Joey had planned.

Riding around on the twisting, turning, up and down of the roads throughout the Great Smoky Mountains, are like a kid to candy. Fun and exhilarating, *this ride was nothing like Irish Hills*, Carmen thought. And the sights along the way were not only breathtaking, but created a challenge, just in paying attention to the road without being too distracted.

After a while, Joey pulled into a long turn off to a gravel road, Carmen read the sign on the way in, "Cade's Cove, how sweet," she said. After a while, they came to a gravel parking area where they parked and prepared to hike. Joey carried a backpack, Carmen carried the water. As they made their way from the parking area to the trail, Carmen read the next sign,

"Abram's Falls 2.5 miles"

"Oh, only two-and-a-half miles," said Carmen, "that's not so bad."

"Sometimes it ain't about the distance, but the direction." Joey returned, ominously.

Carmen soon realized what he had meant. From the moment

the trail vanished into the woods, it began its upward climb toward Abram's Falls. Although only a little more than two miles, the trail changed elevation 675 feet! A hike indeed!

Just as Carmen was about to give in to her impulse to be the whiney child, and ask, 'Are we there, yet?', Joey pushed through to a clearing at the edge of Abram's Creek, "We're there, yet!" he said, anticipating her looming complaint.

"How cool!" she said as she spied the rushing rapids, "Do we have to cross this?"

"No, but we could." Joey jumped onto one of the many fallen trees along the creek, and traversed from tree, to stone, to tree, and back to stone, dodging the rapids.

"You know you've got my lunch in that pack. You go in the water with it and I will be very put off!" Carmen warned.

"No worries." Joey jumped back over to the shore and continued until they came to the falls. "Cool! It's still here!" Joey said as he quickly tossed the backpack down on the ground, and took off his shoes and socks, "C'mon!" he said. Carmen took off her pack and shoes, putting them with his things.

"What's still here?" she asked, and was immediately answered as Joey stepped out onto a fallen tree that extended out over the falls, "What are you doing?!"

"C'mon! Don't be scared!" Joey took her hand and guided Carmen out onto the timber, "Look in my eyes! Don't look down!" Joey edged out, towing Carmen with him, her eyes locked on his. Joey came to a stop, Carmen was all too ready to stop.

"This is, different," she said, as excited as she was nervous.

"We're only about thirty feet up, but the falls more than make up for it with the massive amount of water that poured over the falls and crashed into the pool below with the sound of thunder. Look around you!" Joey slowly nudged Carmen back until she was arm's length away, then slowly dropped his grip, as she loosened hers. As they released their contact, Carmen looked around, her heart pounding in her chest. She turned around slowly to get the full effect.

As she finished her revolution, she noticed Joey was further away, now, almost at the edge!

"And the cool thing is, it's perfectly safe!" Joey started pushing on the log, and it began to bob up and down, making it tough to keep balance, and Carmen had to react quickly, "WHAT ARE YOU DOING?!"

"Oh, just playing. It's OK!"

"Enough, OK? Knock it off!"

"As you wish." Joey stopped his jumping, but the log was still moving, and he lost his balance, "WOAH! CARMEN!!" Joey screamed as he tumbled backward off of the log, flipping out of control until he hit the water with a "SPLAT!" before sinking below the surface!

"JOEY!!" Carmen screamed as she looked down at the water, constantly being churned by the falls, with no sign of her boyfriend. After a moment of no result, Carmen dove into the water. She swam under the surface, trying to locate Joey, but the churning water made it difficult. After several tries, Carmen had to give up and swam to shore.

Exhausted, Carmen, caught her breath while she pondered what could've happened. Just before she was about to hit the panic button, she had a thought. She stared at the water pouring into the pool from the falls. She bent over and picked up a few polished stones, about the size of an orange. Studying the falls, she picked her target and fired three into the heart of the waterfall.

Although the pounding water from the falls was pretty loud, a faint "OW" could be heard, and diving out through the falls came Joey, his forehead gashed from one of Carmen's strikes. As he swam toward Carmen, she sat on a rock and panted.

"What did you do that for?" he asked, as he took off his drenched T-shirt and wrapped it around his wounded scalp, "I didn't know you had such an arm."

"Shortstop of the Varsity Softball Team the last three years. I don't just dance, you know. And you got what you deserved, trying to scare me like that."

"It usually goes over a little better than that."

"Maybe you're just out of practice." The two made their way back up the falls, where they had left their things, made their way back down, and set up for lunch, with the waterfall in the background.

"Why is it that guys do what you do? I mean this whole pissing match, why does everything have to be junior high drama?"

"What do you mean? The waterfall thing? I've been doing that…"

"No, the whole thing with Dagar's gym. Why does it have to be about beating those guys? Can't you just do your thing, and let them do theirs?"

"I don't know. Of course, in this case, it is about the come-upance, fer sure, but I guess it's about the rudder."

"The rudder?"

"Yeah, Coach Lowery used to talk about short term goals being like the rudder of a boat."

"I don't get it."

"OK, there always has to be a plan, right? A way to get to an ultimate goal."

"Like NTI's?"

"Perfect. Let's say my goal is to get to NTI's. If I don't know the path, which goals to set, I may get there, but it may take me too long to figure it out. Well, every time I go off in a direction that's not getting me to my goal, it's like going upstream without a rudder. You know?"

"But what does that have to do with your war with Dagar's, can't you just focus on being, I don't know, *better*?"

"Yeah, but something has to serve as the carrot?"

"What?"

"You know, 'Little Rascals'. Spanky hangs a carrot on the end of a pole and sticks it in front of the goat that's tied to his wagon?"

"What? Spanky? Goats? A wagon?"

"It's a metaphor. The goat doesn't want to move, but he thinks he can reach if he just…LOOK, the carrot is the motivation, the training is the pole. Get it?"

"So, hating on these guys is not about them, it's about motivating you? How self-serving of you!"

"Exactly, I don't hate those guys. I haven't even known them long enough. Maybe if I made a better effort to know them?"

"Are you kidding? Screw them! They thought nothing of setting you up to ruin the rest of your life!"

"But they didn't, did they? This was done out of fear. How can I be mad at fellas that are just scared and insecure? They serve a purpose as targets to get me to the next step?"

"And why is that so important?"

"Are you kidding? That's all that's important!"

"I'm sorry you lost me. What is so important?"

"Getting to the next step. It's about living every day like it's your last. Why do you think I do gymnastics?"

"Because you're good at it, and you're fearless?"

"No, because it's hard, and I'm not fearless. Gymnastics is the only sport where you have to be good at six different things, in a sport that changes so fast, that they rewrite the rules every eight years or so, because the coaches and athletes figure out and exceed the code of points as fast as they change the rules! And unlike most other sports, gymnastics has a very short lifespan. There is an awful lot to do to reach your potential, and you can't do it if you keep getting sidetracked, or you find yourself reinventing the wheel. That's why it's so important to have a great coach, that knows the most efficient way to maximize the athlete's potential!"

"I didn't realize you were so committed!"

"Look, two years ago I was just a slug freshman on the Pioneer's team. We had a great bunch of guys, led by four seniors; Patrick, Dallas, Mackee, and a guy named Chris McClure, who came to us from California for his senior year. The four of them rocked. We won NTI's, but the whole experience was, somehow... bittersweet"

"What do you mean?"

"Well, you would've loved Chris."

"Loved?"

"Yeah, you see, Chris didn't let us know, but he was dealing with a defect in his head, Berry's Aneurysm, and he, uh, collapsed in the middle of the meet, and passed away in the hospital while we were competing."

"You weren't by his side?"

"No, he wouldn't let us. His dying wish was for us to finish what we had started. He knew what was coming, but wanted to push right to the end, and passed knowing that we didn't let him down."

Carmen processed while Joey contemplated a rock formation next to him. The roar of the falls was soothing to both the ear and the eye. Carmen walked over and sat next to Joey who was lost in thought, tears welling in his eyes recalling his good friend. She put her arm around his huge shoulders, and he responded with a hug that led to a kiss.

"Live each day, baby!" he said, as he gave her another kiss and rose to his feet.

"At least the walk back is all downhill," she said.

"Yeah, but that tends to hurt my knees just as much as the way out."

"Now who's whining?"

The pair made the trek back down the trail and to their bikes. Joey took his phone from his pack and dialed his mother, "Hey," he said as she answered the phone, "have you made supper plans?... Great! Don't. Let's meet at Calhoun's!... No, we're done here... Yeah, no, she wasn't amused, and I have a gash to prove it... no, I'll tell you all about it over supper.... Ok, see you there in an hour.... bye, mom."

"How sweet. You're gonna take your mama out to eat. What a dutiful son."

"Well, she's buying, so I don't know how dutiful I am."

"You wanting to spend time with your mom is dutiful enough, and another reason to like you, You're so ADORABLE!!" Carmen gave him a peck on the cheek before putting on her helmet and starting her bike. Soon both were leaving Cade's Cove in a cloud of gravel dust.

After a pleasant evening with his mom, and plenty of stories of Joey's childhood to embarrass him, while amusing Carmen, it was soon time to get to bed to rest up for the trip back the next day. The gym may be closed Monday, but school most certainly would not be.

Again, the next morning, Shirley set the pair up with a hearty breakfast and plenty of snacks to eat on the way back for the eight-hour ride back to Michigan. It was Carmen's first trip so far south, and she was hoping it wouldn't be her last.

18

Immediately after school on Monday, Joey rode over to Taylor Center to see how the floor resurfacing was progressing. Even if he couldn't train, he could get some conditioning in. As he made his way to the gym, he noticed that the floor had not been resurfaced.

Great! These clowns are gonna cost us even MORE time! He thought. Then he noticed a commotion coming from down the hallway, in the direction of the cafeteria. As he walked through the doors his jaw dropped at the sight before him.

What on Friday was a cafeteria, now was a complete gymnastics training facility. Along one wall was a wooden elevated platform, at least seventy-feet long, and six-feet high, ending at a ten-foot wide, loose foam pit, around which was set of Parallel Bars on one side, and a High Bar aimed from the other, and opposite the vault runway, a sixty-foot tumbling strip also accessed the huge, foam-filled hole. On the other side of the room, a Ring Tower and a High Bar sat on 32-inch platforms, on either side of the familiar waffle-patterned foam landing mats, with a trampoline on one end and another raised tumbling strip on the other. The rest of the equipment was set up in the middle of the floor, including a brand new 40' x 40' competition spring floor, and up on the new vault runway, a new vault table.

"You know, it does look like a tongue!" shouted Don, as he approached a dumbfounded Joey with a familiar friend in tow.

"Coach Lowery?" Joey was about as confused as his head could possibly be, "How? What?"

"It's really not all that magical, Joe," insisted Coach Lowery, "Don called me right after Gene showed his ugly mug here."

"But the equipment. Is this…?"

"Pioneers equipment? You betcha. Not much market for my old equipment, so when Don called, I thought, what better fate for my gym than to help you continue your quest."

"But you're here! We need a coach, BAD! I mean, if Don won't do it, you certainly could! Please, please, please stay, at least for a while!"

"I had actually planned on being gone before you got back. You weren't supposed to get back until tomorrow. Once I return this truck, I'm on a 6am flight to the coast. I've been invited to work with several other coaches to examine our whole competitive structure. While I'd love to help out, this is an opportunity that doesn't come my way every day, and I'm excited to still be a part of the sport. After that, I have an RV reserved out there, and I'm finally gonna see the country. Not to worry, I'll be back here in March to see how you boys fare for State."

"Yeah, that sounds great. What an opportunity. I totally get it, and wish you luck. You got any ideas?"

"Actually, you do, Joey."

"Huh?"

"You know the process you went through, it's the same for them."

"What do you mean?"

"The same process I took you through to get where you are, did more than prepare you to be a gymnast, it gave you an understanding of how to get from point A to point B. Just repeat it with your teammates."

"Yeah, but what if I get it wrong, or lead these guys down the wrong path and we're not ready?"

"Who says there's only one path? It's different with each guy, each time out. Trust me, what you know about training, conditioning, motion mechanics, and the preparation process will not let you down."

"And now you can stop bitchin' that your gym ain't up to snuff!" added Don, "Since we never use this cafeteria much, and Carmen is the only one using that stage, I figured between me and Jimbo, here, the least I could do is get it done."

"I don't know what to say," said Joey.

"Well, then that was well worth the investment," added Don, "but if you're still fishing for words of gratitude, why don't you try something like, 'I'm so pumped, I can't wait to kick everyone else's butt into a respectable gear'?"

"I was actually thinking I couldn't wait to train in this gym!"

"Well, we still have some finishing to do," said Coach Lowery, "But yeah, go ahead, get reacquainted with your old equipment." Joey tossed his jacket and shoes off to the edge of the Floor Ex carpet, and looked up in time to see Carmen entering the café, equally dumbfounded at the sight.

"What the f....!"

"I knew you'd be a bit steamed, Carmen," said Don, approaching apologetically, "but we didn't touch the stage, that's still yours."

"But what about performances?"

"We only had two performances all last year."

"I know but you promised..."

"I know, but your boyfriend really needs this, plus, it's set up in such a way that we can breakdown most of it, and still have a decent audience seating. It's not like we need hundreds..."

"I get it. I'm not that mad, really," she said, settling down and watching Joey warm up, "besides, I think this will be much better to look at during practice than an empty room."

"That's the spirit!" Don rejoined Jim to continue finishing the equipment layout.

Carmen watched Joey. He was like a kid in a candy store, moving from one event to the other, taking advantage of the new systems in place; vaulting and tumbling into the loose foam, doing dismounts and releases on High Bar, sometimes intentionally overdone, just to crash into a soft landing. She could see he was finally unbridled, cutting loose for the first time since leaving Dagar's Edge over four months ago! Joey was back in his element!

The next day, as each guy entered TC, they were met with a sign at the gym door,

"Wet floor. Report to the cafeteria," and a poorly drawn arrow, pointing down the hall.

Each entered the newly renovated café/gym, with the same sense of disbelief and wonder. In its way, it was even superior to Dagar's, with some crafty, personal touches by Don and coach Lowery.

"Well, what do ya think?" Joey said as Alex, Rod, Bobby, and the Baker boys looked around the new gymnastics factory, "I think y'all are gonna love this."

"Joey, how?" asked a dumbfounded Alex.

"I'll explain as we go. Y'all get your High Bar grips on!" and Joey led them around their new home, showing off the highlights of the different training devices most had never seen before!

"Alright y'all, here's your first lesson about a pit," Joey stepped onto the piston-actuated platform that allowed him to hop onto a support on the High Bar, atop the six-foot deck, a total of over fifteen feet above the floor, with about the same distance between he and the ceiling, "there are four ways you don't land in the pit," Joey casted up to a swing, and started doing giants, speaking at the bottom of each swing, "your knees...your head....your belly.... Or your teammate!" Joey compressed his shape on top of the bar, setting up a dismount that looked like it could challenge that clearance. Joey flipped twice, twisted twice, and disappeared into the foam cubes, feet first.

Alex was next to bend the bar and cut loose with a little more torque than he had used in quite some time! Bobby, and the Baker's picked up the swing and tap technique fairly quickly, but Rod was having trouble creating the action and managed to ping out, horizontal, with only half a flip, landing him head first in the foam.

"I DON'T GET IT!" Rod could be heard even though he was buried, upside-down, to his waist in the pit.

"It's 'cuz you're weak, Rodney!" shouted Joey. Rodney twisted and contorted his body until he had extricated himself.

"Whachu mean I'm weak? Check 'dis!" Rodney flexed his growing, but still developing, biceps.

"Great, but I'm talking about your core!"

"My core?"

"Yes, your core. That part of your body that makes you strong enough do what you want the rest of your body to do!"

"What?"

"Here's the part where you start getting stronger, Rod," said Joey, "Let's start running, y'all." And the team began jogging around the gym.

"I have an idea," said Alex, "Indian Runs!" Joey glanced to the back to see Bobby pulling up the rear.

"BOBBY!" yelled Joey.

"What?"

"You have to sprint to the front!"

"Why?"

"So, Tommy can pass you!"

"Huh?"

"Just do it!" Bobby picked up his pace to a near sprint and passed the team to get in front.

"TOMMY!" called Joey. Tommy picked up his pace to get ahead of the others. By the time he got to the front, everybody had the idea. Rodney sprinted to the front, then Timmy, then Alex, then Joey. As Joey closed in on Alex, Alex picked up his pace, putting more distance between he and Joey, making it harder for Joey to catch him, much less pass.

"C'mon, Joey!" shouted Alex. Joey found another gear and passed Alex.

"Dick," Joey said upon passing Alex. Alex chuckled. Once Bobby saw Joey hit the front he took off. The boys continued to pass each other all the way to the last lap, then it was down to Joey again. As he broke out to start his move, Bobby picked up his pace to prevent Joey's move. In turn, Tommy picked up his pace to prevent Bobby's pass. Within seconds, the entire team was in a full sprint around the gym.

"Alright, boys, bring it in!" shouted Joey, "Walk a lap, get a drink, and then we'll start pre-strength!"

"What's pre-strength?" asked Timmy.

"Shape conditioning," answered Joey, "basics done with perfect form."

The team finished pre-strength and went to work on events, starting with basic swings and building up to their hardest skills. Don was impressed with the Baker Boys, who were able to hold their own on P-Bars and High Bar, they had a full line up for floor and vault, but Pommel Horse and Rings would be the most critical events. Don hadn't seen Bobby break dance so he was surprised to see what the sophomore could do on the floor.

"Wow. Bobby, can you put that on a horse?"

"I don't know, I've never tried!" Don took the pommels off of the horse so he only had to concentrate on his swing, and not worry about hitting wood.

"I want you to start at the end, do a few circles, then get into flairs and see if you can travel across the horse." Bobby jumped up and started swinging, then moved to flairs. He wasn't sure how Coach wanted him to travel, so he accelerated and elevated his flairs until he was doing Air Flairs, almost in a handstand, turning and hopping, eventually going from end to end effortlessly, finishing with a pirouetting handstand and dropping to the mat. Don, Alex, and Joey were stunned..

"Dude, are you kidding me?" said Alex, "That is the most wicked combo I've ever seen!"

"Can you do that with pommels on the horse?" asked Joey.

"I don't know. Do I have to do it on them?" asked Bobby.

"No, not that combination," said Don, "you will have to learn how to swing up there, but I want to see that same combo around the pommels!" Joey and Alex put the pommels back in place and secured the bolts that held them in place. Bobby hopped up and repeated the combination, exactly the same way!

"Do you have any idea how amazing that combo is?" asked Alex. Bobby shook his head.

"Okay," said Joey, "now let's learn some basic requirements to set up that set!" Joey demonstrated some basic circles and scissors and, after a few turns, Bobby had figured it out.

Don added his two cents, "When your right hand hits the pommel, push your hip real hard and that will accelerate you through the circle and into the next one. It will also make it easier to get up into that Air Flair combo." Bobby went to work on his new routine.

At the end of the workout, Don stressed the importance of not only being strong, but having the endurance to get through a tough, complex routine. Then he proceeded to exercise the team to the point of exhaustion.

"THAT'S what I needed!" said Joey as he fell into a pool of his own sweat.

"Me, too," said Alex, "probably the best workout I've ever had!"

"Best I've had in a year, at least!" said Joey.

"So that's what a real workout feels like?" asked Bobby, "I am spent."

"Yep, now you gotta clue, Bob," said Joey.

Timmy and Tommy dragged themselves to join the group.

"You know, I remember working hard at Dagar's," said Timmy, "but I don't think I remember a single day that I enjoyed it."

"Being goal directed and having guys around that, genuinely want you to be better makes a big difference," said Don.

"Does that mean you'll coach us?" asked Joey.

"Nope. I'll be glad to do little lecture deals like today, but you are gonna have to do most of the heavy lifting."

"I guess we'll take whatever we can get, Coach!" said Alex.

"That's 'Don', or better still, 'Mr. Wheatley' to you!" he responded, somewhat seriously.

"Whatever, Coach, I mean Don, I mean Mr. Wheatley!"

The guys picked up their things and dragged their way back to the locker room.

As the team wrapped up their showers, Don poked his head in to the shower room, "Hey guys, can you come to my office when you're done?"

"Sure thing, Don," answered Joey. Once they were dressed the team went to Don's office.

"Ok, good, follow me guys." Curiously the six followed Coach Wheatley through the gym, into the hallway and through a door marked 'custodian'. As they entered, it was apparent that they were now in the school's boiler room. Following Don down a set of stairs, the team found themselves gathered around a set of boxes.

"With all of what has happened," said Don, "I've notice you haven't taken time to consider uniforms."

"We still have plenty of time to get them," said Joey, "We'll just order stock stuff."

"That's what I thought you'd say. I'd like for you to consider an alternative," Don bent over and opened one of the boxes. Inside was several gold colored step-ins. In the center of the chest was the familiar overlay TC of the Taylor Center logo.

"Are these the uniforms you guys wore?" asked Alex.

"Indeed, they are, Alex. I'm not sure how many we have, or how many are worth wearing, but you could use these. I mean, if you want."

"It would be an honor," said Joey, stunned as he pulled up a step-in.

"Not exactly Lycra," said Alex, "a bit out dated."

"Perhaps, but can you imagine the look on Dagar's face when we walk in with these on?" asked Joey.

"I think he'll probably laugh," said Timmy.

"He'll laugh," said Tommy.

"Well, they're here if you want to use them," said Coach Wheatley.

"Thanks, Don!" Joey felt honored to be holding the uniform that his coach had worn to win State Championships, thirty years ago. Then he put the jersey back in the box.

"What's the matter, Joey?" asked Coach Wheatley.

"I don't know, it's like … we haven't earned the right."

"Are you kidding?" demanded Alex, "Who but us deserve to wear these?"

"But we haven't done anything, yet."

"Well, what do you assume we do for a uniform, if not these?" asked Timmy. Rodney picked up one of the gold warm up jackets "Taylor Center" across the back.

"Are these, polyester?" asked Rodney.

"Back to plan A, we order stock uniforms."

"But that costs money, Joe," said Alex, "not only are these very cool, they're free!"

"Alex, these jerseys are over thirty years old! We don't even know if they'll hold up!" added Don, "I'd sure hate for you guys to get into the middle of an important meet and have your uniforms fall apart."

"Yeah, but Don," said Alex, "I don't think you've fully embraced the entertainment potential!"

"That may be true, Alex," said Joey, "but do we really want to take a chance on becoming disrobed in the middle of a competition?"

"We'd certainly make the news," said Rodney, "and the only guys brave enough to be seen in polyester since the 70's!"

"Yeah, for all the wrong reasons," conceded Joey.

"So, stock it is?" The team agreed and placed the jerseys back in the box they came from, "they'll be here if you boys have a change of heart," Don assured.

The team climbed the steps and filed out of the boiler room, then went their separate ways. Joey, of course, walked back to the café to see if Carmen had finished.

19

By the time the last golden leaves had given up their hold on Michigan elms, the Taylor Center boys had figured out how to train in their new gym. The new pits, both the six-foot deep, loose foam and the three-foot deep soft-land, made progressions easier, and awkward landings much more forgiving, which accelerated the learning process. It had only been three weeks since Coach Lowery created 'Pioneers North' with his equipment, but the results were paying dividends; Rodney's tumbling and vaulting were becoming much more streamlined, more powerful, more predictable and repeatable, and considerably more difficult. The Baker Boys were making significant progress on the swing events, Rings, Parallel Bars, and High Bar. The only one who really didn't benefit from the move, was Bobby and Pommel Horse. While the pits, spotting apparatus, and new gizmos, were great for speeding up the learning process on all the other events, there really wasn't much that could make Pommel Horse any easier. Since Pommel Horse didn't require pits, and is rather portable, the station was located closest to the front of the café/gym. But it didn't matter where the horse was located, its riders would still get bucked.

"OWW, DAMN IT!" Bobby was able to scream between his collision with the pommel and his impact with the landing mat.

"You didn't put a dent in my favorite pommel, did you, Bob?" Joey teased.

"No, but I assure you there plenty of divots in my shins to make up for any damage I could've possibly done to that friggin' piece of devil wood!" Bobby checked for any sign of blood. Nothing this time.

"So, what's the issue, you think?" asked Joey.

"Well, swinging on the leather I think I have figured out, and stepping up onto the pommel hasn't been terrible, but once I try to do any turning on the pommel, I slow down and hit stuff!"

"Have you tried swinging a bigger circle with your shoulders to build some speed?"

"Yeah, but then I usually end up off balance, and BANG, face-plant!" Bobby replied, rubbing his shins.

"Have you thought about creating more torque?" came a voice from the entry.

Joey looked up to see a visitor in the doorway.

"Logan Merwin," said a surprised Joey, "mind if I ask what you're doing here?"

"I need a place to train."

"What makes you think this is that place? After all, you and Keith made sure I didn't have a place to train, and set yourselves up pretty cushy with Coach Dagar."

"Yeah, about that."

"Look who it is!" said Alex, joining the group, "Whatchu doin', Merwin? Doin' a little ReCon for Herr Dagar?"

"We got booted, me and Keith." Logan said, his head down.

"WHAT?" mocked Alex, "THIS IS RICH! You guys plot to screw us over, nearly put my drug dealer friend in jail..."

"I'm not a drug dealer..."

"...the stunt gets us kicked out, and you guys, you got sack to come here?"

"Wasn't my idea. I just drove. I told him it was dumb. I thought it was stupid. I wanted to compete straight up with you guys, and Pitts didn't want to hedge his bets against you guys."

"So, what happened to Keith?" asked Joey.

"When the judgement came down, and Dagar lost those titles,

he went ballistic! Called us into his office and chewed us out for an hour. Screaming about all he had done, how we could've ruined him and kicked us out on the spot, but not before berating us in front of everyone, screaming about traitors and fate, all the way to the door, where he escorted us out, and actually kicked Keith in the ass as we left."

"Quality human being, there," said Alex, "Oh, to have been a fly on the wall."

"And what about Keith? Where is he going to go?" asked Joey.

"Why do you care?" asked Alex, "Dude, he deserves whatever fate comes his way!"

"I wouldn't worry too much about Keith," said Logan, "I'm sure once Coach Dagar brings his blood pressure to acceptable levels, he'll find he's short at least one decent score, and Keith will find his way back to Dagar."

"You think so?" asked Joey.

"Man, you know Keith, no one else in this town wants his attitude in their gym, even with his talent. He and Dagar were made for each other."

"Think Dagar will ask you back? I mean, your gym is a bit better than Keith, I could tell from the mock meet. You sure he won't come to you first?"

"Yeah, no. Keith is the third Pitts to train under Dagar, they have history. Me, I'm as foreign to him as you guys. Besides, why would I want to go back to that? I dig gym, but my happiness and well-being come first. And Dagar's gym was a necessary evil. That is, until you guys dressed this place up. Nice job, I might add."

"Thanks," said Joey, "So, you want to train here? We don't even have a coach."

"I think you sell yourself short. You got Keith to add a bunch of difficulty for the mock meet. Dagar had been trying for a year to get him to do that. I saw you cheer us all on, regardless of how you did, which was friggin' phenomenal, by the way, and you put Dagar and his whole team of Hitler youth in fits. I don't care if you don't know a kip from a Kohlman, I'd rather train and lose with you than give up my soul to those vampires!"

"Joey, tell me you're not buying this?" pleaded Alex, "this smells of a set-up, pal. We are finally headed in the right direction, we just got all this stuff and the other guys are figuring out. We don't need this guy, or that drama!"

"But we sure could use a solid third score..." said Bobby, "especially on horse!"

"Your pig is just fine, Bobby," said Alex, "what we *don't* need is more drama!"

"Like the kind you're creating right now, Al?" said Joey. Silence.

"Look, I'm not looking to create trouble, I just want to train. Trust me, don't trust me, I don't care. Let me train off in a corner if it makes you feel better. You may have haters out there, but I'm not one of 'em. But, if it's more important to ..."

"Welcome to Taylor Center," Joey interrupted.

"Wha...?" Alex was stunned.

"Look, Logan, as much as I want to see you burn for what y'all did to me, you seem sincere."

"He *seems* sincere, Joe, but it could just as well be a trap!" conspired Alex.

"To what end, Al? Is he gonna sabotage the gym? Give away our training secret of total disorganization? Maybe throw the meet when we need him most? Maybe. Maybe not. Maybe Logan is just as much a misfit as the rest of us. Which do you think is most likely? That Logan got caught in a stupid plot that cost him his gym, and now he probably wants just as much to get back at them as us, or that he is some hired plant, whose sole mission is to pretend to be our friend so we will count on him, and at just the right moment, bails on us just in time to spoil our plans of beating a team that doesn't think we have a chance to begin with?"

Alex furrowed his brow, "Most likely? The second option sounds truer."

"You gotta stop reading tabloids, Al, they're rotting your brain.

At the very worst, we lose. So, what. The more I think about it, the less I care about Dagar and his crew. We are doing an awesome thing here, and I think we should consider this a sign that what we're doing is much bigger than just revenge."

"Dude, I'm supposed to be the hippie-idealist, you're supposed to be the pragmatic realist."

"So? Can I join, train, compete, you know, um, be a … *a Ram?*" Logan asked.

Joey called the others, "Y'all! Bring it in!" the team gathered at the Pommel Horse, "Y'all, this here is Logan Merwin. He was the guy who drove the car in the little plot to frame me. Now, don't go judgin', he's here with hat in hand, sayin' they kicked him and Keith off the team and Logan could go about anywhere, but he thinks he wants to train, of all places, right here with us. As I'm willing to extend the olive branch to bring him on board with us, I just don't feel comfortable about accepting him if anyone here has a question about my call. So, we know how Alex feels, does anyone else have any questions for Mr. Merwin, or me for that matter?"

The team thought about their concerns, none were significant enough to be voiced.

"Can you swing pig?" asked Bobby.

"My start value is close to 15," he replied.

"He can stay," Bobby concluded.

"Well, if no one has a problem…" Joey looked around, "Logan Merwin, welcome to Taylor Center!" Each of the guys welcomed Logan to the crew, even Alex, who conceded a solid, third Pommel Horse score was worth the risk.

"Now, what was it you were saying about torque?" asked Joey.

"Sure," replied Logan, pulling off his shirt and shoes, and approaching the horse, "if you turn your shoulders a little quicker going into the turn on the pommel, you can create a little more tension between the shoulders and the hips…"

"That, in turn, you can pull the hips and legs around faster," added Joey, "increasing the speed of the circle without having to get the shoulders out of line. Brilliant!" Bobby watched as Logan exaggerated the example, and followed him with his own version, quickly making the correction, and easing into balanced, turning circles on the pommels!

Now, we are set! Joey thought.

As the workout came to a close, and the team began to disperse, Joey stayed out on the spring floor to do standing back tuck to stick.

"What are you doing?" asked Logan.

"Just thinking of my workouts back in Tennessee. We would finish with what we called the 'Pioneer Circle'. We would yell, "PIONEERS!" and back tuck stick until there was only one left."

"Sounds good," replied Logan, "I'm in, but we can't chant Pioneers."

"Go, Rams?"

"Sounds good to me."

"Fine," chirped Alex, "you guys go ahead and flip 'till you puke. I'm hungry, how about you, Rod?"

"I'm always hungry, but are we gonna do this?"

"C'mon, guys," pleaded Alex, "can't we do this tomorrow?"

"If you're in a hurry, just punk out early. No one will judge," said Logan.

"Yeah, right, if you're not already judging me. Let's get this over with."

The team circled the floor. Joey, Alex, Logan, Bobby, Rodney, Timmy and Tommy shouted in unison, "GO RAMS!" followed by simultaneous back tucks to stick. Joey shouted "AGAIN!"

"GO RAMS!" all flipped, all stuck.

"AGAIN!"

"GO RAMS!" all flipped, all stuck.

"You sure you wanna go through with this, Joey?" asked Alex.

"AGAIN!" Joey shouted.

"GO RAMS!" all flipped, all stuck, although Alex was a half-beat behind.

"AGAIN!"

"Wait, wait, wait," said Alex, "Let's save some time. How about back tuck, punch front, stick? It's harder and more impressive. Instead of flipping, over and over, we go until everyone sticks?"

"Dude, I like it!" said Logan.

"Of course, you like it, Merwin, it's a good idea, and you're a suck up. The question is, does Joey like it."

"It is a great way to separate us from your past, Joe," added Bobby.

"Fine. Let's do this!" The boys prepared and Joey chanted, "GO RAMS!" The team replied, "GO RAMS!" and did back tuck to immediate punch front tuck. Only three of the seven stuck, Rodney ended up on his bottom, "I thought this would be easier," he said.

Once Rodney got to his feet, Joey shouted, "AGAIN!"

"GO RAMS!" back tuck, punch front. All stuck.

"Yeah!" shouted Rodney, "that was cool!" the guys high-fived and started toward the door. Alex stayed back and got Joey away from the rest.

"Are you sure having Logan on team is a good idea?"

"Al, what else are we gonna do?"

"What if he does bail?"

"Then he bails. I don't see how having him is an issue. Even if he does let us down how are we any worse off than if we just boot him out?"

"It's not leaving that I'm really worried about, it's what could be done with a little destructive social sabotage."

"You really need to lay off the Conspiracy Theory Channel," concluded Joey.

"Yeah, well I guess you have nothing to worry about."

"What does that mean?" Joey looked at Alex who was looking at the reunion on the other end of the gym.

"Are you taking me out to eat or..." Carmen burst into the

gym and directly into the chest of Logan Merwin, "I'm so sorry... Logan?"

"Hey, Carmen."

"What are you... how did you?... Does Joey know you're here?"

"Haha, yeah we just finished."

"We? Are you... here, now?"

"Yeah, after you guys got Dagar in hot water, Keith and I got booted, and Joey was kind enough to take me in."

"So, you're not mad about the whole car thing? By the way, I am so sorry I treated you so mean. I mean, you're really a nice guy, but..."

"Forget it. You actually did me a big favor. I was trying to find a way out as soon as that stunt got out of hand. I think I knew you were scamming me. As soon as I pulled away it occurred to me why you would do such a thing, but then I was relieved at the thought, and just let the wheels of justice turn."

"So, no hard feelings?"

"Are you kidding? I'm relieved. I was so worried that you guys wouldn't accept me."

"Well, I'm sure as long as you are an asset, and not a liability, you'll be welcomed!"

"Thanks, I think?"

Carmen gave Logan a big hug, "All is forgiven...for now," she said.

"First day and I have to question your intentions, Logan?" said Joey as he and Alex approached.

"Not at all, Joey, just burying the hatchet over the car ride I gave Carmen, when she grabbed that note that led to Keith's, and my, downfall after he tried to frame you."

"I wouldn't consider it a downfall, more of an upgrade," exclaimed Joey, "You're in high cotton, now, boy!" Joey flipped the breakers that killed the lights, and locked the doors behind him, "I think we need to go get some food and get reacquainted. What do you say?"

"I got no other plans," said Logan.

"No way I'm missing this," added Alex, "you're buying, right?"

"No, I'll get Carmen's, the rest are Dutch Treat."

"I can always eat, but I don't know…" said Alex.

"How about my treat?" said Logan.

"Even better!" exclaimed Alex, "Sports Games and Grub?"

"Sounds perfect!" agreed Logan. And the group dispersed and headed toward Detroit.

Located within view of Joe Lewis Arena and the Renascence Center, "Sport Games and Grub" was a magnet for hungry sports enthusiasts, especially when the home teams were on the road, and quite crowded for a Monday night. Joey grabbed a table, as Alex roamed around the game floor, examining all of the different video games, as well as the Skeet-ball, Corn-hole, and other activities that required more than just a quick, joy-stick reflex. While Alex examined the quality of the games, Joey and Carmen sat with Logan, to hear his story.

"So, how did you become a gymnast?" asked Carmen.

"Well, my folks thought it would be a good idea to toughen me up."

"So, they put you in gymnastics?" asked Joey.

"No, dance actually."

"And your parents thought dance would make you tougher?" asked Carmen.

"No, my folks thought they were giving me culture. Once the kids in the neighborhood found out that I was dancing, that made me tougher."

"So, you got into some fights?"

"Only one. The boys had been running me pretty hard, teasing as boys do, and Jamal Preston, my best friend at the time, crossed a line, and I hit him. Hard. He dropped like a rock on one punch! Jamal was kinda the neighborhood leader, and the other kids looked up to him. Once he woke up and told the other guys to leave me alone. All was good."

"So, how did you end up in gymnastics?" asked Joey.

"After that encounter with Jamal, I decided I needed more of a challenge, so I started working out at a little storefront gym. They weren't very progressive, they didn't even have a program for boys at the time, but they gave me enough with basics, and I kept moving from gym to gym to try to get what I wanted. I really thought Dagar's Edge was the pinnacle of what I was shooting for."

"And now?" prodded Joey.

"Pfft. What a joke. He can get guys to produce, but not the most wholesome environment."

"You can say that again," added Joey.

Logan continued, "Naw, what you guys are doing at Taylor Center is awesome. This is what I envisioned when I was looking for something better: a place where I could train on my own terms, with a bunch of guys just as jazzed about my progress as their own. I think, once you get a full-time coach, someone really good, like Don, this place will take off! You'd be surprised how many good guys are out there, that just have a bad taste from Dagar's, that would love to train in what you've created. And, now that you've got new equipment and all, I wouldn't be surprised if you have guys lined up out the door!" As Logan finished his comment, the wait help, dressed as football officials, delivered drinks.

"I don't know about that," replied Joey, "but it sure has been an adventure to get to here!"

"Well, here's to the future of Taylor Center Gymnastics!" Logan said, raising his Coke in salute, quickly joined by Carmen and Joey.

"What are you guys doing?" asked Alex, arriving at the table, "there are games to be played!"

"We are trying to get to know Logan a little more," answered Joey.

"There's only one thing you need to know about this guy; can he play Air Hockey?" suggested Alex.

"Air Hockey?" asked Logan, "I've never played."

"Perfect. We will get a real good idea of who you are after you take the drubbing coming your way!"

"Probably not the best way," suggested Joey.

"Who died and made you smart? C'mon Merwin." Alex grabbed the sleeve of the newest Taylor team member, and pulled him from his chair, as he grabbed one more gulp of cola before being dragged to the Air Hockey table.

"Y'all go ahead, Carmen and I will enjoy the show from here." Alex led the way and supplied the hands full of quarters it would take to play several games. Alex loaded the required number of coins, and the game came to life, the sound of air being forced through pin-holes in the table surface.

"You know how this works, right?"

"Um, it's hockey. Score more goals."

"Bingo, Merwin. You ready? First one to ten." Logan nodded to signal such, and Alex quickly executed a two-wall bank shot to score the first goal, "Sorry, that was quick. Were you ready?"

"Yes. Good shot." Quickly, Alex was three goals in front. With each goal, Alex became louder while Logan became more focused. Within minutes, the score was tied at five each.

"Now, you're catching on!" exclaimed Alex, "I'm gonna stop holding back now. You ready?"

Alex's query was answered in a heartbeat, as Logan scored a quick two goals to take a 7-5 lead.

"Are you sure you haven't played this before?" asked Alex.

"I'm sure, but it does have a pretty flat learning curve," he replied as he scored another goal.

"Hey! I wasn't ready for that! The goal shouldn't count!"

"Shouldn't count? Why?"

"You distracted me!"

"How?"

"You're talking! How am I supposed to concentrate?"

"Kinda the same way I've been concentrating during your trash talk."

"Trash talk?! You haven't seen the beginning of my…" Logan scored another goal, raising Alex's blood pressure.

"WAIT UNTIL I'M READY!" Yelled Alex, now only one goal away from defeat.

"Are you ready, now?" Logan asked, waiting for Alex to calm down.

"Yes," replied Alex. And before the 's' sound in 'yes' came out of Alex's mouth, the puck landed in Joey's goal. Deciding the outcome.

"GAME!" shouted Logan.

"Best two-out-of-three!" shouted Alex.

"Nope. I see what this game does to you. Perhaps you should pick a less intense game. Maybe Skee-ball." If Logan was sincerely trying to help, it didn't work. The only thing that would satisfy Alex was to see Logan lose it, which the more they played on, the calmer Logan was, and the more unhinged Alex became.

"THAT'S IT. I'VE HAD IT!" announced Alex, "I'm out of here!" and Alex stormed out the door, without ordering anything.

"I thought he was hungry?" said Carmen.

"He probably forgot about that," said Logan, returning to the table, cheeseburger and fries waiting for him, "excellent," he exclaimed, jamming the sandwich into his face.

"You have to forgive Alex," said Carmen, "he's very competitive, at times."

"I've not seen that side in the gym," said Joey.

"The competitiveness or the temper?" asked Logan.

"Both," answered Joey, "he's a great gymnast, but most of the time he waits for others to do something before he tries harder. It's almost like he's content with where he is, as long as he is better than the pack. As soon as someone looks like they're closing in on him, he steps up, creates some good gymnastics, and then it's back to just maintaining."

"Hmm," wondered Logan, "I wonder how that affects his competing?"

"It doesn't seem to," replied Carmen, "I've been watching him for years and he doesn't seem to get rattled."

"But has he ever been in a 'make it or else scenario?" asked Joey.

"He didn't have a great State meet last year," she added, "come to think of it, he hasn't had a good State meet since he was young boy."

"I've seen this before," said Joey, "he's content as long as he is the top dog. Once someone looks like they are gaining ground, he steps up another level, all to stay above only the guys in the gym. Once they are in a meet that matters, they tend to choke."

"Not a good sign going forward," said Logan.

"Well, we are just going to have to keep him pumped."

"Like, let him win?" asked Logan.

"No, not that, maybe just be that thing that makes him up his game without frustrating him to quitting."

"And how do we get him to compete better?" asked Logan.

"I'm still working on that one," replied Joey. The three dove into their meals, while sharing anecdotes and experiences that had brought them to where they were. *This guy is the REAL DEAL!* Joey thought.

20

If Alex was holding a grudge, it didn't show. Back in the gym, the work continued. While Alex had become less social, and more focused, he wasn't beyond cutting up to break the mood. While Joey could feel the uncomfortable tension, he knew it was what Alex really needed to stay on task. Today was a floor day, and Joey's mission was to teach Rodney how to use a pit.

"That was terrible!" Joey said.

"Is that any way to encourage me?" asked Rodney, after pulling himself from the loose-foam pit.

"You don't need encouragement, Rod, you need a brain. You're using this pit all wrong."

"How so?"

"Dude, you're trying to do a double-back, right?"

"And I'm getting I around to my feet!" Rodney defended.

"But you're barely head height, and traveling ten feet back into the foam!"

"But, I'm getting it around!"

"IN THE PIT! You are not going up at all, just trying to get to the pit."

"Because it would suck if I didn't make it to the pit."

"That's my point! You think it's about making it to the pit. Nothing could be less important."

"You expect me to miss the pit?"

"NO, dummy, I mean that trying to get to the pit should not even be a consideration, much less a priority."

"You wanna kill me?"

"Not at all. You know how we have that strip of tape on the floor as a target for your hands in the round-off?"

"Sure."

"THAT'S what gets you to the pit! When you get to the end of the floor, your ONLY JOB is to go up. Everything you do in front of the punch is what makes it go up, makes it rotate, and gets you to the foam."

"But..."

"No 'buts'. C'mere," Joey motioned for Rodney to join him on the floor. Joey positioned a large mat, 32" tall, at one end of the diagonal, and placed a strip of athletic tape about 15 feet away. "OK, tumble up onto that," he said. Rodney did a couple passes to make sure the spacing was correct, and gave it a go. Straight up, without much rotation, landing him, mostly, on his head, sinking into the mat.

"Good," said Joey, "direction is right, but you need to stand up faster, so we have some rotation!"

Rodney tried three more times, until he figured out how to go up and create the height and rotation he would need to over-rotate one-and-three quarters, to land on his shoulder blades.

"THAT'S IT!" yelled Joey, "Now, let me see two more like that!" It took four turns to get the required two, and Joey took Rodney back up to the elevated strip, leading to the foam pit. Rodney walked back to the edge of the strip, Joey took his place next to the pit to have the best angle on Rodney's take off. "Now, just like down there," Joey said, pointing down at the drill station they had just left. Rodney took a deep breath, focused on mark on the floor for his first hand of his round-off, and leaned into a jump to start his run. The adrenaline kicked in, and the increase in speed made it hard to control. By the time he got to the pit, Rodney had rotated too much to make the punch go up, instead he shot back, almost to the back of the sixteen-foot pit, never rising more than his waist, but made two flips around, disappearing in a fetal position into the loose foam.

"I'm guessing not quite it?" Rodney said as he pulled his head from its impingement.

"Roger, Rod," agreed Joey," let's try again." Joey reached down to lend Rodney a hand out of the pit.

"Dude, you would think that in this day and age they would figure out an easier way to get out of a pit. Like a rope or somethin'?"

"Well, it's much easier getting out if you don't start from a cranial perch."

"I dig."

"You ever play golf, Rod?" asked Joey.

"Is this a racial thing?"

"No, no, seriously, have you played golf before?"

"Yeah, I swung a club."

"Like, a driving range?"

"Yeah, that."

"Ever been on the links? Played nine holes?"

"Once or twice. What's your point?"

"How are your drives at a driving range?"

"Not bad, I guess. I can smack a ball."

"How many in a straight line?"

"What's your point, man?"

"Do your drives out on the course, in a match, match what you do at the range?"

"Not usually."

"That's right, because when it matters, you try a little too hard, which is not the same."

"And?"

"Believe it or not, you're gonna get more power from slowing down."

"WHAT?!"

"Do what you did down there, no different. When you get to the punch, get your arms and chest up as fast as you can, but tumble with power and position, not just speed you can't control." Rodney made his way back to his starting point. Joey jumped down from the platform and grabbed a small mat, and brought it up on the strip.

"What is that for?" asked Rodney, suspecting he was going to be a Guinea pig for something. Joey opened up the panel mat and made a four-foot wall at the edge of the pit.

"Just pretend this is the drill. This mat is just as tall as those mats stacked, so you know you've already cleared it. Once you have, THEN tuck."

"Right…" Rodney doubted. He checked his mark, took a breath and tried to imagine not dying in the attempt. Rod jumped into his start, and all looked well, until he broke down in the handspring, plowing into the mat, taking it with him deep into the back of the pit.

"I guess not like that," Rodney surmised from a much more comfortable place in the pit, on his back on the panel mat.

"Not quite. First, you're gonna have to trust what you're doing. What are you afraid of?"

"Dying?"

"How?"

"I don't know. It's just so…"

"Different, unusual, sure but unsafe? Think about it, you know you can clear, easy. Just get to that part. If it feels weird, just don't grab your knees, just drop into the pit on your back. You just need one of those to get it."

Rodney marched back to his mark, more pissed than scared, he wanted to break the floor with each step, but choose instead, to focus on control through the tumbling, and maximize the punch.

"You got this!" said Joey.

Rodney jumped into his run, controlled, but purposeful, gaining speed through the hurdle, he pushed into a strong round-off, back handspring and shot straight up! As soon as he knew he had cleared the mat, he drew his legs into the tiniest tuck he could manage.

One-two-THREE flips before vanishing again into the blue pit-foam!

"WAS THAT IT?! WAS THAT IT?!" yelled Rodney as he pulled his head up, like a groundhog on February second.

"Heck Yeah, man! You got any idea what you did?"

"A double, I think."

"Try triple!"

"What?"

"Yep. I mean, you will likely never compete that, but it sure will make the doubles easier."

"Why not do the triple?"

"Risk-reward. You have so much to do, besides this pass, to be competitive. This skill is easy two years away. The time you take working this skill is time taken away from everything else."

"What if I get "everything else" done first?"

"Then, of course, this is one thing you could work on, but your fundamentals have to come first."

"I know, I know, I just hate it when you put barriers on a man. Regardless of whether I can ever compete it, you didn't have to shoot it down on day one."

"True that. Sorry man. My point made, that was friggin' awesome!"

"So, let me try it."

"Rodney," Joey pleaded, "don't you think you should figure out how to land two before you think about doing three?"

"Aw, C'mon, I'll work on two, but I just want to try."

"OK. Rod, a couple tries, just for fun."

"AWESOME!" Rodney jogged back to his start point and Joey took his place at the edge of the pit.

"I'm gonna give you a bump on this one, just remember, 'when in doubt, ball out'!"

"Huh?"

"Don't try to figure this one out, just stay tucked until everything stops moving."

Rodney checked his mark and eyed the edge of the pit, where he planned on exerting the most force. With a hop and a step, he drove his frame across the spring floor, stretching his round-off, back handspring into a tight, long explosion through his point of attack. As Rodney stood up, Joey gave him a boost, pushing his lower back, sending him higher than he would've achieved alone. One-two-three! Rodney disappeared into the foam, still tucked in a ball.

"Awesome!" he exclaimed, "let's throw in a mat!"

"Seriously? It took both of us to get that around! You might want to do a few more into foam, first."

"I got this." Rodney proclaimed as he marched, defiantly, back to his starting point.

"Right." Joey tossed the mat he used as a wall, and grabbed an eight-inch thick mat, one he knew would be very forgiving, in the event of an errant turn, which Joey was all but sure it would be.

"You want another bump?" Joey asked.

"Nope, got this."

"Roger, Rodney. You are cleared for takeoff."

Rodney took a huge breath and puffed it out, shrugging his shoulders, then exploded into his run. Although it had all the energy and angles of the previous turn, lacking Joey's help, it didn't have quite the height or rotation, causing Rodney to land face first, in a fetal position, as the vinyl covered mat folded up around him.

"Hahaha. That was a lot closer than I thought it was gonna be, Rod!" Exclaimed Joey, lowering his intertwined fingers from covering his eyes.

"Wait a minute, I got this!" Rodney shouted as he climbed out of the pit.

"Are you sure you want to put yourself through this, Rod?"

"Two more tries."

"Think you'll live through two more tries?"

"Watch me."

Rodney tried twice more, but faced both turns before turning to Joey, "Okay, I'll work on landing two."

"Good man."

Joey gave Rodney a high five and Rodney went back to his start and Joey jumped down off the platform to get to his own training.

As Joey arrived at Pommel Horse, Logan and Bobby were just finishing up.

"You wanna see my new combo?" asked Bobby.

"Sure."

Bobby jumped up on the horse, and began swinging flairs on the leather on one end. After three flairs, he popped up into his air flairs, hopping around one pommel, before pirouetting to a handstand on both pommels and dropping down into a scissor.

"NICE! You figured out how to get out of the air-flair! Sweet!"

"Thanks, Joey!" Bobby grabbed his gear and headed for the showers.

"I could use a little of that," said Logan.

"What's that?" asked Joey, strapping on his wrist guards.

"Figuring it out."

"I don't read, man. Figure what out? Pommels? I think you have that worked out."

"No, Floor. I saw you work with Rodney, and I could use some help."

"No offense, but I think we're thick on Floor. Between me, Alex, and Timmy, or Tommy, whichever one tumbles so well, and Rodney coming up, I think focusing on Pommels and the swing events will help the team best, right now."

"Yeah, but I need to get better at Floor, it's my weakest event and really puts dent in my All Around."

"I get that, but look at it like this, the time you spend trying to fix Floor could be time spent on beefing up the events where you are more likely to count for team, AND increase your All Around and the team score at the same time."

"I guess you're right. I just wish there was a way to increase value without such a long learning curve."

"Have you thought of the non-acro element group?" asked Joey,

"You have a dance background. Why don't you get with Carmen and the Code of Points and see if you can dance your way into a higher start value." Logan glanced up at the stage where Carmen was going through her routine. She was working on leaps.

"You sure you're good with that?"

"As long as it's just dancing, and it doesn't detract from the other priorities."

"I'm sure you'll let me know."

"You know it. Now, unless you got something to show me here, I'm gonna let this horse beat me up for a while."

"Naw, I've paid my pound of flesh, literally, it's all yours!" Logan grabbed his water bottle and headed toward to back of the gym, where Carmen was into turn and leap combinations.

Just as Joey jumped up into his first set of circles, Don appeared in the doorway and watched the junior swing. Joey moved effortlessly from part to part on the horse, doing five fast circles on each, pushing to stretch and speed up each circle, ending with pommel loop to handstand and pirouette to the end and drop.

"'Five on five', is what my coach called it," said Don.

"Funny that's what my coach called it, too," replied Joey, knowing his coach's coach and Don's coach were one in the same.

"It was a great warm up 30 years ago, and you make it look easy."

"Thanks, like I said, I had a great coach."

Don looked out into the gym as Joey jumped up for another endurance turn of Pommel Horse. Rodney was up on the strip, working on his double back, already progressing to a big mat in the pit. The Baker Brothers were both on Parallel Bars, working giants, Alex was working his in-bar combinations on High Bar, and Bobby was finishing up leg lifts on the wall bars. The newest member, Logan, was making small talk with Carmen.

"Looks like you have the makings of a pretty good team, here, Joe," said Don as Joey dismounted from his turn.

"Thanks, Coach, I MEAN, Don!"

"No worries, son, I get called dad, mom, coach, and worse. How's it looking from your side?"

"Not too bad. We actually got lucky with Logan showing up. Between he, Alex, and myself, we could probably take on the Edge guys."

"So, you gonna dump on the misfits"

"Misfits? Naw, these guys are doing fine, I just don't think we are as desperate as before. I think it'll be great to see these guys build up and break into the team score on some events."

"Are you sure you can trust all of your parts?" Don asked looking at the stage where Logan was still talking to Carmen.

"I don't know. Logan thinks he needs more on floor and I suggested he pick Carmen's brain for ideas to add some difficulty with some dance."

"You suggested? Don't you think that's like lettin' the fox guard the hen house?"

"Pfft. It's just dance, Don." Joey looked at the stage as Carmen and Logan were just getting into seeing where his dance knowledge lined up with hers.

"Until it's more than just. But that's none of my business. What I do see here is a pretty fine operation, Joey. You done good. Jimmy'd be proud of you."

"Well, we haven't done anything yet. Season is only a couple weeks away and we're nowhere near ready to start the season."

"And yet you will. I'm gone for the night. You got lock up?"

"No prob. Thanks, Don."

"No, thank you, Joey. You breathed life into this old place. Keep it up and all this may be yours one day."

"Is that a threat?"

"Depends. G'nite, Joey."

"G'nite, Don." Don withdrew and Joey went back to his workout, but first glanced around the gym and got a really good feeling that he was doing something meaningful and important, and it was good to know he was not alone in that sentiment.

Across town at Dagar's Edge, another tension-filled workout was coming to a close, as usual, with laps around the gym. Danny Dukes and James White, the newest members of the team, were bringing up the rear.

"Guess who... I saw... yester...day," Danny said in a gasp.

"Who...?" replied James, as they came to a stop after the final lap, collapsing against the wall and sliding down to the floor.

"Logan... Merwin! He was at 'Sports Games and Grub'... with Johnson and Story!"

"What?!"

"I was there with my folks... I don't think they saw me." James grabbed a drink from his water bottle as Tom Shultz, the team captain approached the pair.

"Did you say Logan was with the Taylor guys?" asked Tom.

"Yeah, they were kinda pals, it looked."

"After what he did with Keith?" asked James.

"I guess after Coach Dagar kicked 'em off team."

"The enemy of my enemy, is my friend!" said Tom.

"You think he's training at Taylor?" asked Danny.

"I would be," said Tom, "They've got three solid All Arounders, if he is! We better tell Coach Dagar." And the team converged on Gene's office to tell him the news they knew he didn't want to hear.

21

With the first test only weeks away, it was a good time for an intersquad to see where the team stood. The uniforms had arrived and it was the perfect opportunity to see what they had. Don and Carmen played the role of judges, really just saluting and going through the motions. There would be no scores, just evaluation of start value, hit routines or parts, and determining what was still missing.

By the end of the scrimmage, it was up to Joey, Alex, Don, and Logan to determine the results.

"Well, that could've been better," said Alex.

"I don't know, I think we look pretty good," said the ever optimistic, Joey, "we still have some hitting to do, but I think we've got some depth."

"Really? Looks like it drops off after the three of us," said Alex.

"Yeah, but these guys are close," encouraged Logan, "Bobby's Pommels, Timmy and Tommy on P Bars and High Bar, even Rodney is putting together a floor routine that could break the line-up."

"True that, but can they stand up to the three and four guys for Dagar's?" A moment's pause while they reflected.

"They do look good, but they are each gonna need another skill or two to match up with Gene's boys," said Don.

"So, we are gonna have to be on, in case they take longer to get ready."

"They'll be ready," assured Joey.

Two weeks passed quickly. The first snowfall surprised Joey as he walked out of the house. It was much earlier than he ever remembered seeing snow, but it drove home the point that the season was just around the corner.

As the time for the first meet neared, there was a sense of trepidation, "We're not ready!" Alex said constantly. Joey was feeling the pinch, too. He and Alex and Logan were ready to start the season, but the newcomers, with as much as they had grown over the past few months, were still a long way from being able to stand toe-to-toe with Dagar's guys.

"What do you think, Don?" asked Alex, "Are we ready?"

"Well, if you wait until we're ready, we'll never compete," he said, "these guys are gonna have to be thrown to the wolves to see what they can do. There's a lot of good gymnastics out there, but there's no way of telling if they will be able to handle it until they have to salute a judge and do a routine that counts."

"Fortunately, the meet this weekend is in Ann Arbor, where nobody knows us," said Joey, "any mistakes made shouldn't have a major impact going forward, just another lesson to get us ready for State."

"One would hope," said Don.

Don was able to borrow one of the city school buses for the drive over to the competition. That Saturday morning the team met and filed onto the bus. The biting chill of Michigan in December was still something Joey hadn't gotten used to.

"Hey Don, can we postpone this meet until it warms up?" asked Joey.

"You mean April?" replied Don to the chuckles of the rest of the team, "You'll get used to it."

"I doubt it."

"Hey, Coach," said Alex, "I have a question."

"Shoot."

"What name did you enter us as?"

167

"Taylor Academy of Gymnastics" said Coach.

"TAG, eh? I guess that works."

The bus pulled into the parking lot of the small gym in Ann Arbor, 'Ann Arbor Marauders' was a, relatively small gym club, but held a decent meet to start the season with.

"Joey," called Alex as he stepped off the bus, "Do you see what I see? I thought this meet was supposed to be under the radar?"

Joey looked in the direction of Alex's gaze and saw the familiar mini-van, with 'Dagar's Edge' painted on the side. *This is unexpected,* he thought.

"I wonder how they knew we were here?" asked Alex.

"Perhaps it's just a coincidence?" added Joey.

"I doubt it," replied Alex.

"Well, if it isn't Don Wheatley and his puppies!" taunted Gene as he approached, "when I heard you guys were starting your season here, I just had to enter. I wouldn't, normally, come to a meet this small, but it will make a nice little scrimmage before we head to the Big Apple next week. Oh, this is gonna be fun!"

"Have a good meet, Eugene," said Don, trying not to appear surprised. Gene laughed, "Of course we will! And I can't wait to see what you've done with all these strays, Don. Haha." Gene guided his team toward the entrance.

"So much for being incognito," said Joey.

"Don't let it get to you, Joe," said Don.

"C'mere, guys," Joey gathered the troops, "Ok, we weren't expecting Gene and his mutants here, but this is what we've got. It'll be a good test of your concentration. They are gonna try to intimidate you. Remember, you can't be intimidated unless you give your permission. We have a job to do today, and it has nothing to do with those jokers. Your task is to stay focused and concentrate on your duty. Hit your sets. Anything we accomplish today is one step closer to State. If mistakes are made, you have to do your best

168

to find the lesson, take it back to the gym, and fix it. Don't let these guys get to you."

"That might be easier said than done, Joey," said Rodney.

"You can only do your best. Let's take it inside." The team walked into the small gym that was set up for the competition. It was cramped, but enough space to get the job done.

"Where do we start, Joe?" asked Logan.

"Pommel Horse." Joey and Alex dropped their things by the pommel horse seating, and the team followed suit, and followed them to the floor exercise carpet to start their warm up. As they jogged around the 40' x 40' border of the floor, they could feel the gaze and hear the chuckles coming from the Edge Team.

"Block it out guys," Joey said as they gathered in the middle of the floor to stretch, "stay on task."

"Did you see who they added, Joe?" Alex asked, gesturing toward the pack of Edge gymnasts, revealing Keith Pitts in the middle.

"I guess Dagar's principles go only so far," said Joey.

"I can't say I'm surprised," added Don, "Gene's word is only as good as his options."

"Can't I just go over and punch Keith in the teeth?" asked Alex, "just one punch."

"Sure, Alex, if you want to blow everything we've worked for," said Joey.

"But it's so damned tempting!"

"Is it gonna help your All Around?" asked Logan.

"No, but I'll feel a lot better."

"Then can it! Get your head straight."

"Roger that." Alex directed his attention to his team and their preparation. After introductions and National Anthem, the teams reported to their first events. Dagar's started on Rings.

"At least we'll know what scores we need," said Alex.

"Somehow, I don't think that'll matter," said Joey. Pommel Horse is the hardest event to start or finish on, as it is the hardest to hit and the pressure can be immense. Timmy and Tommy struggled through weak routines, while Dagar's Edge was hitting Rings sets.

"Ok, Bobby, let's see what you've got," said Don. Bobby jumped up on the end of the horse and began swinging circles that moved into Flairs. As he popped up into his Air Flair, his right hand completely missed the leather, and Bobby found himself on his back on the mat. He looked at Rings to see the Edge Team in mid-belly laugh. Bobby reapplied his chalk and picked up where he left off, only to find himself spinning on the horse, wildly, coming to rest on the mat once again. With little left to do, Bobby saluted the judge and swung a circle into a handstand dismount.

"That sucked!" Bobby said as he plopped down next to Joey.

"Don't sweat it, Bob, this is why we compete. We have to work out the kinks. Competition brings a whole different set of distractions that aren't there in the gym."

"Like the Dagar guys laughing their asses off."

"Yeah, that, but also the pressure of only getting one chance, having to salute a judge, wanting a good score, those are all distractions that, if you don't learn to control them, control you!" said Logan.

"Tough lesson," said Bobby, as he watched the rest of the competition.

"Hey," Joey said, slapping his leg, "it's December! Nothing will be settled until March. Learn from this moment and come back stronger! C'mon, Alex!" Alex jumped up and hit a strong Pommel Horse routine, which worked to quiet the Edge hecklers. Logan followed with another strong routine, keeping pace with the Edge team. Joey followed with a strong set, as well. As he dismounted he noticed Keith clapping as he waited for the Rings judges to salute him.

Keith saluted and was assisted to the Rings by Coach Dagar. After a complex strength combination, Keith did several double-flipping swings that ended with him in a handstand, followed by a full-twisting, double-tuck dismount.

"You really think we got a shot at beating these guys in three months, Joe?" asked Alex.

"We have some kinks to work out."

"Kinks? We're only through one event and we're over three points behind! That's a lot to make up!"

"Have faith, young Alex. There's more meet to go and we got pig out of the way first!" The teams rotated in Olympic order; Dagar's boys to Vault, TAG to Rings.

"Alright, Bullet, let's see what you got!" Don lifted Rodney Rodney to the Rings and supported him while he adjusted his false grip.

"Keith look!" said Danny, well within earshot of Rodney, "They have a mascot!" Both laughed while standing at the end of the Vault runway. It was enough to frazzle Rodney, leading him to not hold his strength parts that he had worked for so long, and so hard to get. To top things off, Rodney over-rotated his double-back dismount, landing him squarely on his bottom, which brought another round of guffaws from the Edge Team.

"Rodney, where are you going?" said Don, as Rodney, instead of returning to the seating area, headed toward Vault, and Keith and Danny.

"I didn't know we were going to have a sideshow for entertainment!" laughed Keith at Rodney, standing a good six inches shorter than Keith. As Keith doubled over with another laugh, Rodney met his chin with an uppercut that put him on his back. Keith tried to jump to his feet, but found himself restrained by his teammates. Rodney spit in his general direction before returning to Rings.

"That's it, Wheatley," said the meet director, "that kid's gotta go! He's done. We'll not have unsportsmanlike conduct at my meet!"

"Sorry, Sandy," said Don, "go wait on the bus, Rodney."

"Wait! Aren't you gonna do anything about those guys?" pleaded Rodney.

"None of them threw a punch, son," said Sandy, the meet host.

Bobby, who was only competing Pommel Horse, walked Rodney out to the bus.

"Those guys were acting 'unsportsmanlike', too!" cried Rodney.

"Yeah, but you REALLY crossed a line," said Bobby, "by the looks, I would say that was probably a gymnastics first! Dude, don't you see? That's their game. They know we are getting better, maybe not good enough to beat them yet, but enough to be a threat. So, if they can get us off our game, they don't have to work so hard."

"I feel so bad. I sure hope Mr. Wheatley doesn't kick me out, although he'd have every right!"

"We'll just have to see. What you and I need to do is come up with a plan to get better."

"Or get even."

Inside the gym, Taylor and Edge traded sets. Once Pommels and Rings were out of the way, Timmy and Tommy provided solid scores to back Alex, Logan, and Joey's routines. When it was all said and done, Dagar's Edge had won the meet with a convincing score, while TAG came in a distant fifth, over eight points behind the leaders.

"So that's the group you're gonna put on the floor at State, Don?" asked Gene, sarcastically.

"They're rough around the edges, but we have three months to smooth them out."

"If none of them wind up in jail between now and then!" Gene chuckled as he rejoined his charges.

"Looks like we may have bitten off more than we can chew, eh, Don?" asked Joey.

"Actually, I think you have them right where you want them."

"Eight points ahead of us?" said a confused Alex.

"They aren't really eight points better than us, boys," said Don, "obviously Bobby and Rodney had a rough day, but hit sets from them on their events, and a little better performance from the four of you, and we stand a pretty good chance."

"Are you serious? We looked like a joke in there!" said Alex.

"Yes, but now they think they know us, and they'll be over-confident."

"Eight points worth?" added Joey.

"Heck, you can just about make that up just in falls! It's a long way until March, Joey." Don and the team climbed onto the bus.

"Joey, I am SOOOO sorry!" pleaded Rodney, "please don't kick me off the team!"

"Believe me, Rod, nobody is getting kicked off this team. We didn't do well, but we didn't embarrass ourselves either, other than your uppercut to Keith. You have to direct that energy in a more positive direction, like your training! We have a ton of work to do but we got this out of the way, now we can get back in the gym and get back to work. We've got three months!"

The twenty-minute bus ride passed in silence as each considered what must happen next.

22

In the weeks that followed, the team made significant progress in hitting routines, but still had many spots that needed quantum leaps to catch the, more experienced, Edge gymnasts. The next test would be in Toledo, a week away.

When Don arrived to open the doors for Monday's practice, he found the doors already open, with Joey and Carmen sitting on the Floor Exercise carpet. Carmen had her laptop and Joey was feeding her data from the Ann Arbor fiasco.

"Find a magic bullet?" asked Don as he approached.

"Not really, but you were pretty close. We're starting to close that gap between mistakes and difficulty."

"Yeah, it appears that hitting more routines certainly improves your odds," said Don.

"But, even still, this group has a way to go to be competitive," surmised Joey, "not only do we need to be hitting routines, but we need to be hitting better routines. Dagar's guys beat us by almost a point-and-a-half on each event with start value alone!"

"So, where can you add some beef?" asked Don.

"Well, we're actually pretty close on Floor, Pommels, and Vault," said Carmen, crunching the numbers.

"And we're close to putting a little more strength up on Rings," said Joey.

"But High Bar and Parallel Bars are the biggest deficits in start value," concluded Carmen.

"You got any ideas. Don?" pleaded Joey.

"Hmm," Don thought, "what do releases look like on pipe?"

"Well, Alex, Logan and I each have a release. Timmy and Tommy are close."

"Well, they're gonna have to get closer, and you boys need to look at going bigger."

"Bigger?"

"Yep. Straddled skills are gonna have to be bigger and laid out, to increase the value, plus combinations of two releases will get you some bonus."

"YOU'RE RIGHT!" cried Carmen, after factoring in some variations in start values, "If you guys can add a release and the Bakers can get a release or two, you guys are almost dead even with Dagar's!"

"Then I guess that sets the emphasis for today. Releases it is! Care to hang out and help make some magic happen?" asked Joey.

"Naw, you got this just about figured out. I have other fires to put out. You just keep on, keeping on. I got a nice seat right over here." Don walked over to a stack of panel mats and had a seat, opened his newspaper and began to read, just as the others were arriving for practice.

"So, what's on the menu today, Joe?" asked Alex, walking in with the Baker Boys.

"Today it's all about releases. Dagar's guys beat us pretty bad in start value on pipe, mainly because they are loaded and we are still lacking."

"What's wrong with my Tkachev?" asked Alex.

"Nothing. It just needs to be bigger, or connected to another release so we can beef up that start, Al."

"This should be fun," said Alex, as Logan entered the gym.

"What should be fun?" asked Logan.

"Joey, here, thinks we need to step up our releases on High Bar, today."

"Sounds like fun," said Logan.

"For you, maybe," said Timmy, "Tommy and I are just figuring this out. It's not the releasing that bothers me, it's colliding with the bar!"

"Oh, quit it," said Joey, "get warmed up and get your grips on. I'll see you guys at the pit bar." The guys went to work with the usual warm up routine; a little cardio, a little stretching, some body shape conditioning, and some pre-strength and they were ready for the bar.

"OK," started Joey, as the guys strapped on their grips, "it's all about using the bar and timing." Joey jumped up on the bar and was soon into giants, "Understanding…how the bar works…is the key." Joey spoke as he swung around another giant, then modified his shape to create more flex in the bar at the bottom of the swing, resulting in a release directly above the bar! Joey looked over his left shoulder as his body rotated thru the half-turn and catch, executing a text-book Geinger.

"Ok," asked Tommy, "how do you make that bigger?"

"There's a couple things," said Joey jumping off the bar, "I could put it up a little higher and add a full-twist…"

"Or, you could release a little later and take that Geinger the bar and turn it into a Gaylord 2!" added Alex.

"Or if you can sneak in another half-twist, you've made a Kolman!" chimed Logan.

"It's about timing and influence," said Joey, "there's got to be more momentum behind the swing, that turns into torque on the bar, and then it's just about timing!"

Alex jumped up on the bar. On his second giant, he pulled the bar and closed his hips to accelerate the swing and put torque into the bar. He then pushed his body from closed to arched, right at the bottom of the bar to give just the right flex. Then, on the upswing, Alex drove his heels down while thrusting his chest upward to release and fly above the bar. In mid-flight, Alec piked his hips, and straddled his legs, to front flip his Tkachev. Upon the catch, Alex loaded up for a second, consecutive Tkachev! Hands dead on and continuous swing through the giant was met with cheers and applause!

"Nice, Alex!" said Logan, "I think you just added some bonus and another skill to your set!"

"That was easy!" said Alex, surprised at how quickly he added the new release.

"My turn!" said Tommy, jumping up to the bar. While Timmy and Tommy had been getting close to their releases, re-catching was still an issue. Tommy cranked the same set up as Alex, but Tommy released the bar before getting his feet down and his chest up, resulting in him flying over the bar, back first, with no rotation, bringing him to rest on his back on the 32" deep mat.

"That was close," said Joey, "but you've got to throw and kick a bunch more before you let go or it won't flip!"

"Like that, you mean?" asked Tommy. Timmy got up for his try, doing the same release. Although he was more patient than his brother, his throw was not as aggressive, which put his Tkachev on top of the bar, where he bounced off of his thighs and back flipped to a fetal position crash on the big mat.

"Wow," said Alex, "put the two of you together and we have one good release!"

Logan jumped up to the bar for his turn. Taking a cue from Alex, Logan tried the Tkachev-Tkachev combination. To add a wrinkle, Logan crossed his hands and turned his shoulders so his second release half-turned on the catch, swinging through the bottom back first, making the combo slightly more valuable than Alex's.

Alex, not to be outdone, jumped to the bar, and put more power behind his swing which launched his Tkachev high enough that he could keep his legs together and did a layout Tkachev, followed immediately by a straddled Tkachev!

"Wow!" yelled Joey, "That was insane!"

The Baker boys realized in that moment that if they were ever going to break into the team score, they had better catch up. Within minutes, Timmy and Tommy were catching their Tkachevs and almost able to continue to swing giants out of them. In the meanwhile, it had become a battle between Alex and Logan. As Alex added releases together, Logan was only doing two, but kept adding twists and stretching the shape, until they both settled in on what their competitive combinations would be.

"That was a clinic!" Joey said as the guys took their last turns, "Al, are you gonna be able to do Layout Tkachev, straddle Tkachev, Geinger in a set?"

"We're gonna find out in just a moment." Alex was feeling accomplished, getting a big release combo ready, even before Logan.

"Mr. Merwin, have you decided your combo?" asked Joey.

"Yeah, Layout Tkachev to Tkachev-half!"

"Outstanding," said Joey, "I think we just closed that gap in start value."

"What about us?" asked Tommy.

"You guys are doing great," said Joey, "you can see the gap. The more you guys do, the closer you get, who knows? You might knock one of us off the awards stand!" Timmy and Tommy were not as encouraged as Joey thought they should be, not realizing the back-handedness of his comment.

"Yeah, but none of this stuff is ready to compete," said Alex, "Maybe by State, but I would forget about unleashing any of that any time soon."

"But it's getting' to do the big stuff that makes the rest tolerable," added Tommy.

"If there was only a way to put the Edges on their heels…" added Joey.

"Back in my day," came the voice behind the newspaper, "we used to throw our biggest skills in warm up, just to try to get a psychological advantage." Don folded his paper, "These guys haven't seen you in a while."

"So, you think if we throw insane skills in warm up the Edge's might be intimidated?" asked Joey.

"It has to be believable," added Don, "but you guys don't have the difficulty yet, and you might as well try to get in their heads."

"It's worth a try," added Alex, "How many times have you 'won warm ups'?" Alex added rhetorically.

"What's the competition format?" asked Joey.

"One hour open warm up, then compete," replied Don.

"Guys! Fall in!" Joey shouted, and the team gathered around him, "look, we still aren't up to the Edge guys, but we're close. And I think we're close enough to scare them. Rodney, you think you can put that triple-back on your feet if I gave you a big bump?"

"You want me to compete the triple?"

"No, just warm it up! We are gonna do our sets the way we've practiced, but before we do, I think we can get the Edge's to feel a little pressure. It can't hurt."

"Unless one of us gets killed in the warm up!" pleaded Tommy.

"We don't have to be incredible, just credible," answered Joey, "So, here's my plan." And Joey laid out his scheme for the upcoming trip just over the Ohio State line. Don excused himself to his office for another cup of coffee while the boys finalized the plan.

"This sucks a little bit," exclaimed Don as he returned from his office, a letter in his hand.

"What's up, Don?" asked Joey.

"Well, it appears you guys will have just one season to accomplish all you have planned."

"One season? What do you mean?" pleaded Joey.

"In my hand, I have a notice from the Taylor School Board. They plan to close this place as soon as the season is over," said Don, through moist eyes.

"WHAT?! HOW CAN THEY DO THAT?" cried Joey.

"Every year the school board has tried to sell this place off. It's, kinda, an albatross for them, with the operating costs constantly rising and, as you can tell, there's not a ton of people taking advantage of this place, and it's just too much for the Board to justify the upkeep."

"Let's go talk to them," said a desperate Joey, "Maybe they will give us another year?"

"No good. I've already tried. They wanted to close immediately, but I was able to talk them into letting you boys finish the season, first."

"Mighty nice of 'em," replied Alex, "And what are we supposed to do with all the new equipment?"

"Well, you have until the end of season to find a new facility."

"How are we gonna do that?" exclaimed Joey, "With school and gym, when will we find time? And besides, a new facility is gonna cost money. Where are we gonna come up with that?"

"Not to panic, Joseph, I will be on the watch for a new spot. Since the car industry took its hit, many businesses have shut down, leaving plenty of empty spaces. It's a buyer's market when it comes to warehouse space. We should be able to find a decent spot, with a manageable rent, in plenty of time. According to this letter, we have until June first. After that, they will start their plan to raze the site by the end of June."

"Wow," said Joey, "so much history here. Why would they tear this place down and lose all that history?"

"I'm afraid nostalgia takes a back seat to the bottom line. It's all about money."

"Hey, maybe we can pool our resources and buy the place from the school board."

"Tried that. Number one, they want to clear this site to make way for a new park. Second, I offered to buy the place, but they want waaaaaay too much."

"How much?"

"Half a million dollars." Every head dropped.

"That really does suck," added Alex, "That seems like a lot."

"It is, by about a factor of three. But, that's the point. They really don't want to sell. They know that anyone who could afford to buy it, won't because there seems to be no way to see a return on investment. They've already contracted architects, demolition, and contractors to turn this place into a park. I'm afraid the days of Taylor Center are numbered." They boys looked at each other, hoping someone had an answer.

"Then, I guess we should go out with a bang!" exclaimed Joey, "If this is the last year for TAG, it's up to us to make it memorable!" The team nodded their heads in agreement.

23

Don pulled the Taylor School District bus to the front door of the Toledo Sports Arena, a relic built in 1947. He pulled the lever, splitting the doors, "Alright, gentlemen, here's your first step toward beating those guys. Now go get 'em!" The team stepped off the bus and headed toward the entry doors.

"Great, look ahead," said Alex, "it's almost like those guys were waiting on us." Most of the Edge gymnasts were just outside the doors and couldn't resist the opportunity to dig at their favorite foils.

"Well, if it ain't the Hillbilly and his misfits," said Keith as the team approached.

"Well, if it's not a future fugitive in training," replied Alex, "hope that suspended sentence doesn't affect you getting into college." This stopped Keith in mid-breath, and the team entered in silence.

The TAG team took their place on the floor exercise carpet and began their stretching and loosening up. Once stretch was concluded, the team split into two groups, Joey, Rodney, and Bobby went to the corners of the floor, while the rest got their High Bar grips on. From the first turn, the warm up took on the atmosphere of a circus, Taylor guys cheering each other, much louder than normally during a warm up, and the skills were just as loud. While Timmy, Tommy, Alex and Logan ran a release clinic, doing gigantic release combinations, Joey and Bobby warmed up big double backs. After his turn, Joey jumped up onto the carpet to prepare for Rodney's big pass. Joey stole a glance toward High Bar, where the Edge's were warming up, to make sure that they were watching. He gave a nod to Rodney.

"Let's go, Rod!" yelled Alex from High Bar, and all attention turned to Floor. Rodney exploded out of the corner and turned his round-off, back handspring as fast as he could, and hit the floor just right. Joey gave the bump Rodney was looking for, and catapulted into the air before drawing in his legs for the tiniest tuck he could manage, and turned his triple. ONE-TWO-THREE! Joey grabbed Rodney's shoulder, allowing his feet to get under him. Rodney pushed the floor as hard as he could to keep the landing on his feet. A smile came to his face as he stood and faced Joey, to the cheer of most of the athletes, and a bit of bewilderment from the Ring Tower.

"Don't get any ideas, Rod," said Joey, trying not to move his lips, "Stick to the script."

"Oh, you can count on me. I just thought how cool it was to do that."

"Right. Well, it sure looks like we got their attention, now the second half is us hitting."

"Wow!" shouted Billy Hopkins, to his Edge teammates, "Looks like the Taylor guys are out for blood!"

"Looks like a bad meet to hold back, Coach!" added Keith.

"You may be right, Mr. Pitts," said Coach Dagar, as he assessed the situation, "alright, boys, warm up your releases!" and the Edge's began warming up their big release moves, those they had planned to hold out of routines until the hit/miss ratio was more in their favor, were now being tried with the intention of rushing them into today's routines. As they rotated from event to event, the TAG boys warmed up over their head and the Edges, as inconspicuously as they could manage, tried to keep pace, adding difficulty with each turn, so that, by the end of warm up, the Edge's had spent a little more energy than they had intended.

As competition began, it was evident that the warm up had had the right effect. With Taylor starting on floor and the Edges starting on High Bar, they had a front row seat to the Edge's breakdown.

Between the first three routines, the Edge's had four falls, While Rodney, Timmy, and Logan hit solid sets, Rodney opening with a gigantic, open-tucked, double-back, not the triple the Edge's expected to see.

"Did you see that!?" exclaimed Keith to his team's captain, Tom Shultz, "that kid warmed up a triple-back!"

"How observant, Keith," said Tom, recognizing the ruse, "it appears we've been played. Looks like we have ground to make up."

As the competition progressed, the TAG boys gained confidence with each routine, while the Edge's couldn't figure out why they were having such a tough go. The more they tried, the more they missed. The more they missed, the angrier Coach Dagar became. The more he fumed, the more they missed. In the meanwhile, the Taylor boys did their stock routines. By the third rotation, the Edge's realized the damage was done and there would be no coming back this meet.

Although the competition had been settled, early on, the final landings told the story of the day; Joey sticking his full-twisting, double-layout off of High Bar, to win the All Around, at the same time that Keith struggled to finish his Parallel Bars routine without landing on his face, putting both hands on the landing mat. On the strength of three of the top five All Around, and event winners on all six, TAG not only won their first competition, but also managed to keep the Edges off of the team podium, finishing fifth to TAG, and three Ohio clubs.

When the final dismount hit the ground, the Taylor boys jumped as if they had won NTI's, not just a small invitational. As the cheers and back slapping ceased, Joey noticed some of the Edge guys coming their way.

"Nice job, Hillbilly," said Keith, "you got us with our pants down."

"Well, it's nice to see y'all are human after all," replied Joey.

"I saw the rest. You guys only won because we shot ourselves in the foot. We still out-value your routines, and you can expect us to hit in Cincinnati."

"Of course. But, at least we both know it won't be a walk for you at State. Now, if you don't mind, we're just gonna go gloat for about an hour, and then get right back to the job of disappointing you. Besides, looks like y'all have unfinished business here." By the look on Coach Dagar's face, it was apparent that the Edges would have at least an hours' worth of conditioning before they would leave Toledo.

"I hate it when he makes the hired help wait around while he conditions the crap out of us," said a dejected Keith, "I better get over there before I make it worse."

"You could leave."

"Ha, not likely," his sneer returned, Keith turned toward his team, "this was a fluke, Hillbilly. You will see in three weeks." Keith jogged to join whatever punishment was coming their way.

"He sure doesn't look happy," said Alex.

"Yeah, we had the advantage today, and they are a little shook, but we may have awakened a sleeping giant."

"I think you give them too much credit. Forget about Dagar's Edge for about an hour or so, it's time to celebrate!" Alex mussed Joey's red hair, and put him in a headlock, and dragged him from the arena where the bus was waiting.

"How'd it go?" asked Don, as he opened the bus doors, "Rodney punch anyone?"

"Haha, no, no punches were thrown, but 'winning warm ups' worked like a charm," said Joey, as he and the others climbed on board, "by the time they figured out what was going on they had already blown the meet. So, yeah, that worked, but it's not likely to work again."

"Doesn't have to," replied Don, "you planted a seed of doubt. Sometimes that's all that's needed."

"I hope you're right. We still have a long way to go." Joey took the seat directly behind the driver's seat.

"One goal at a time. That's what Jimmy would say," said Don.

"Yes, he would. Can't wait to give him a call and let him know how we did!"

Don closed the doors, his full complement on board, and pulled the bus out into traffic for the quick hour-long ride back to Taylor.

24

The victory over the Edges served as a springboard for the TAG team, motivating each to give that much more, adding difficulty, perfecting technique, and sticking landings. As the Cincinnati meet approached, Don took note on just how good the boys had gotten, without his help. As he opened the doors for the Monday workout prior to the meet, he couldn't help but think of a time when he and his teammates were just as excited about their potential. He only wished he could do more.

"Hey, Don!" called Alex as he entered the gym, "have you heard from Joey?"

"No, should I have?" he replied, as he unwrapped and dropped a new block of chalk into the chalk bucket at High Bar.

"He wasn't at school and he's not answering his cell."

"What about Carmen? Has she heard from him?"

"Dunno, haven't been able to reach her, either."

"Well, I'm sure there's an explanation. You'll have to make sure the guys get started on time until Joey does show up."

"Of course."

As the rest of the team arrived for workout, each was quizzed as to what they might know about the absence of their leader. Throughout the warm up, each racked their brain to think of the last things they had said, as if that would somehow be a clue to his disappearance. Just as they had concluded that they had no clue as to where and why, Joey arrived. Barely able to stand, supported by

Carmen, Joey was obviously exhausted, and his red eyes gave away that he had been crying for some time.

"Joey! What's wrong?!" asked Don.

Through tears Joey answered, "Coach Lowery!...He's gone!" Joey collapsed into a heap.

"WHAT?" cried Don.

Joey tried to gather himself, "We got the call this morning. He was on his way back home from out west. Somewhere in Utah, an eighteen-wheeler crossed the double yellow line...He was hit head on...killed...instantly." Joey collapsed once again, sobbing. Don had to sit down and process the news.

"Guys, we can't have workout today," said Don, through tears.

"Don," said Alex, "I understand, and we are all hurting for you guys, but, no offense, but we do have a meet this weekend."

"Not me," cried Joey, "he's being brought back here. Service is this Saturday."

"So, what are we supposed to do?" asked Alex.

"You guys will just have to do the best you can without us," replied Don.

"That doesn't sound promising."

"So maybe winning isn't the goal this weekend," Don suggested, "regardless, Joey, you don't need to be here. Go home. I'll get with your folks about arrangements."

"But, I need to..."

"You need to rest. Anything you try to do today can only end up bad. Go home and get some rest. You'll be better off and tomorrow is another day."

"Okay." Carmen helped Joey to his feet and led him to his bike.

"As for the rest of you," Don addressed the team, "you're gonna have to step up to make up for Joey's scores this weekend, so there's that."

"But, that's gonna be hard to do," said Alex.

"Regardless, that's the task at hand. And, depending on how

long it takes for Joey to grieve, you may have to take the reins for a while, Alex." Alex's eyes widened at the thought of being the leader.

"True that," replied Alex, "don't you worry, Don. I got this."

"Well, let's hope so. I've got to go to my office and start making arrangements myself. You got this?"

"I got this. You go do your thing and I'll take care of these guys," said Alex, confidently.

"Great," Logan said under his breath, "Story on a power kick is just what we need."

"Maybe he could use your help?" said Rodney, "I mean, where is it written we need only one leader? Like, haven't we all been leading, at some point?"

"I have no idea what you're saying, Rod," said Logan.

"Or maybe no leader. Like, we all lead, and we all follow..." meandered Rodney.

"What?"

"Like, we work together, so there isn't really a leader?" Rodney circled the wagons around his point.

"I'm the leader," demanded Alex, "for now, I mean."

"Right, so start the leading, Al," demanded Logan.

"Alright, let's get to work! Twenty-five laps around the floor!" and Alex proceeded to guide the rest through one of their, less than optimal, workouts.

"C'mon, Tommy," screamed Joey, at the High Bar, "be patient!" Tommy closed his hips as he came over the top of the bar to set up his dismount. Opening from the hollow to an arch before bottom, Tommy's preparation for his double-back looked correct, but like his previous turns, as he hit the bottom of the swing, he pulled his head out and released only thirty degrees out of the bottom, and shot almost straight down into the pit.

"It's a good thing that pit is deep, Tommy," said Alex, "otherwise you would be a LOT shorter!"

"Very funny, Story," said Tommy, "just let me get back up on the bar so I can..."

"Peel at the bottom again?" teased Alex.

"Dude, give it a rest," said Logan, "you want to chase these guys off? They have been working very hard, without much support, just so you can ride them? We kinda need them."

"Really? So far it has been the 'You, me, and Joey' show. I don't know if they'll ever catch up."

"So, why chase them off? We've come a long way to get here. Seems a shame to discount them now."

"I'm not trying to chase them off, I'm trying to teach them something."

"What? Like, how irrelevant they are?"

"No, like, how far they have to go to catch up before State."

"Yeah," added Timmy, "we've been doing this for months without much chance to beat you guys, much less beat Dagar's"

"You get many more bees with honey, than vinegar," said Logan.

"Haha, yep, you would be hard pressed to get close to Dagar's without us!" bragged Alex.

"Is this really the fight you want to fight, Alex?" asked Logan.

"Why not? You've spent a lot more time helping these guys than getting better yourself."

"Perhaps, but if we don't help these guys get better, what do we do if one of us gets hurt?"

"We lose! Just like we have all along, just like we will when we get to State, regardless of how much they improved. It's still gonna come down to you, me, and Johnson."

"Exactly," added Logan, "which is why we need these guys to be ready in the event the three of us aren't perfect. We still need a forth score. Each one of these guys make it possible for us to contend. You want to chase them off and have no chance, at all."

"Which, at best, only increases our odds from zero to a thousand-to-one."

"At least there ARE odds with us," said Tommy, "Of course those odds get even better..."

"... if we had a REAL coach," said Timmy, finishing his brother's sentence.

"Well, we don't!" said Alex, his voice raising, "I'm it! You knew that when you came in. It doesn't take a great coach to do what you have to do, just keep busting your ass trying to figure it all out."

"And if you get stuck?" asked Timmy.

"You break it down more, Tim. Construction comes from deconstruction. At least that's what Joey says..." The group went back to work, Alex barking orders, the rest, mostly, ignoring him.

25

Joey tried, and failed for the third time, trying to tie his tie, with more tie sticking out from the back than the front. He sat down on his bed as his dad entered his room.

"You gonna be ok, son?"

"Yeah, just a stupid tie. It's just so hard…"

"I know, son. Coach Lowery meant the world to you."

"Not just that, dad, I can't stop thinking, maybe if I had stayed in Tennessee…"

"How would that have helped? He was closing the gym, anyway."

"Yeah, but if I had stayed, he would've stayed open, at least for a while, and he would've postponed his trip, and…"

"You can't go beating yourself up, Joey, there is nothing you could've done."

"But, now… I don't know if I want to go back to the gym. I don't know what I would be doing it for. Ever since I started gymnastics, my goal has been to impress Coach Lowery. Now, I just don't know…"

"Well, it's probably not smart to make any important decisions while you are still shook up. Maybe give it a while and see. Certainly, you didn't go through all you have, just to impress him. You have to do it for yourself."

"Yeah, I hope I figure that one out."

"You will," Jonas replied, just as the doorbell chimed.

"That'll be Don," said Joey, "I guess it's time to go."

Although Jim Lowery had spent more than half of his life in Tennessee, his roots were still in Michigan, so it was no surprise that there would be a crowd to pay their last respects.

"Looks like Coach Lowery was a popular guy, eh Coach?" said Joey.

"Oh, yeah, by the time of Johnny's accident, Jim and I had already started making our mark as coaches and, somewhat of innovators when it came to drills and coaching technique. Even though we were just Sophomores in college, we were being asked to lecture at camps, clinics, and coaching congresses. Then the accident happened, and we all went our separate ways; Gene and Jim continued to coach, I just got as far away from the sport as I could." A long pause, "I guess it was good while it lasted." Joey understood that his desire to keep training had put a crimp in Don's plans to become a hermit.

As the pair made their way to the chapel, Joey could recognize several faces. Coaches from all over were there. Coaches from Tennessee, and all around the South, were there. Coaches Joey recalled hanging with his former coach, sharing laughs and gymnastics. It was immediately apparent that Jim Lowery had an enormous impact on many, many more than the small groups of boys that, like Joey, shed blood, sweat, and tears for. Before he could grab the doorknob of the chapel, Joey was spun around in his tracks.

"JOEY!!!"

Joey regained his balance and focus to see the frame of Patrick Goodman, former Pioneer captain.

"PATRICK!!" Joey shouted and grabbed his former teammate into a tight bearhug, "How? What?"

"I'm just up the road in Ann Arbor. Knocked me down to hear about Coach Lowery. How long have you been in Michigan?"

"Since we tanked State. I came up almost the next day."

"Are you training?"

"Ha, yeah, funny story. By the way, Patrick Goodman, this is Don Wheatley. He runs the Rec Center where we train."

"Nice to meet you, Patrick. Believe it or not, I've heard of you," said Don.

"Oh yeah?"

"He and Coach Lowery were teammates back when our gym was an actual high school."

"The old Taylor Center High School?"

"Yeah, how'd you guess?"

"Are you kidding? You guys have drawn some attention. It's not just anyone who can put a dent in the Dagar's Edge. Wow, that all makes sense, now."

"How did you know...?"

"News travels fast in the gymnastics community. You made news. We knew you guys existed, especially after taking those guys down in Toledo, I just had no idea it was YOU!"

"Yeah, but don't be fooled, it was all smoke and mirrors. Let's get inside, I'll bring you up to speed."

The trio entered the chapel to a full house. Once everyone was seated the minister delivered a fine sermon about a life spent in the service of shepparding young men to adulthood. At the close, an invitation was extended to anyone who wanted to share. Don immediately stood and made his way toward the pulpit. After a few friends and family paid their respects, with memories of a life filled with laughter and love, Don took his place at the podium. With no notes, Don stared at the top of the lectern while he gathered his thoughts.

"I wanted to be Jimmy," he began, "he was the one of us that had talent. While my teammates and I were trying to figure out gymnastics in the '70's, Jimmy was always one step ahead of us. He understood motion mechanics like none of us, but on top of that, he knew how to say just the right words that could calm the most frightened gymnast, and get him to gladly step outside his comfort zone to try something new. He understood that accomplishment leads to confidence, not the other way around. I understood the physics, but Jimmy, more than anyone I've ever known, knew how to get to the psyche, and always knew how to trigger the "want to" in every athlete he worked with." Joey sat in tears, recalling every moment that Don was alluding to. Joey realized that he was not the only one for whom Jim Lowery was so important. Don continued, "Many of you know that Jimmy ran a successful gymnastics program in Tennessee after leaving Michigan. For the last quarter-century, Jimmy helped young men realize their dreams, and two of his charges are here, both of whom helped Jimmy realize his greatest dream, to win the National Team Invitational. I just want to recognize two of the many that Jimmy meant so much to. So, would you please stand, Joey Johnson and Patrick Goodman." The boys stood, "Patrick is a Sophomore on the U of M team, and Joey is Junior at Kennedy. These two gentlemen have spent the last couple years under Jimmy's tutelage, absorbing everything he gladly provided, and look at the result. Not just fine athletes, but fine gentlemen.

"I always wanted to be Jimmy. When we were just a couple years out of high school, an accident happened that changed our paths. While Jimmy continued to coach, I withdrew from the sport. I couldn't bare another tragedy, but Jimmy bravely continued, not just to coach, but to advocate for changes in the sport that made it safer. For over twenty-five years, Jim Lowery gave of himself. Not for accolades and awards, but for the love of the sport, and the kids he got to coach. Just look at the number of folks here that have had their lives enriched by knowing a true, positive force in this universe, in the form of James Lowery. Good bye, my friend, I know now that I could never have been you." Don thought for a moment, figured he'd said enough, and surrendered the podium to the next speaker.

As Don took his seat, Joey could see he was fighting tears.

"That was...special," Joey said.

"Jimmy was special," he replied, as he searched his pocket for a handkerchief, "I was just thinking of the boys that will never get to experience what you and Patrick did, being coached by him."

"Excuse me," came a female voice from the isle, "Donnie

Wheatley?" Don and Joey looked up, both curious as to who would refer to Don as "Donnie".

"Mrs. Banister!" Don exclaimed.

"I'm surprised you remember me, Donnie. I don't mean to intrude, but I'd like to speak to you, in private, when you have the chance." Don excused himself, and left Joey with Patrick, and followed Barbara Banister outside the chapel. Once outside the couple moved to a bench, situated under a budding Cherry Blossom tree.

"It's been a long time, Donnie," she started, "I always wondered what happened to you. You kinda disappeared after Johnny passed."

"I was miserable," Don explained, still on the verge of tears, "I felt so responsible for what happened. I had no idea how to tell you how I felt."

"But you should've tried, Donnie. Johnny adored you. We know you aren't responsible for what happened, yet you've carried this guilt with you for so long."

"I couldn't bear the thought of another accident, and I know I'm not directly responsible for what happened, from that day on I couldn't trust what I was doing. I just couldn't coach anymore, so I just... withdrew."

"What a shame Donnie."

"I know. I owe you an apology."

"Not me, young man," Don looked through puffy eyes at a woman, ten years his senior, "you should apologize to all of those boys who never got a chance to be coached by you. I can show you letters we got from Johnny, about how awesome you were as a coach. How he could see the other coaches coming to you during that camp. You and Jimmy were very similar back then. You both were very passionate about your craft, and you respected your athletes and the process above your ego. Unlike someone else we both know."

"Gene?"

"Of course, Eugene Dagar. You weren't the only one we lost

contact with after the accident. Notice you don't see him here, do you? He wasn't at Johnny's funeral either."

"He's another reason why I haven't coached around here. Every time I'm around him, he drives me crazy, bragging about everything, making everything about himself. He's never taken responsibility for what happened."

"Well, you need to get over all of that, Donnie. Holding a grudge with Eugene is like taking poison and expecting *him* to die!"

"How do you suppose I do that?"

"Start with forgiveness. Believe me, Donnie, it took a long time for me to crawl out of that hole in time. I held so much contempt, not for Eugene, but for his lack of empathy. You know he actually blamed Johnny for being so reckless. It dug at me for a long time. It destroyed my marriage."

"What did you do?"

"I forgave him."

"What?! After all he did?"

"He did nothing, compared to what I did to myself. It took a long time before I realized how pointless it was to wait for him to find a conscience, so, after all else failed, I forgave him. He wasn't trying to hurt my Johnny, he was trying to make him better. He may be guilty of putting his ego ahead of his good sense. But regardless, I have no control over how he feels, only myself. And the world looks so much better when you purge yourself of that guilt, Donnie." Don had no words.

"It's not too late, Donnie, you can still be the coach you were meant to be. Who is that boy you came here with? Joey Johnson? Didn't you say he was one of Jimmy's boys?"

"Joey? He moved up to Taylor last summer after Jim closed Pioneers."

"Who is training him now?"

"No one, actually, he and a few others are training out of TC."

"Really? How did that come to pass?"

"Well, he started over at Gene's, but ended up in my lap. He decided his quest should be to beat Gene and his guys at State, to keep Gene from qualifying to NTI's."

"Was he slighted by Eugene?"

"You could say that. Joey is an outstanding talent, and the other boys felt threatened, and they were able to get Gene to bounce him before he got the chance to know him."

"Seems like Eugene's loss."

"Oh, I don't know, he has a pretty big stable of boys over there."

"Still, it seems these boys need some guidance."

"They've done pretty good on their…"

"DONNIE!" Don stopped midsentence, "It has to be you! YOU need to coach these boys!"

"I don't know Mrs…"

"Are you gonna let a boy finish a man's job?" Again, Don had no words, "These boys need a coach, and in my estimation, YOU need these boys as much as they need you! They need direction and you need to get back to doing what you were meant to do, coaching boys!"

"Gee, I don't know if I …"

"I won't hear of it, Donnie. You don't owe me a thing, but you owe it to yourself to put all of this behind you, and do what it is you were MEANT to do! I will be paying you a visit next week, so do not let me down, Donnie!" She gave him a kiss on the check and walked away, leaving him stunned. Joey and Patrick emerged from the chapel ahead of the crowd and found Don at the bench.

"You Okay, Don?" asked Joey.

"Yeah, I guess, I just got scolded by a sixty-year old woman. I feel like a kid told to pick his own switch."

"Well, I wish it were under different circumstances," said Patrick, "but it was nice to meet you, sir."

"Nice to meet you, too, Patrick."

"Good to see you, Patrick," said Joey.

"I'll be back. Where is state this year?"

"Lansing. In two weeks," replied Joey.

"I'll be there. You keep up the good work." Patrick gave Joey a big bear hug and headed back to his car, and back to Ann Arbor. Joey looked at Don, still seated on the bench, his head down.

"You gonna be okay?" Joey asked.

"Oh Yeah, just got some thinking to do."

"Me, too. Speaking of thinking, how do you think the guys are doing?" Don shrugged his shoulders.

Alex and Logan led the rest of the team into Duke Energy Center. As soon as they entered the hall, they are met by Keith and Danny Dukes.

"I guess Johnson was too scared to show," Keith suggested.

"He just lost his coach, you dick," said Alex, "he's at the funeral now. I see you have your coach with you. You think he would be there, it was his friggin' teammate!"

"Coach says he barely knew the guy," said Keith.

Alex knew better, "At least we know your coach's priorities. Any meet is more important than a friend's funeral. Nice."

"Regardless, Story, it looks like it's up to us. It almost seems unfair. You guys without your best gymnast. It'll be a mercy killing."

"We'll see, Pitts," Alex stormed off to find a spot to stretch out, the rest not far behind.

"You know, Alex," said Logan as they arrived at the corner of the floor carpet that wasn't already occupied, "it really is dumb to try to get into a pissing match with the Edge's this meet. They out gun us, out start-value us by miles. We really should just focus on hitting our sets."

"There's a reason they put me in charge, Logan."

"You actually assumed that. No one really appointed you…"

"That's how you see it. I say we attack! Go big! Pull out the stops! We can beat these guys!"

As the competition got underway, the TAG boys had trouble right out of the gate. Starting on Parallel Bars, Timmy and Tommy both missed skills in the middle of the routine, and touched out their dismounts. Both came back to the group only to receive a tongue-lashing from Alex.

"WHAT WAS THAT?" he screamed, "You guys haven't thrown sets that lousy since you joined the team! WHERE'S YOUR BRAINS?!"

Logan stepped in, "Cool it, Alex."

"Cool it? These guys are throwing the meet!"

"No, they're not, they just missed."

Alex stormed over to the chalk dish to get ready for his turn, imagining a pending mutiny. Instead of focusing on the routine coming up, Alex could not shake the thought that the rest were trying to sabotage his chance at leading them to greatness! Alex blew off the excess chalk and saluted the judges. Alex jumped from the springboard to grab the bars to start his routine with a glide kip, swing to handstand. It was in the handstand that Alex realized that he hadn't set the bars for his routine, the bars still set for Tommy, almost three inches narrower than Alex's setting. His only option, try to swing his routine on the narrow setting. From the handstand, at the end of the bars, Alex swung down and through the bottom, expecting to rise above the bars enough to throw his hands from the end to the middle of the bars, to swing to another handstand, before the difficult segment of his routine. But, instead, when Alex swung up through the bars, his body came to a complete stop, as his latissimus dorsi muscles wedged into the narrow setting. After a moment, Alex's weight pulled him down and he found himself on his back, staring up at the narrow-set rails. *I guess I can reset the bars now*, he thought. Alex set the bars to his setting, and walked over to the chalk dish to re-chalk and gather his wits. As he rubbed his hands in the magnesium carbonate, he could hear the chuckles coming from the direction of the Edge team. Rather than start from where the fall took place, Alex started over. Although he was mad, frustrated, beat up, and embarrassed, he hit his routine like he had a thousand times, but Alex knew his score would be at least two-and-a-half points low to account for his fall and the comedy that led to it.

Alex walked back to the team, his lips tight, fighting the urge to explode.

"Helluva set, Al! Seriously," said Logan, "No way any of us could've pulled off that set after that start."

"Glad I could provide some entertainment for you guys."

"It was kinda gratifying," said Tommy, "at least that first part. It's good to know that even you, gym lifers, are mortal out here."

"Well, don't expect me to let up on you guys!" Alex said, still trying to convince himself that he was supposed to be leading, "we still have five events to go."

And with each event, each mistake activated Alex's anger reflex.

On the last event, Floor Exercise, Rodney opened his routine with his gigantic open-tucked, double-back, but misjudged the landing, and over-rotated, ending up off the floor completely. Rodney recovered on the second pass, but was drained by the end of the routine and landed on his hands and knees on the last pass. It was the straw that broke Alex's patience. Rodney was barely off the floor before Alex laid into him.

"WHAT THE HELL WAS THAT, ROD? You tumbled like you never learned how!"

"Dude, you best get out of my face," exclaimed Rodney as he took a seat next to Bobby.

"We're trying to win a meet, here, Rodney."

"No, we're not, Alex," said Logan, jumping in between the two, "we're trying to do our best."

"Really? You call what we did today our best?"

"No, I said we were TRYING our best. It's been a tough day."

"Not for the Edge's, they went six-for-six! We lost by seven points!"

"You're really reading too much into this, Alex," added Bobby.

"IT'S ALL YOUR FAULT!" Alex exclaimed, "You guys aren't serious!"

"Who's not serious!?" said Rodney, rising to his feet, "we are all busting our asses out there!"

"You guys aren't gymnasts! You're freaks! You wouldn't be anything without me and Joey!"

Silence.

"Fine," said Logan. Without another word, each gathered up their grips, wristbands, and other belongings, and silently headed for the door.

"Oh, I couldn't let you guys leave without telling just how grateful all of us are for the show you guys put on," said Keith as he cut off the TAG boys from the exit, "I seriously cannot recall when I have laughed so hard!"

As Keith prepared to launch a belly-laugh, Rodney stepped between the two and put Keith on his butt with stiff right-cross to the chin. As Keith hit the ground, the TAG boys stepped over him to exit the hall.

26

Don made sure the gym was all set to go for workout on the Monday following the funeral. With only two weeks before State Championships, he knew it would take hard work and all kinds of luck for his team to be ready.

The 4:00 start time came and went. The first person to arrive was Logan, at well after 5:00.

"Where is everybody?" Don asked.

"I guess you didn't get a report from the weekend?" said Logan.

"No, I was waiting to hear from you guys. What happened?"

"You know how they say a little power can be a dangerous thing? Well, I'm afraid Alex went postal when things weren't going right."

"He does have a temper."

"Yeah, but he really melted down. I'd be real surprised if you saw any of the others back."

"Are you kidding?"

"Nope. It was historic. Alex made an ass of himself and alienated his whole team in, like, a heartbeat." Logan's remarks were punctuated by the opening of the gym door to reveal Alex.

"Where is everyone?" asked Alex. Don and Logan looked at each other.

"Well, Mr. Story, it appears that everything you and Joey have worked toward has gone up in smoke over the weekend."

"Don, I can explain," started Alex, "I tried to get these guys to try harder, and they just folded."

"So, it's *their* fault?"

"Like I said, I was trying to get them to try harder and they just gave up on me!"

"And this, young Alex, is why you will never become a great coach."

"Like you, you mean?" Alex said, condescendingly.

"Well, we're about to find out," said Don. Alex and Logan looked at each other, puzzled.

"You mean, you…?"

"That's right Mr. Story, I'm gonna see if I can fix what you've messed up and see if I can't get you guys ready to take on the Edge's in just two weeks. No pressure."

"Does Joey know?" asked Alex.

"Nope. I thought about it a lot over the weekend and just decided, it's time."

"Speaking of Joey," asked Logan, "where is he?"

"I'm sure he's home. His coach's death has hit him hard. It's gonna take a lot to get his head back."

"And the others?" asked Alex.

"Oddly enough, I'm sure they are at the battle downtown," said Logan.

"C'mon boys, we'll pick Joey up on our way downtown."

The three piled into Don's truck and headed for Joey's.

"Hello, fellas," Said Jonas, opening the door to Don, Alex, and Logan, "Joey's in his room. He seems inconsolable." The trio made their way back to Joey's room, where they found in lying on his bed, starring at the ceiling.

"Hey, guys," he said, "what are y'all doin' here?"

"We have unfinished business," said Alex, "State meet is just two weeks away."

"So? Who cares? I'm done with it all."

"Really?" asked Don, "all that work. Was it all for naught?"

"Don, you know we don't stand a chance against the Edge's. Why bother?"

"That's 'Coach Wheatley' to you, young man, and I've never thought you didn't have a chance."

"Coach Wheatley? Does this mean?"

"Yes, yes, I'm gonna try to be a coach. As long as I'm willing to try, I can only do it if you're willing to try, too."

"Are you kidding? It's what I've hoped for since the first day we opened that stupid closet!"

"Great, now get up, we have work to do," said Coach Wheatley.

"It's kinda late for a workout, isn't it?" asked Joey.

"It's not that kind of work," said Logan, "we kinda have to clean up Alex's mess."

"What mess? Where are the others?"

"I'll explain on the way," said Logan, "You're gonna love this." Alex punched Logan in the arm.

Don pulled his truck up to the group of cars parked in front of the warehouse where the tricking event was taking place. No signs advertising the event or pointing the way.

"They like to keep these things small," Joey said, observing that Don had noticed that lack of marketing.

"Almost invisible," replied Don. The quartet made their way into the warehouse and the seating area surrounding the marked area where the fun would take place. Joey searched the audience and spotted Rodney, sitting by himself.

"Hey, Rod!" announced Alex as they approached.

"Great! You want me to punch you again Story?"

"Rod, I'm sorry for being a dick, dude."

"How can you be sorry for who you are? You are who you are. You guys can just keep moving on."

"C'mon, Rodney," exclaimed Joey, "Alex can't help it he's a jerk most of the time."

"Fine, just shut up, the battle's about to begin." The fellas took seats around Rodney just as the lights came down. Over the next hour, the group sat, slack-jawed, as Bobby, Timmy, Tommy, and a dozen other guys and girls, flipped, twisted, and flew across spring floors, from bar to bar, doing elements that even surprised Don, who though he had seen as much momentum as the human body could produce.

"Wow, this gives me some ideas," he said.

After the battle was over, and a few awards presented, the space began to empty as the acro trio rejoined Rodney, to find the rest of TC with him.

"What are you guys doing here?" asked Bobby, "didn't Alex tell you? We're not gymnasts."

"We're freaks," said Timmy.

"About that," said Alex, "guys, I can't apologize more. I was a dick, of the highest order. I didn't mean what I said."

"Yeah, you did," said Tommy, "you still see us as something less than you because we haven't spent four hours a day, for most of our life, doing gymnastics. We may not have as much gym experience as you, but we have trained just as hard at what we do best."

"And I want you guys to bring that back with you," chimed Coach Wheatley, "what's gonna happen, is gonna happen. I'd like the chance to get you fellas ready for what you've worked all year for; a chance for redemption. A chance to show all of those who have written you off that you are much more than they imagined. You guys have worked as hard as any athletes I've ever seen. Why would you not want to see just how good you can become."

"That's all fine and good, Don, but, we still don't have a coach," said Bobby. Alex, Joey, and Logan grinned at each other as Joey told them the kicker.

"Don's gonna coach us."

"Don?" asked Rodney.

"Coach Wheatley, to you, Bullet." The trickers looked at the gymnasts, and then at each other.

"Can we start now?" asked Bobby.

"You guys just finished an epic battle, and it's close to 10:00," said Don, "You have to eat, so, it'll be close to midnight before we can start."

"Perfect," said Tommy, "we're actually better then."

"Alright," said Coach Wheatley, "let's get this party started. Let's head back downriver."

27

The look of the gym when the metal halide lights warm up, casting a violet hue over everything, reminded Joey of Tennessee, and training on Saturday mornings, when he was almost always the first one there. Once again, Joey had that feeling he had had back in the day, filled with optimism.

"Alright, boys," said Coach Wheatley, "It's time you fellas learned a little something about momentum." Don brought the guys together, "Gentlemen, you have a goal, to deny Dagar's Edge entry to their 21st consecutive NTI. And the only way to do that is to deny them a State Championship. And to do that, you are gonna need solid gymnastics from each of you. Problem is, you guys depend so much on your massive muscles, you can do some pretty hard skills, but your form is atrocious! You're not gonna beat Dagar's guys just with difficulty, it has to be spotless!"

"We've been trying," said Bobby, "we're just having a hard time picking it up, we've been so used to our way, and it has worked for us."

"Oh, I don't know, Bobby, after what I saw tonight, I think you boys know more than you realize!"

"How so?"

"Simple. Take that triple full I saw you do. How do you create it?"

"I don't know. Jump real high, twist real fast?"

"Very funny. Actually, your technique is quite unique. When

you take off, you kick your right leg almost to a split. At the same time, you are creating tension in your chest. So, when you 'release' into the wrap, you use a ton of momentum and torque! It's motion mechanics 101! You guys already know, inherently, what to do!"

"Yeah, but what about form?" asked Rodney, "I can do stuff, but it ain't as pretty as these boys."

"Perhaps you are looking at it from the wrong perspective Rod. You look at form as something you have to add to your difficulty, I see it as the root of your difficulty." Don walked over and picked up a 2' section of PVC pipe, "It's about efficiency. See this PVC? It has no desire to do big gymnastics. In fact, it is completely content doing nothing, but even without trying, this is the most efficient body in the gym!" The team looked at each other, bewildered, "Look gymnastics, like tricking, is all about creating and manipulating momentum. The winner is the guy who can do the most with that momentum, in the most efficient way possible." The team, except for Joey, who had heard all this before from Coach Lowery, were still confused.

"Ok, watch," said Coach Wheatley, "this pipe is an excellent tool for transferring momentum. All I have to do is add some horizontal speed and a little rotation, and the shape does the rest!" Don took the PVC and tossed it, with a little rotation, and it flipped across the panel mat several times before popping up to do a double back before coming to rest on the mat."

"How'd you do that?" asked Rodney.

"Easy, Rod, all I had to do was put a little gas and some rotation behind it, at just the right angle of contact and it'll do that just about every time! Mechanics of gymnastics are very predictable, as long as the shape is consistent, the results will be the same. The closer you can get your body to resemble the PVC, the more efficient, and stronger, your gymnastics becomes. It's not that hard to figure out. And it all begins with a strong core to tie both ends of your body together!"

"Sounds easy enough," said Timmy.

"In explanation, yes. In practice, it takes discipline! You guys have different, inefficient shapes every time you go. So, every turn is impossible to predict, or correct. You have to be diligent to condition your body to do everything with the right shapes, every time, so it is predictable. And you have to be strong enough to do it A LOT, to the point it's the only way you know how."

"Where do we start?" asked Bobby.

"Where it always starts, Bob, with conditioning."

"I was afraid he was gonna say that," said Tommy.

"You better start liking conditioning, Tom, it's what's gonna get you where you want to go and you won't get there without loving it. Watch." Don turned to Rodney, "Hey, Bullet, let's see what just six months of conditioning has done for your Rings." Rodney jumped up on the Rings and did an effortless muscle up, 'L' seat, press handstand. He then lowered down with a straight body and lowered into an Iron Cross.

"When he started, he couldn't do the first skill, but he has been in here every day doing just that. And after he got the muscle up and the 'L' seat, the press handstand came next, and finally the cross. It took him six months, but he's got it. And he has a long way to go to get close to Gene's guys.

So, every day for the next two weeks, you've got lots of conditioning and lots of training. The first thing you have to do is make your body strong enough to train hard and long. So, we'll start with a dozen laps around the gym. GO!" The boys took off running, but, unlike when they were running at Dagar's, it wasn't out of punishment or discipline, it was to get somewhere!

It was almost 2:30 am before the boys reached a point of diminishing returns.

"Alright, boys, pack it in," shouted Coach Wheatley, "you guys need rest, too."

One by one, the team filed out, with Joey being the last.

"Thanks, Joey," Don said, just as Joey's hand hit the exit door.

"For what, sir?"

"Everything. Your heart, your drive, your friendship. If you hadn't shown up with Alex back in the summer, I would probably never have come back to this sport."

"Oh, I don't know, Coach. You obviously still love the sport, I'm sure you would've found your way back."

"Not as long as I stayed cooped up in this gym. Who else would've shown up and make me open this gym?"

"I'm sure there would've been someone."

"Yeah, perhaps, but I'm glad it turned out to be you!"

"Fat lotta good it'll do. They're gonna tear down the gym this summer. Then where will we be?"

"Somewhere else for sure, Joe, but you need to not worry about the gym. Just focus on your training, let me worry about the rec center."

"Gotcha, Coach. Regardless of how all this turns out, I'm really grateful for the way it went. If it hadn't been for Keith and those jerks at Dagar's Edge, I might never have found you!"

"It's Kismet," said Coach Wheatley, "It was meant to be. Whatever, you need to get home and get some rest. You and I have much to do, and only ten days to get it done."

"You bet. Thanks, Coach!" Joey punched the bar on the exit door and disappeared into the night, Leaving Don mesmerized as he soaked in Joey's words. *Coach*, he thought, how long I have missed being one. Don smiled as he thought about the events that had brought him to this place. He killed the lights and locked up for the night.

28

Momentum, that's what Don said was so important, not only in creating gymnastics, but momentum is also key in development. Each step, taken immediately after a previous step, creates momentum, too, the kind that Joey, Alex and Logan had hoped for, for Rodney, Bobby, Timmy and Tommy. How much momentum they could create in the next week would be critical for the team to succeed. And if there was one person who could pull it all together, it would be Don Wheatley. Although removed from the sport for almost three decades, most would agree that he had forgotten more than most coaches knew. Not just the mechanics, but Don still had an uncanny way of getting kids to do whatever he asked. If he wanted five hit routines, the boys would bust their hides to hit five routines. The same if he wanted ten, or a new skill, or a new variation of a skill. All he had to do was ask. What seemed like pulling teeth to get them to condition for Joey, all Don had to do was say the word, and all seven would push themselves to exhaustion.

It was the Monday before State Championships. With only five workouts before the NTI qualifier, the TAG team was working like a well-oiled machine. Most often, routines are settled early on, so that the time leading up to competition is focused more on hitting than figuring out a new skill to add, or re-arrange the set. As the boys finished their pre-strength, Don brought them together to put their collective brains on the right path for the week ahead.

"Alright guys, bring it in. Before we get going, and so I don't

212

muck up the works before State, I just wanted to tell you boys what it has meant being a part of this, uh, project. I know you all come to this for different reasons, but you all have trained extremely hard to get to this point, and I want you to realize something. You are not doing this for revenge or payback. Everything you boys have done over the past few months has been for you. No one else. Let that sink in."

"But, Coach," said Alex, "I reeeeally *DO* want revenge!"

"Yes, you do. In fact, you go around the room, and we each have an axe to grind, but that is not the reason, just a motivator. I'll tell ya, I hate competition."

"WHAT?!?" cried Joey.

"No, I do," Don continued, "There's nothing like being in the gym and creating magic. It's just a shame that we can't just stop there. Why do we need to compete?"

The boys looked at each other, trying to make sense.

"It's a necessary evil," said Logan, "If we didn't compete, there would be little motive to take such risks."

"And I doubt we would see the level of gymnastics we see now if there weren't some hot shot, phenom, kicking our butts, forcing us to keep pace," added Joey.

"Exactly," agreed coach Wheatley, "it's competing, not training, that pushes the sport forward. So, now it's up to you to decide if this Saturday you are the 'pusher' or the 'pushed'. Who's a pusher?" All seven raised their arms.

"Capital!" exclaimed Coach, "Herein marks the beginning of State week. Let's get those High Bar grips on, fellas!" As though shot from a cannon, the boys made their way toward their first event. Don detoured to his office to pour up a fresh cup of coffee before first event.

"Alright y'all, you heard the man," exclaimed Joey, "Let's see if we can finish our warm up turns before Don comes back!"

"NOW PATIENT!" yelled Joey to no avail. Again, Tommy peeled into the pit.

"Dude, are you ever gonna do this right?" prodded Alex.

"Maybe if we had a little less criticism?" said Tommy.

"Or maybe if you had a clue," jabbed Alex.

"This won't do, Al," said Joey, "you gotta give them some slack. They're new to this."

"Is that what you're gonna tell the judge when he lands on his face?" added Alex.

"You know," said Tommy, climbing out of the pit, "you're not making this any easier, Alex. Maybe some encouragement and a decent correction."

"Maybe try not yanking your head out at the bottom of the swing!" yelled Alex.

"Maybe try not being a dick, Alex," replied Tommy.

"I think, maybe, you're a little used to that stiff bar you used to tricking off of," suggested Joey, "A High Bar has a ton more flex, which means it takes longer for the swing to develop. Can you spell Patient?"

"P-A-T-I-E-N-T!" Tommy replied, pausing to make sure he knew the next letter.

"Exactly. Be patient. Dude, take as long as it takes to load up the swing and catapult your bod into the stratosphere!"

Tommy hopped up on the bar and went through his routine again, this time taking the time at the bottom to push his hips through the bottom, creating more flex, and more torque.

PIIING!!! This time, instead of peeling at the bottom and ejecting straight down into the pit, Tommy's body rose high above the bar, giving him plenty of time and rotation to complete the two flips and full twist, before sticking his landing on the in-ground resi-mat.

"WOW! That felt GREAT!" exclaimed Tommy.

"Nice job, Tommy!" yelled Joey.

"Nice job yourself, Mr. Johnson!" Joey turned to see the familiar frame of Barbara Banister.

"Mrs. Banister! Hello. Thanks. Just sharing what I've learned."

"You've had good teachers. Is Donnie around?"

"Yes, Ma'am. He just ducked out to grab a cup of joe. I'm sure he'll be right back."

"Can you point me to his office?"

"Sure, go through the gymnasium, toward the guys locker room and is office is the door on the left."

"Thank you. We'll talk soon, Joey." Mrs. Banister turned and walked out of the gym toward Don's office. As it turned out, he met her right at the door to the gymnasium, nearly spilling his coffee.

"Mrs. Banister! What a nice surprise. What can I do for you?"

"It's what I can do for you, Donnie." Don looked puzzled, "You may have been separated from the sport for a while, but I never left it. Johnny was one of four children, Donnie. My daughter, Kelsey, competed all through high school, and even in college, she was a four-year scholarship gymnast for State."

"That's great, Mrs. Banister, but"

"Barbara, Donnie."

"Barbara. That's' great but what does that…"

"Well, if you would let me finish." Don closed his mouth, "I had to pay their way, Donnie, so I started producing my own line of Leotards. I've been at it for years."

"Again, that's great, but I still don't…"

"You need to get back to your boys, Donnie. I'll be right back, and all will be known."

Somewhat dumbfounded, Don made his way to the gym, just as the boys were putting a wrap on their High Bar workout.

"Hey, Coach," said Joey, "I hope you don't mind, but we went ahead and did routines. Alex is up and the last guy to hit five sets."

"You guys have already hit five sets each?" Don was amazed.

"Well, once we fixed Tommy's tap, we all started with cold sets, and, well, I guess there's something to that momentum thing."

"Right."

"So, what did Mrs. Banister have to say?"

"Um, curiously, I'm still not sure…"

"DONNIE! Can you give me a hand, sweetheart?" Don turned to see Barbara with a box on a two-wheel dolly, "Why don't you call your boys over?"

"GUYS!" called Coach Wheatley, "fall in!"

The team gathered around just as Mrs. Banister opened the box.

"You boys don't know who I am," she began, "but I'm sure you're all familiar with what happened to my son years ago. Well, I just wanted to let you boys, and Donnie, know that you have REAL fans out there, and I didn't want you boys going into competition looking like any other gymnast."

Barbara pulled the first garment from the box. A screen-printed design, incorporating a Ram's head in abstract. The Black, Gold, and White step-in was nothing like any had seen before.

"Those are BAAAAD!" said Rodney, "by which I mean very cool!"

"Wow. This is too much, Mrs. Banister," exclaimed Joey, "I mean, they're awesome, but I don't know if we can accept…"

"Shut up, Johnson," said Don, "just say thank you."

"Thank you, Mrs. B!"

"My pleasure, boys. Your coach holds a very special place in my heart, and this was the least I could do. Why don't you boys try these on. I guessed at sizes, which I'm pretty good with, but let's see how they look on." The team went through the box, grabbing a step-in and a pair of black competition pants, and headed for the locker room.

"Barbara, thank you so much."

"No Donnie, thank you. You taking these boys on is the answer to this old lady's prayers. Every time I watch one of your boys, I'll be thinking of my Johnny. And that's a good thing, Donnie."

The team emerged from the locker room, one by one, and lined up. Both Don and Barbara shed a tear.

"You guys look…AWESOME!" concluded Don, "What do you think?"

"Can we train in these today?" asked Alex, "I just feel like my sets will be better sporting a new uni!"

"I don't know," said Don, "You have to wear them this weekend."

"It's not like we all don't own washing machines," added Alex.

Don looked at Barbara for the call.

"They'll be fine, boys," said Mrs. Banister, "just be sure to use cold water and turn them inside out before you wash them!"

"Okay, great!" the team fell out and headed for their next event.

"Would you like to stick around and watch, Barbara?"

"I thought you'd never ask."

Workout continued and Barbara was glued to every movement and quizzed Don on almost every aspect of creating gymnastics, from motion mechanics to child psychology. As fascinated as she was with the actual gymnastics, she was just as impressed with their focus. Over the course of the four-hour workout, she saw gymnastics she had not seen before, and many, many more hit routines, than misses.

"I've always admired consistency, in the midst of so much going on, how can they stay so focused?" she asked.

"It's all part of the process," Don began, without taking his eye off the workout, "First, you have to learn the skill. Then you have to learn how to do it the right way. Then you just have to do it over and over again, until you only know one way to do it. Then repeat the process with combinations, and eventually, full routines. Great gymnastics, by the time it hits the competition floor, should actually be...boring!"

"Boring?"

"Sure. Here's an example: I've been out of the sport for almost three decades. So, these kids are doing skills we weren't even dreaming of back when we were doing it."

"How have you managed to keep your senses? It all looks so scary."

"At first, but after you've seen so much, you get used to it. And understanding how the mechanics work, makes results predictions easier, so you know what's coming up."

"Well, it is, by far, the most fascinating thing on this earth!"

"When it's done right, I agree with you. RODNEY! Turn your legs over more so that low back doesn't get loose!"

"By my estimation, you do, do it right Donnie."

"Why, thank you, Barbara. I just hope we don't let you down this weekend."

"You've brought life back to this school, and this sport. You've impacted these gentleman in a way no one else could. How could you possibly let me down? In my book you have already won, Coach Wheatley."

Don cut a small smile, noticing that, for the first time, she hadn't referred to him as 'Donnie'.

"Barbara, what are you doing this Saturday?"

"I have no plans."

"How would you like to be on the floor with me in Lansing?"

"Is that allowable?"

"I'll expedite membership for you, you'll be my assistant coach! Guys! Bring it in!" The team finished up the last routines for the day and gathered around Coach Wheatley.

"Boys, how would you feel if we brought Mrs. Banister to State Meet?"

"I think that is absolutely awesome, Coach," said Joey, "we would probably still be tripping over ourselves if she hadn't come along. And these uniforms are top notch. We owe you so much, Ma'am. I think I speak for the rest, that it would be an honor to have you on the floor with us!"

"Oh, boys, you're bringing a tear to this old woman's eyes. I would be just tickled to be there with you."

"Then it's settled, Coach Banister. Welcome to the team! We leave from here at noon, Friday!"

"Oh, I never imagined! Bless you boys, especially you, Donnie. After all these years, I just imagined what my Johnny would've become, and I can see so much of him in you boys. It will be my honor and pleasure!"

After several hugs, and each saying thank you, Mrs. Banister excused herself and left the gym.

"Well, guys," said Coach Wheatley, "that was well done."

"It's the new uniforms, Coach!" said Alex, "not only do these fit like a freaking glove, but they are Bad-Ass looking! How could you not do great gym in these togs? Heck, I bet *you* could do gym in these unis!"

"I think you'd be surprised what I could do, Mr. Story. And I don't need a snazzy step-in to do it!"

The group shared a chuckle, but each knew inside, that he was probably right, "All you boys need to do is have three workouts just like this one and you are about as ready as you could possibly be!"

The team high-fived each other and made their way toward the exit. Joey hung around to wait for Carmen. Joey sat on a spotting block with a pad and paper and started crunching numbers.

"Whatcha doing?" asked Carmen as she entered the gym.

"Trying to see if there is any way we can win this thing."

"I thought you guys were ready?"

"As ready as we'll be. Nobody is adding anything from here out. When I look at it, on paper at least, we are a good three points down to those guys. I don't see where we can make it up."

"So, you are going to have to count on them making mistakes…"

"…and us being perfect. Kinda looks bad from this point."

"So, what is important?"

"Doing our best, of course."

"I doubt that that is your number one priority."

"Of course, beating Dagar and his boys is the number one, but that doesn't seem likely now."

"So, everything you've done, everything you have gotten the others to do, that's all a waste if you don't beat Dagar's?"

"Of course not."

"Then don't make it a priority. Remember, you can only control what's within your power to control. Other athletes? Your scores?

Their scores? None of it is in your power to determine, so why not readjust your goal?"

"To what?" asked Joey, not sure what could possibly replace the fire that was ignited when Dagar kicked him out last May.

"How about just doing your best and let the results speak for themselves."

"Are you kidding? What kind of goal is that? Whatever you do is going to be the best you can do, that day, anyway."

"No, the goal should be to put on display the awesome dedication these guys have shown in following you. Besides, regardless of the result, if you don't beat the Edge's, you guys could easily think that the whole year has been for naught, but that's not so. Just think about how far these guys have come, especially Rodney. Holy cow! If there ever was a guy not built for this sport, it might be Rodney Joiner, but for some reason, he and the other guys have been more dedicated than you could've possibly imagined or counted on. You need to put THEIR contribution on display. You've spent the last 10 months empowering these guys, and now it's time to make THEM the subject of the spotlight."

"Golly, I hadn't even thought about it from that perspective."

"Which is why you have me."

"So, how do I go about shifting the emphasis with them? For some, like the Baker boys, are only in it for the revenge factor."

"I think you are missing something. Sure, they only came to you when they found they could exact a little revenge on Dagar, but there's no way that feeling has carried them this far. Somewhere along the way, I'll bet they have evolved their motivations, too. Just give them a chance."

"Of course, you're right. You're always right."

"Of course, I'm right. Now let's get out of here. I'm starving and it's your treat."

"Somehow it's always my treat." Joey and Carmen shut off the lights, locked the door, and headed for their bikes, and the local pizzeria.

29

"C'MON, JOE, BRING IT HOME!" shouted Alex, as Joey cranked his swing over the top of the High Bar, to set up his dismount. The bar pinged as Joey used every bit of potential energy created by his tap to finish the full-twisting double-layout. Joey sunk his feet into the blue vinyl and pushed to resist the force of his impact, to a motionless stick.

"Nice job, Joey!" said Coach Wheatley, "way to finish up the workout guys. Bring it in!"

The team discarded their grips and gathered around Coach Wheatley.

"That's the way you finish up your preparation for State! This whole week I think we only had, what three falls? I'll take that hit ratio any day!"

"So," asked Alex, "do you think we're ready?"

"Good question, Al. If you're asking if you guys have done enough to do your best this weekend, then the answer is yes, but..."

"There's always a 'but'," said Alex, "but, what? You don't think we can beat Dagar's guys?"

"Well, that's what I wanted to talk to you fellas about."

"So, you don't think we can beat them?" cried Logan.

"I didn't say that. Hold on. Stop. Everybody take a couple of deep breaths. Alright, look, if your only measure of success is beating the Edge's, you're missing the big picture, and you may be in for a big disappointment."

"So, you don't think we can win?" added Alex.

"I didn't say that. In fact, I think you guys have a really good shot at surprising everyone, but you have to see the bigger picture."

"There's a bigger picture than beating those jerks?" chimed Tommy.

"YES! A much bigger picture. First, the focus cannot be on winning or losing this meet. That's a result you don't get to control. I think you guys have a great shot, but a lot of things have to go your way. So, winning, or the thought of winning, takes your focus off of the one thing you CAN control, what you do."

"But, getting even with those guys has been what's pushed us this whole year," said Joey.

"Really? You mean to tell me that the only reason you and the rest have worked so hard is for revenge?"

"It's a pretty strong motivator," added Alex.

"So, if you hadn't been framed and kicked off the Edge team, you would've had no reason to push as hard as you have?"

"I'm sure getting to NTI's and trying to make a national team would've replaced my need to beat those guys."

"But, beating those guys, whether they were your teammates or the 'enemy', would've been part of the plan anyway, right?"

"I guess so," Joey conceded.

"Then let's look at it from that perspective. You all came to this place for similar reasons, but not the ones you may think. Rodney, what do you have against the Edge's?"

"Um, I don't know coach. I know I don't like 'em. And the others have enough against them, so I gotta back my brothers," surmised Rodney.

"But is that why you want to put that triple-back on floor? To beat them?"

"No, huh-uh, I want that for me."

"Explain."

"Since the first day you guys let me try this stuff, I have just wanted to do more! I've always been just an average guy. Not the last guy picked, but certainly not one of the first. But, like, every day in here I find I can do something that that I couldn't do yesterday, and I can do stuff that none of my other friends can do! No, I could care less about those other guys. I'm selfish. I'm in this for me!"

"Exactly," said Don, "regardless of the motivator you used to get in here, it was really just a means to an end. You each had a question as to what your body could do, what physics you could defy, and limits you could push. This was never about them. It's about you, and what you want out of this sport.

"Everything that you have done over the past year to prepare for this weekend will last long after you've hung up your grips for good. Unlike every other sport, where the challenges of the sport, throwing, catching, running, and what-not, come in learning how to play the game, gymnastics challenges you every day to be stronger, smarter, and BRAVER than you were the day before, or even the turn before.

"When you boys step foot in that arena, I have every confidence that you each will put your best gymnastics on the floor, and the challenges you've overcome, from having no equipment, to no coach, is a testament to your dedication to your goals. Your gymnastics is legit. You could not have prepared better, but you need to understand what REALLY motivates you. What do you think *really* motivates you?"

The boys looked at each other.

"Making you, and Coach Lowery proud," said Joey.

"I couldn't be prouder than I am, Joe. I only wish I had come to my senses a long time ago, but this is what I'm talking about. I let something someone else did keep me from what I really love. I realize it actually wasn't Gene's fault, it was my own. And you can bet that Jim Lowery is looking down with pride. Besides, I couldn't let a boy finish a man's job!"

Joey smiled and thought of Coach Lowery, and how similar the two coaches were.

"Alright, that's it, fellas! Go home get some rest. We leave from here tomorrow morning at ten a.m., with a workout on the competition equipment tomorrow night. Then competition is Saturday at four. You guys get out of here, and I'll see you in the morning. Good job fellas!"

The team gave each other high fives and headed for the showers. Carmen was waiting at the door as the guys came through.

"Good workout?" she asked.

"Awesome, actually. Everybody is hittin' on all eight cylinders! It's looking kinda good!"

"So, do you think…"

"It's gonna be what it's gonna be. All I know is we've prepared as best we can, and we are gonna go out and hit sets, and let the rest take care of itself."

"This is a new approach."

"I know, but it's so liberating! For so long I've had this chip on my shoulder, and for why? 'Cause Keith Pitts felt threatened and framed me? 'Cause Coach Dagar was afraid I'd ruin his reputation?"

"Yeah, something like that."

"Well, in that case, why don't you let your recently liberated shoulder carry me to dinner!"

"Of course. I didn't know liberation could make me so dang hungry!"

Joey let the door close behind him. The sound bounced around the gym and into Don's ears as he looked over the numbers he had crunched all week. As the sound of the door faded out, until the only sound was the hum coming from the metal halide lighting in the gym, Don punctuated his calculations with a subtle fist pump, and a percussive, "Yes." Don looked around at the gym, and dreamed of what it would look like filled with hungry athletes. After one more look around, he killed the lights and headed home.

30

"Do we really need to wait for Mrs. Banister?" asked Alex. All were packed, with their bags on the bus, just waiting on Mrs. Banister before heading to Lansing.

"Of course, we're going to wait," answered Coach Wheatley, "she's the one responsible for those kicking uniforms you guys are sporting. Plus, I owe her a ton, so this is a small sacrifice."

As the words escaped his lips, Coach Wheatley could see the shiny sedan pulling into the school lot.

"There she is!" exclaimed Joey, anxious like the rest, to get to Lansing and get this show on the road.

"Sorry I'm late, Donnie," she exclaimed, "but I had to wait until my cookies were finished." Barbara produced a sack full of home-baked goodies, which the boys grabbed and boarded the bus to divvy up the spoils.

"Thanks!" said Joey, "It's been a while since these jokers discovered their manners."

"Haha, Mr. Johnson, no less than I had expected from a group of growing boys. Enjoy!" Joey retreated into the bus to join the other fellas in dividing up their booty.

"Boys never change, Donnie," she said, "they still love cookies."

"Yeah, these guys are a team of regular garbage disposals! I don't think any of them have missed a meal!" Don motioned for Mrs. Banister to climb on board. Once on board, Don took his place behind the wheel and Barbara sat in the first seat behind him. Don put the bus in gear, and they were off.

"If you don't mind me asking, what is the order of activities?" she asked Don.

"Well, we have a workout when we get there, and competition starts, in earnest, Saturday, working our way from the young fellas up to these guys. Then it's kinda simple, everyone does their sets, and the best three out of six scores on each event determines the team score and who wins and who has to look to next year."

The trip over to Lansing went quickly, each person preoccupied with their tasks for the weekend. Athletes lost in music on their devices, Coach Wheatley continued to crunch numbers, as if some magic combination could assure a victory.

The bus pulled up to the host hotel, several other gymnasts were meandering about.

"Alright guys, let's get in and get settled." Coach Lowery went to the admit desk to check in while the fellas pulled out and organized luggage.

"Here we go, fellas," called Coach Wheatley, as he distributed room keys, "Johnson and Story, here, room 201. Rodney and Bobby, room 203. Timmy, Tommy, and Logan, suite 205. Mrs. Bannister is in room 207, and I'm right down the hall in room 209. Let's get in, get your stuff stowed and get ready for workout."

"Coach," asked Joey, "we gonna eat first?"

Coach Wheatley looked at his watch. Workout wasn't for another 90 minutes.

"Good idea, Joey. You guys put your other stuff in your room, bring your workout stuff, because we'll go from there to the site, so don't forget your grips and stuff." The boys made their way towards their respective rooms, downloaded their bags, grabbed their essential training gear, and headed back for the bus.

After a satisfying meal, the team headed for the competition site, Breslin Center.

"Wow, this place is huge!" commented Bobby.

"Win a few national basketball titles and the alumni will throw money at the university. MSU has fared well," said Coach Wheatley. The boys entered the main arena to a bit of a shock. It was easily the biggest venue any of them had ever been in before.

"Pretty high ceiling," noted Timmy, "could get lost in a High Bar dismount.

"That's part of why we're working out tonight, Bobby," replied Joey, "to work those bugs out."

The boys made their way to a part of the floor that wasn't already occupied by athletes, starting their warm up. While stretching, they noticed the boys from Dagar's Edge walking into the arena.

"Alright, boys, keep your cool." Coach Wheatley could almost see the smoke coming out of the boy's ears. "You guys have a job to do, so let's stay on point and keep those guys out of mind for a bit."

The Rams did their best to disregard the Edge's and focus on their own responsibilities. However, it's hard to ignore them when they walk right up and start the conversation.

"Oh, lookie, boys," said Keith, condescendingly, "the Rams of Taylor Center are here. I guess we should pack up and go home now."

"Are you ever not a jerk?" asked Joey.

"It's a gift," he replied.

"Well, you gents just focus on your job, and we'll stay focused on ours," barked Joey.

"But what fun is that? Oh, well, I guess the Rams don't want to play, fellas, let's get after it." And the Edge's moved to another part of the arena to start their warm up. Gene followed his charges and walked up to Don.

"Well, here we are Donnie," Gene said.

"Indeed. It's been an interesting year," Don replied.

"Enjoy it while you can, Donnie. From what I hear, the schoolboard has decided to razz your gym this summer."

"How did you...?"

"Who do you think pushed to expedite the demolition? It's in the city's best interest to get that financial albatross off the books as soon as possible, so money that's being wasted on your gym, can go to more beneficial things."

"Why does that not surprise me?" replied Don, trying not to lose his cool. "There's still time to find a buyer."

"Not likely," said Gene, "but, good luck with that. And, good luck tomorrow." Gene delivered his parting shot and turned to catch up with his team.

"What was that about, Donnie?" asked Mrs. Banister, "Is the schoolboard closing the gym?"

"Yeah, it turns out that the rec center isn't doing a good job of justifying its existence, and they want to tear it down as soon as we finish our season. So, yeah, if we don't move on, the demo could start next week. Even if we do move on, it will only delay the inevitable."

"Oh, dear, why didn't you tell me?"

"You've been so supportive, and I thank you, but I didn't have the heart to tell you."

"Donnie," she scolded, "You should know better than that. You just put that out of your mind, and coach those boys. You never know, they might just have a future!" She pat Don on the back and shooed him back to the team. Then walked out into a quiet corridor to place a phone call.

"Those guys just burn me up," said Joey.
"Then it's working," said Alex, in mid-stretch.
"What's working?"
"You don't think Keith knows he's in your head?"
"He's not in my ..."
"Yes, he is. Constantly."
"What makes you think..."
"Just start training, and try not to think of the Edge's, OK?"
"I'll try. Should be no big."

However, it was. As long as the Edges were there, Joey could not find his rhythm, falling several times on Horse and missing connections on High Bar. And with each miss, Joey could see the Edges snicker, which only made matters worse.

"Dude, you have got to get them out of your head!" exclaimed Alex, "You will be worthless tomorrow, if you don't!"

Joey tried to shake his thoughts, but each attempt to shift thought always led back to thoughts of how the Edges had his number, which only added to the frustration, and caused more mistakes.

Joey finished his workout, if you could call it that, and stormed out of the arena. Alex watched as Joey disappeared through the exit doors, then turned to see the Edge's, snickering. Having taken their last turns, Alex bolted out the door to look for Joey. It didn't take long as he was parked on a bench, just outside the arena. Joey was staring into space.

"You ok, pal?" asked Alex.

"I don't know. I don't know why I let Keith get to me."

"Aw, I think you're just too good a person, Joe."

"What?"

"Face it, you try to see the good in everyone. And when you're done wrong, you go nuts."

Joey pondered the idea.

"You just gotta find a way to ignore him."

"How do I do that?" Joey asked.

"Heck, I don't know. Picture Keith competing in his underwear."

Joey furrowed his brow.

"Complete with visible skid marks!" Joey exploded with laughter. Just what was needed to bring him out of his mood.

"Thanks, Alex. That was really funny."

"No problem. Glad to be of service."

The rest of the team, Coach Wheatley, and Mrs. Banister emerged from the arena.

"You gonna be ok to eat some pizza?" asked Coach Wheatley.

"I was kinda hopin' you might let me spend some time with Carmen," Joey said, as Carmen joined the group.

"Well, you hoped wrong. I'm responsible for you and you need to stay with the group."

"Yessir. Do you mind if she comes with us?"

"Can't stop the girl from eating at a public establishment. Of course, she can join us. She's been as much a part of this team as anyone. Climb aboard!" replied Coach Wheatley, as the bus pulled up.

"I'd love to join you guys, but I'll have to meet you there, my bike is here."

"Fair enough. Just follow us."

After a hearty meal, the check paid, the group started making their way toward the door.

"Alright boys," said Coach Wheatley, "we'll have about an hour before lights out, so when we get back you guys can get some spa time."

"Coach, can Carmen give me a ride back," asked Joey.

"I thought we covered this?"

"It's just a ride. I promise I won't be more than an hour late."

"If you're not back a half hour after we get to the hotel, you'll be scratched from the meet. I'm serious!"

"Forty-five minutes?"

"Thirty. Not Thirty-one."

"Okay. Thanks Coach." Joey and Carmen headed for her bike.

"So, if I bring my girlfriend can I take off, too?" asked Alex, sarcastically.

"I know it breaks with protocol, but if Carmen can get Joey's head back on straight, it'll be thirty minutes well spent." Coach Wheatley followed his troops onto the bus, closed the door and headed for the hotel. Joey and Carmen headed to Crego Park, a little faster than the posted speed limit.

Carmen slowed her bike and came to a stop at a nice quiet spot,

Pulling a blanket from her saddle bag, the two had a seat facing the lake, the sun setting across the way. They stared at their surroundings in silence for a moment before Joey opened up.

"I don't get it. Why can't I get Keith out of my head?"

"Because you expect him to change. You have to forget about him."

"Yeah, that's what I've heard. I've tried. Got any ideas?"

Carmen thought for a moment. "Have you thought about forgiving him?"

"What? After all he's done?" cried Joey.

"I think your problem is thinking this about you!"

"What?"

"This not about you, it's about Keith. He's the weak one. He's threatened by you. The only way he wins is by you falling apart. It's pitiful, so, pity him."

"Should I forgive him or pity him?"

"It doesn't matter, pity him, forgive him, or both. Just try for once to see that it's his weakness, not yours, that has brought you to this point. If you can't see him for the sorry soul he is, and that when you make this about you, he wins!"

Joey thought long and hard, "You know, you're right. I see now."

"See? That wasn't so difficult."

Joey gave her a big kiss, "What would I do without you?"

"Something stupid, I'm sure." Both laughed, "I better get you back before you get scratched!"

"Do you really think he would scratch me?"

"Do you really want to find out?"

"No," he replied, "I'm actually a little excited to get back. I got this."

Carmen gave him a peck on the cheek and hopped to her feet, tugging at the blanket, rolling Joey off. She wadded the blanket and pulled Joey to his feet. She secured the blanket and they hopped on her Honda and headed back to the hotel.

Five minutes early.

31

The next morning, the boys gathered for breakfast, each locked into his personal space in preparation for the battle ahead. They continued in silence until Coach Wheatley tapped his water glass to get the attention of his charges.

"Gentlemen, as we get ready to see if your year of training will be enough for the task ahead, there's a few things I'd like to leave you with before the meet. First, and foremost, I want to thank you boys for bringing me back to the sport I love. I let a lot of things that were out of my control lead me, not only away from the sport I love, but down a dark hole that I may never have crawled out were it not for you boys. Most specifically, Joey, who, somehow, brought all of these different kinds of guys together. Regardless of how this all turns out today, know that I am extremely grateful for the effort and passion you boys have shown. You are to be commended for all you've done to get to this point. Although this is a team sport, it is up to you, as an individual, to find your focus and apply what you've learned.

"Each of you have been given certain gifts, and your task is to trust your training, trust the process, and give it your all, without reservation. You've all worked very hard to get to this point, and now is the time for you to unleash the beast. But, regardless of the result, you've all worked extremely hard and my hope is that the fruit of your labor shows in your efforts today.

"I want to also thank Barbara Banister for her support. You guys never got to meet Johnny, but he reminds me a lot of each of you. He was hungry for the next step and worked extremely hard to achieve his goals. Not unlike each of you." Coach Wheatley took his seat as Joey rose.

"I want to thank Coach Wheatley for coming to our rescue and provide the guidance I only wish I could give, to get you guys where you are today," Joey said, "All of you have bought into the idea that, together, we can do almost anything, and today we get to find out if our work was worthwhile. Like Coach said, regardless of the result today, I am pretty darn proud of what we've done in such a short time, and grateful for each of you, for believing in the cause, and going along with me to create something that will stay with us the rest of our lives. I'm proud of y'all, and proud to be a part of this team." Joey took his seat to the applause of his teammates and coach.

After a few minutes of silence, while the boys finished breakfast, Alex spoke, "I gotta say, fellas, this has been one weird trip. At first, I was pissed to get booted from Dagar's Edge, but what we've done since last summer has been more gratifying and rewarding than anything I could've gotten from the Edge." Alex turned to Coach Wheatley, "Do we know where we start, Coach?"

"We start on Pommel Horse, Edge starts on Floor Exercise. Since Pommels is traditionally a low scoring event, versus Floor, where the scores are higher, we may be playing from behind after first event. But don't let that worry you. We should know a lot after the first few events. Edge will have to get through Pommels and Rings, while we should be able to make up ground on Vault. So, halfway through we should have a good idea where we stand." The boys pondered the possibilities, ranging from being out in front after three events to being out of contention halfway through the meet.

Coach Wheatley settled the check and the Rams, with Coach Wheatly and Barbara Banister, boarded the bus for the short drive to the arena.

The bus pulled up to the front of the arena. Coach Wheatley stood at the front of the bus, "Alright guys, here we go. If I know

Gene, they will be trying to into your head to gain an advantage. Understand that that is an act of desperation, like pounding their chest to show dominance. Don't be fooled, stay focused, stay on task. Their antics will only work if you give permission. I suggest you don't. Let's get in, get focused, and make the most of this moment."

The team filed out of the bus and entered the arena. They walked directly to the seating area designated for Pommel Horse, and dropped off their gear, then made their way to the Floor Exercise carpet to begin their stretch.

After setting his bag down, Joey looked up to see Carmen and his parents enter the arena. Joey quickly jogged over to see them.

"Mom! You made it!" shouted Joey.

"Of course, son," she said, "I got in last night. You know I wouldn't miss this!"

"Now don't screw up, Joe, I'm recording everything!" said Jonas, sporting a brand-new camcorder.

"You don't have to shoot everything, dad," said Joey, "Just the routines will be enough."

"It's my camera, I'll record as much as I want. Besides, some of your best turns happen in warm up!"

"Whatever you say, dad. Knock yourself out." Joey gave Carmen a kiss on the cheek and hurried back to join the team.

No sooner had they finished a light jog around the Floor border and settled into an open space on the floor to stretch, that Dagar's Edge entered the arena with an arrogant swagger, as if they had already won.

"Ignore those guys, Joe," said Alex, "They're just gonna try to get into your head again."

"Not gonna happen, Al. I got this figured out." Joey popped to his feet and made a bee-line toward Keith Pitts.

"Hey, Keith, good luck today," Joey said, extending his right hand to shake his.

"Sure, Hillbilly, let's have a good show."

"I just wanted you to know that I forgive you, Keith."

"Oh, really?"

"Yep. I've decided that regardless of all the nonsense you've pulled, that this was less about me, and mostly about you. So, I'm tired of feeling like my troubles are your fault. So, I just considered the source, and figured that you gotta live with you, and I for me."

"How profound, Hillbilly," said Keith, "Tell you what, you guys beat us today, and I'll buy the pizza afterward."

"No need. We are just gonna focus on our sets and see how the chips fall. I forgive you for what you've done to me, but that doesn't mean I'll forget it. In fact, I should thank you. If you hadn't worked so hard get rid of me last year, I would've, likely, never met these awesome guys. And, with every breath, I'm trying to get good enough to beat you. You've been the best motivator for me and my team, so I gotta thank you for that. You're no friend, Keith, so this will be our last conversation. Have a good meet." Joey, having said his piece, returned to his team.

"What was that all about?" asked Logan.

"Oh, I just felt I needed to forgive Keith for all his antics. Carmen and I talked a bunch, and I realized that what I've done, I've done to myself. So, forgiving Keith was the first step to getting him out of my head."

"And what's the next step?" asked Alex.

"Why, kicking his Yankee ass, Al."

"That's my boy." The boys resumed their stretch.

"What was that about, Keith?" said Coach Dagar as Keith returned to his team.

"Johnson was forgiving me."

"Forgiving you? HA! That just shows how weak he is."

"Yessir," Keith replied, although he didn't quite agree with his coach's assessment.

As Coach Dagar finished and sent Keith to join the rest of the Edges in stretch, Coach Wheatley and Barbara Banister approached him.

"Say, Gene, just wanted to wish you good luck today," said Don.

"We don't need luck, Don, this is just a necessary step toward our next NTI. I sure hope you enjoy today. It'll be your last for a while, after they razz your gym next month!" Gene said, condescendingly.

Barbara stepped between the two.

"Eugene, that's no way to talk to old friends," she said.

"But, I don't consider you two friends. You are the enemy. An enemy I'll be happy to watch fall today, and then again when they tear your gym down!"

"About that," Barbara said, then turned to Don, "Did I forget to tell you, Donnie, that Maggy Case is an old friend of mine?"

"The superintendent of the Taylor Schools? No, you never mentioned it, Barbara," replied Don.

"Oh yes, we go way back. And it was surprising how little the school board was willing to settle for to keep the gym open!" she replied. Gene's eyes began to bulge.

"WHAT!?!" cried Coach Dagar.

"Yes, Eugene," she continued, "once I explained what Donnie was doing for these boys, they were quite acceptable to my offer."

"Your...offer?"

"Why yes, Eugene. Ever since Johnny passed, I put his insurance settlement into an IRA that builds quite a bit over almost 30 years. I couldn't think of a better way to invest his money, than into Donnie's program. It's amazing what you can do with half a million dollars."

"So, it's not going to be torn down?" cried Gene.

"Not only is it not going to be torn down, it's now mine. And as such, Donnie will be able to coach as long as he wants and my Johnny can rest easy knowing that his passing wasn't all in vain."

"I guess we'll be seeing a lot more of each other over the next few years, Gene!" exclaimed a joyful Don Wheatley, who was hearing Barbara's bombshell for the first time, "Have a good meet."

Don and Barbara headed back to the team. It was all he could do to keep from giving her a bear hug. Instead, they exchanged high fives.

"Boys," said Coach Wheatley to his team, "great news. As was just told to me, Mrs. Banister, here, has purchased Taylor Center! Not only is it not going to be torn down, but will be our home as long as we like!" The team, not feeling the same inhibition as Don, jumped to their feet and gang-hugged Barbara.

Gentlemen, you may begin warm up on your first event, came the announcement from the loud speaker.

"Well, boys, here's where the rubber meets the road. Let's get after it! The format has been changed, It's now only four up, three scores count." The Taylor Rams headed to Pommel Horse to begin their quest. In the "four up, three scores count" format, Don would have to designate his four athletes for each event, and the order they would compete. On Horse it would be Bobby, then Alex, followed by Joey, and then their anchor and strongest Pommel Horseman, Logan, would be last.

Following the ten-minute warm up, the teams lined up at first event for introductions and the singing of the National Anthem. Following the anthem, the announcer called,

Gentlemen, report to the judges at your first event to present yourselves and begin competition. Good Luck all!

Knowing that they would have their gym for the foreseeable future, the Rams presented themselves to the Pommel Horse judges with a renewed sense of pride. While the rest of the team stood at their seats, Bobby chalked up to prepare for his routine.

"Okay, Bobby," said Coach Wheatley, "we will have one score to drop on each event, so don't feel like it's on you to win this for us, however, your routine will set the pace for today, so relax and hit a good set to get us started!" Bobby nodded to his coach and turned his thoughts inward, visualizing his routine. Once finished, he raised his head and saluted the judges.

Bobby's routine started simply, jumping into scissor work first, then picking up to circles, Bobby did a quarter turn on the pommel to do several circles on one pommel, including several circles that turned and required support in his hands behind his back, to secure some bonus. Once his pommel circles finished, Bobby broke into his flairs. The rest of his routine consisted of circles, travels, and hops from position to position. Then he shifted from traditional flairs to the elevated air-flairs, his hips overhead, turning and hopping from end to end at blazing speed, culminating with a handstand that turned down the horse and back before joining his legs together and dropping to the blue vinyl surface, sinking his feet into the mat for a stuck landing! The Rams all jumped to their feet and joined the chorus of cheers coming from the grandstands.

"Way to set the pace, Bob!" yelled Joey.

"Crap," said Logan, "that set was good enough to be the anchor, Bobby!"

The team watched as the judges had to confer, just to make sure they had all seen the same thing, and to make sure they were in agreement on the value of Bobby's original parts. The team waited patiently for the final score was posted. 14.7, one of the highest Pommel Horse scores of the season!

Bobby's set setup Alex, Joey, and finally Logan for four hit sets on the first event. The Edges, on the other hand, were proving that it has been no accident that they have qualified for the National Team Invitational twenty years in a row, hitting all four of the routines they put up.

At the finish of the first rotation, the announcer called,

That concludes the first rotation. Gentlemen, you may move to your second event and begin your warm up. After one event, in third place, with a team score of 39.6, Melvindale Gymnastics. In second place with

*a score of 41.7, the Taylor Rams, and your leaders after one event, with
an event score of 43.3, Dagar's Edge!*

"Holy cow!" exclaimed Joey, "after hitting all four sets, we're
already a point and a half behind!"

"Yeah, but we started on pig," said Alex, "we'll see a little more
where we stand after the next event!"

"Not only that," said Logan, "Melvindale is just two points
behind us! If we're not careful, we could slip to third!"

"Stay focused, guys," said Coach Wheatley, "we have a long way
to go and you don't want get caught off guard focusing on the scores.
Rings is next. Let's get those grips on!"

The Rams rotated to Rings, putting their grips on as they walked.

"Okay, here's the order," said Coach, "Rodney, you're up first.
Tommy, Alex, and Joey will follow Rod."

Rodney saluted the judge and stood under the Ring tower. Coach
Wheatley helped Rodney jump to the Rings and held Rodney's legs
to bring him to a still hang before releasing and stepping back
to watch the routine. The Edge's, as they prepared for Pommel
Horse, looked at Rings and snickered to see Rodney up on Rings,
remembering his melt down from the first meet. However, their
grins turned to open-mouthed surprise to see how much Rodney had
improved. When Rodney began training with Taylor, he couldn't
do a simple muscle up. But now Rodney showed how much he
had improved by starting with a backward roll into an iron cross.
From there he pressed up and forward to a Maltese (horizontal)
cross, and, after a three second hold, pressed up to a solid, straight
handstand. From his handstand, he dropped into several swing
elements, finishing with a solid double-back, in layout position.

Rodney's hit routine was the cause for cheers from both his team
and the crowd. The Edge's heard the applause and caused their first
fall on the day. Danny Dukes clipped his legs on the end of the
horse, which sent his body over the horse and onto the floor. A full

point deduction. Danny finished his routine, with one more fall and several form breaks, for a 10.2 score.

"They'll likely drop Danny's score," said Joey.

"Ya think?" replied Alex.

Tommy was next. As much as Rodney's routine was centered around his brute strength, Tommy's routine was comprised of mostly swing. From a tucked double front (Yamiwakee) to piked double front (Johanson), finishing with his first strength part, a back uprise to a horizontal, straddled planche. Tommy pressed the rest of the way up to his handstand, then swung a giant forward and one backward, both stopping in a handstand, but with each handstand, the rings had a little bit of forward and backward swing, instead of the still handstand he was hoping for. Once he fulfilled the rest of the routine, Tommy waited for his swing to go forward so he could drop for his dismount, a tucked full-twisting double-back, stuck!

"Way to go, Tommy!" shouted Joey.

Tommy came back to high fives and fist bumps. He looked up at his score, 13.5.

"Great job, Tommy," said Coach Wheatley, "That'll work!"

"How we doin' Coach?" Tommy asked.

"Pretty good. Edge's have to count two falls, so far!"

It was Alex's turn. He blew the excess chalk from his grips, tightened his pony tail, and saluted the judge. Coach Wheatley helped him mount and bring him to a still hang. Although Alex had a more balanced routine than Rod and Bobby, his strength parts were not quite as difficult as the routines that would follow. But the routine was solid, with a fine full-twisting double-back to another stuck landing!

"Way to go, Alex!" shouted the team.

"Nice set, Al," said Logan, "I think we might end up in front after Joey's routine. The Edge's had to count three falls on Pommels!"

Coach Wheatley assisted Joey to the Rings for the start of his set. Joey mounted with a cast to uprise iron cross. Joey pressed hard on the Rings and ended in a Maltese cross of his own. From the

Maltese, Joey pressed his body over the top and swung down and up to arrive in another Maltese cross, then, after a two second hold, Joey pressed his body up to a planche, then up to his handstand. After his hold, Joey bailed forward and did his version of the Yamiwakee/Johanson combination, finishing with a solid swing handstand. After his hold, Joey swung a giant in each direction, and finished with a full-twisting double layout. Stuck! Joey punched the thin air and let out a growl that could barely be heard over the cheers of the crowd. Joey's 14.7 score was flashed as the announcer called for rotation to third event.

Gentlemen, this concludes the second rotation. At this time, you may rotate to your third event and begin your timed warm up. At the end of two rotations, in third place, with a score of 71.4, Melvindale, and we have a tie at the first-place position. Co-leaders, with a team score of 85.2, Dagar's Edge and Taylor Rams!

The boys rotated to their third event, Vault.

"Alright, guys, here's where we can put some distance between us and the Edge's. Here's your order, Timmy, Logan, Alex, Joey."

Rodney furrowed his brow at the fact he would not be competing vault.

"Coach, I thought I was Vaulting today?" said Rodney.

"It was a tough call, Rod, but it came down to who I think can score higher, and Timmy's Tsukahara with a full twist will very likely outscore your Front-handspring front. Not to worry, we will be counting on you down the road." Rodney, while still a little dejected, came to the same conclusion, once he pondered it.

Timmy lived up to his coach's prediction and nailed his Vault for a respectable 14.8 score. Timmy's Vault was followed by hit Vaults by Logan, Alex and Joey, who scored a 15.1 to lead the group. Since Vault goes by so fast, the Rams were able to watch the last two routines from the Edge's on Rings from Tom Schultz and Keith.

Both hit their sets but couldn't make up ground on the Rams. The announcer called out what the Edge's already knew,

Gentlemen, we have reached the halfway point in the competition. At this time, rotate to your fourth event. After three rotations, in third place with a score of 106.6, Melvindale. In second place, with a score of 125.2, Dagar's Edge. And your new leaders, with a score of 128.1, Taylor Rams!

In addition to the crowd roar, the Rams were trading high fives and fist bumps. Coach Wheatley quickly put a stop to the premature celebration, "GUYS! GET FOCUSED. It's great that we are out in front, but there's still three events left and this could easily go sideways if you're not on point!" The boys immediately shifted from celebratory to solemn, shifting their focus to their next event, Parallel Bars.

"Okay, fellas, here's your order, Tommy, Timmy, Logan, and Joey." Ordered Coach Wheatley. And they began their warm up, the team cheering each teammate as they warmed up.

Over at the Edge's bench, the mood was one of panic. For the first time, they were behind in a State meet.

"You guys better figure out something or we will end up watching the Rams on ESPN at NTI's!" cried Coach Dagar.

The Edge's tried to figure out what they could possibly do beyond just hitting their routines.

"I've got an idea! Danny hand me your nail clippers," said Keith.

"Why?" asked Danny.

"Just hand them over." Danny grabbed his grip bag and reached in to pull out his nail clippers.

"What are you gonna do, Keith?"

"Never mind, Danny, just focus on your Vault."

Keith made his way over to the seating area for Parallel Bars, making sure that the Rams attention was on their teammates. He reached over the chairs and grabbed Joey's grip bag. Pulling out one of his High Bar grips, Keith quickly snipped a small cut near the base of the grip and returned them to Joey's bag, just as the Rams were finishing their warm up turns. They were surprised to see Keith standing behind their seating area.

"What are you doing over here, Keith? Don't you have a Vault to warm up?" asked Joey.

"Oh, I'm not in the line up for Vault, so I wanted to take the opportunity to come over and thank you for your words earlier. I've had time to think about and I just want to apologize for all the crap I've pulled on you this year. Thanks for putting it all behind you. I hope we can still be friends." Keith lied.

"Sure," said a confused Joey, "glad you've seen the error of your ways. Let's talk after the meet, OK?"

"Sure, man, have a good rest of the meet!" Keith shook Joey's hand and headed back to his team.

"Well, that was quite out of the ordinary," said Alex, "I don't trust him any further than I can throw him."

"Aw, c'mon, Al, you gotta believe that guys can have a change of heart," said Joey.

"Not this guy. He's trying to get into your head again."

"No chance. I've done my part. I've forgiven him. I'm competing with a clear conscience."

"If you say so, Joe. Right now, you better focus on a P-bars set."

"Alrighty, gents, let's attack P's. Here's your order, Timmy, you're up first. Alex, Logan and Joey," said Coach Wheatley.

Timmy gave the Rams a good start with a hit routine. Not very difficult, but clean enough to get him into the 13's. Alex, Logan, and Joey followed with three more hit sets, none scoring below 13.5. In the meanwhile, the Edge's were putting on a Vault clinic, posting three scores above 14. The announcer called the rotation,

Gentlemen, that's four routines in the books. At this time rotate to your fifth event. At the end of four rotations, in third place, Grand

243

River Gymnastics with a 156.7, in second place, with a 166.8, Dagar's Edge, and your leader after four events, with a 170.1, the Taylor Rams!

"Wow, we have almost a three-point lead with two events to go!" said Alex.

"Stay focused, Alex," returned Coach Wheatley, "it wouldn't take much for that lead to disappear with a couple falls. Keep your head in the game."

"Yessir."

"Here's our order, Bobby, you're our lead-off. Hit a strong set! Following Bob is Logan, Alex and Joey."

The boys warmed up their High Bar routines. Although he didn't notice, the tear in Joey's grip was getting a little larger with each catch of the bar.

Tommy led the way with a solid 13.1. Logan followed with a respectable 14.6. Alex had some trouble with swinging off axis on his Blind Change and Pirouette, requiring him to break form to recover. It wasn't the set he wanted, scoring a paltry 13.2.

"Well, Joey," said Coach Wheatley, "Alex has put a little pressure on you for us to keep up with the Edge's so be clean, be tight, and be aggressive!"

"Gotcha, Coach!"

After Joey saluted the judges, Coach Wheatley helped Joey up onto the bar. Joey began with a pike to the bar, then kicking backward to rise up to the bar, followed by pirouette and turning giants. Joey fulfilled his "in-bar" requirement and then set up for his release sequence. He closed his hips as he came over the bar to set up the first release, a Tkachev back over the bar in layout position, to be followed by another Tkachev, in straddled position, followed by a final Tkachev, straddled with a half turn on the catch. But after the first release, Joey could tell that his grip was getting loose. On the second release, Joey's grip tore through, causing Joey to peel his hand off the bar, followed by the other hand. Joey flew off the bar. In his effort to find the landing mat, Joey landed awkwardly on one foot, and he heard a "pop" in his left knee and he crumbled into the mat, grabbing his knee!

"Joey, are you okay?" asked Coach Wheatley.

"It's my knee. I felt it pop!" Joey grimaced as Coach Wheatley helped him up to his one, good foot, and helped him to the trainer's table. Looking into the stands, Joey could see Carmen, standing next to his parents, shrugging her shoulders, as if to say, *What the heck was that?* Joey raised his hand to show his grip in two pieces, the strap, still attached to his wrist, and the rest, detached from the base, the strap of leather with the dowel and three finger holes, hanging off his middle three digits.

Coach Wheatley dropped Joey off to the care of the trainer while he headed to the High Bar judges' table to see what could be done.

"His grip failed," Coach Wheatley pleaded, "what can we do about it?" Don showed the judges what was left of his High Bar grip.

"Well," said the head judge, "since he had a grip failure, he's allowed to repeat the sequence without penalty."

"If he can compete at all. Plus, we have to find a replacement grip!"

"And," said the head judge, "since his routine came at the end of the rotation, you have very little time to make that decision. We must move the meet along."

"I understand," said Don, "can I get, like three minutes to go over and see what the trainer says? It may be a moot point."

"You may have two minutes, Mr. Wheatley. Otherwise the routine stands as scored, without the dismount requirement."

Coach Wheatley hustled over to the trainer's table where Joey was just sitting up from having an air cast fit to his damaged left knee.

"So, what's the prognosis, doc?" asked Coach Wheatley.

"I don't think the damage is too severe," said the trainer, "I saw the spill/ It's a good thing he has such good reflexes, or it could've been much worse. I think it is only a sprain, but I would strongly suggest seeing your family orthopedic as soon as you get home, to make sure I'm right"

"But, can he finish?"

"You're just in time to see, Coach," said Joey, as he slowly stood from the trainer's table and tried to put weight on his left foot. No sooner did he try to balance, he could feel his knee buckling. Coach Wheatley caught him before he hit the floor.

"I'm pretty sure that means he's done for the day, coach," said the trainer, helping Don get Joey back to the table, "I'll fit him with crutches, and he can return to your team."

Don walked over to the High Bar judges table, "He can't finish, so, no need to hold up the meet any longer." The head judge nodded and pushed the button that sent the final score to the scorers' computer, and up on the display board. Coach Wheatley turned to see the 9.9 post for Joey's score. His score would be dropped, and Bobby's 13.1, combined with Alex and Logan's scores, for 40.9 team score.

Gentlemen, called the announcer, *at this time rotate to your final competitive event. At the end of five events, in third place, with a score of 205.3, Grand River Gymnastics, in second place, with a score of 211.0, the Taylor Rams, and your leader going into the final rotation, with a score of 211.8, Dagar's Edge!*

The Rams walked to their last event, Floor Exercise, with a sense of dread. They now knew the score. With only eight-tenths of a point separating them, and without their best athlete, and no one ready to step up to be the fourth routine, it would be up to Logan, Alex, and Rodney to hit their sets, and hope that will be enough against the Edge's, who still had a fourth score to drop on their last event, High Bar.

Joey, complete with a set of crutches, caught up with his team as they were placing their things at the seating area.

"Coach, I think Rodney should anchor," called Joey, "I think his will be the most dynamic routine."

Coach Wheatley looked at Rodney, "Well, Bullet, think you can handle the anchor spot?"

"I was born for it, Coach!" he replied.

"Alright, then, Logan, you get to lead off. Alex second and Rodney caps off the meet. Fellas, I know we've been dealt a crappy hand, but we are still in this! Just give it your best and we'll let the chips fall where they may. Regardless of the outcome, you guys have done yourself proud. You've worked hard and have earned every accolade."

Joey looked up into the crowd to find Carmen, but she wasn't sitting next to his folks. He scanned the crowd to find her, but no luck. *She must've gone to the bathroom*, he thought.

Dagar's first High Bar set was less than stellar, 12.1, a score sure to be dropped. Meanwhile, Logan saluted the head judge on floor and stepped into the corner of the floor exercise carpet to start his routine. Although his tumbling was not on par with the best, including his teammates, Logan added complex dance elements and connections that few had seen before, full-twisting butterfly, spindling flairs, Tour jete full, and a difficult "swallow" press handstand. At the end of the routine, the judges had to confer to come up with a score. When the 14.8 was flashed the team jumped and high fived Logan.

"Great job, Logan," cheered Joey, "that stuff was cool, man!"

"Couldn't have pulled it off without Carmen's help!" Joey looked back at the stands to find Carmen, but she had not returned to her seat. As Joey swung his head around to watch Alex's routine, his eyes caught the familiar frame of Carmen at the scorer's table. *What is she doing there?* He thought.

The next Edge on High Bar, Tom Shultz, put up an impressive routine, with a stuck landing, to score an impressive 14.8.

Knowing that they were still .7 away from the Edge's, Joey gave

Alex the best pep-talk he could think of, "Get out there and kick some ass, Alex. Remember, you started this!"

"Oh, thanks, pal. No pressure at all," Alex replied, sarcastically.

Alex saluted the judge and stepped into the corner. After a big breath, Alex raised his arms and rose on his toes, and sprinted across the floor to execute a massive, round-off, back handspring double-back in layout position, to a stuck landing! After turning to step to the corner, Alex darted back across the floor to do another double-back, this one tucked with a full twist, to another stuck landing. He then jogged across the side of the floor to do round-off 3/2 twist to an immediate punch-front with a full twist. Alex dropped to the floor and pushed into flairs that popped into a turning handstand, and taking a page from Bobby's playbook, broke into his version of air-flairs before dropping to a front support and popping back up to his feet, turning into the corner. Alex grabbed a breath before sprinting across the royal blue diagonal for his final pass, a layout with three twists. Stuck! Alex returned to the seating area to cheers and pats on the back.

"That's how you close a State Meet, Alex!" said Joey.

"Thanks, pal," replied Alex, "I hope it's enough to make a dent!" The Rams looked to the scoreboard to see Alex's score, which came up at the same time as Edge's third High Bar score. Alex scored a 15.2 to Danny Dukes 14.4.

"Holy Smokes!" Joey cried, "Alex's set brought us to within one tenth!" Joey turned to Rodney, "Alright, Rod, here's the deal. Keith is Edge's best High Bar swinger. He's probably gonna pull of a low to mid fifteen. You have been waiting for this moment to represent. Get out there and give it your best!"

"That's it?" asked Rodney, "That's your pep-talk? Why not just say, 'Good luck, we're all counting on you'?" Joey was trying not to show that the odds were against Rodney, a first year, former backyard tumbler, against one of the best Dagar's Edge has produced. "No worries, Joe, I was born for this!" The pair fist-bumped and Rodney took his place in the corner, his head bowed as he went through his set in his mind and said a little prayer before lifting his head to seek out the head judge to signal his readiness. Rodney stepped inside the 40' by 40 border and took a deep breath.

With the weight of the world on his shoulders, Rodney sprinted across the floor and stretched a quick round-off back handspring and exploded upward. One, two, THREE flips to a stuck landing! Cheers erupted as Rodney, casually, turned to the corner for his next pass. Rod launched a 2 ½ twisting layout into a punch 1 ½! He turned into the corner and did his, obligatory, press to handstand. Stepping down into the corner, Rodney set up for his third pass, a full-twisting double tuck! Then finished his set with a piked double back, to a stuck landing, and the cheers of friends and fans alike! Rodney came back to the team to hugs and congratulations.

"That was outstanding, Bullet!" said Coach Wheatley.

"Thanks, Coach. I hope it's enough!"

The team waited patiently for Rodney's score. In the meanwhile, Keith's score on High Bar came up first. 15.2. Rodney would need a 15.3 to tie the Edge's. After much deliberation, Rodney's score was posted. 14.9

"Crap," said Joey, "I thought we had 'em with that floor set."

"Well, keep your chins up, fellas," said Coach Wheatley, "You boys did great."

Joey looked over to the scorer's table, where Carmen was still talking to the officials, and it looked as though they were looking at Jonas' camcorder. Coach Wheatley made his way over to the table to see what was going on, but before he could reach them, the group broke up and Carmen met with Coach Wheatley to explain as they made their way back to the team. Just as they approached Joey, the announcer broadcast the results

After the final event, in third place, with a 249.9, Grand River Gymnastics, in second place with a 255.9, the Taylor Rams, and your State Champions and qualifiers to the National Team Invitational, with a score of 256.2... Just a moment ladies and gentlemen. The

announcer paused as the Meet Referee reported the new result. *Ladies and gentlemen, due to an unsportsmen act on behalf of one of the Dagar's Edge gymnasts, his scores have been forfeited, and their score recalculated using their dropped scores. Your final results, in third place, with a revised score of 249.6, Dagar's Edge, in second place with a score of 249.9, Grand River, and your State Champions and qualifiers to the National Team Invitational, with a score of 255.9, the Taylor Center Rams!*

The Rams jumped for joy and hugged each other as tears streamed down Joey's cheeks as he grabbed Carmen. "How did you…?"

"And you didn't want your dad to record everything? If he hadn't, he wouldn't have been recording your Parallel Bars warm up and would've missed Keith cutting your High Bar grip with a pair of nail clippers!"

"Wow, you saved me again, Carmen!" exclaimed Joey.

"I guess you should keep me around."

"Indeed." Joey gave her a big kiss.

"I don't mean to interrupt," said Coach Wheatley, "but there is this little thing about an awards ceremony we have to take care of." Don put his arm around Joey's shoulder and led him and the team toward to staging area.

As the third place was announced, the Edge's were nowhere to be found.

"I guess getting your ass handed to you was a bit more than they could bear!" said Alex. Grand River proudly took their position at second. When the champions were announced, the Rams each congratulated the Grand River guys before taking their place on the award stand. After being presented with the first-place trophy, the boys, respectfully gave the trophy to Coach Wheatley.

"Thank you, fellas," he said, "this means a lot."

"It means a ton to us, too, Coach," said Joey, "I don't know if we could've pulled it off without you! Thanks for believing in us!"

"No, Joey, it's you I should be thanking. If not for you and Alex, I may have never crawled out of the hole I dug for myself."

"My pleasure, Coach! Looks like you've got work ahead of you."

Will Joey Johnson report to the officials table, said the voice over the loudspeaker.

Joey crutched his way to the scorer's table, with Alex in tow. As they arrived, they could see that security had Keith in their grasp.

"Mr. Johnson?" asked the head official.

"Yessir."

"We have determined that Mr. Pitts sabotaged your High Bar grips, and wanted to know if you plan to press charges?"

Joey furrowed his brow and looked at Keith, who looked scared to death at the thought.

"Naw. Then he'd just spend the rest of his life blaming me," he replied.

"WHAT?" demanded Alex, "this guy framed you, got you kicked out of the gym, nearly ruined your reputation, then nearly got you killed today. And you're not gonna press charges!?"

"Nope. Nothing he did had an impact on the final result. Besides, he can't help it. Maybe if I show a little leniency, it might rub off. After all, I'm sure he's sorry for what he's done, ain't cha, Keith?"

"Yes, yes, yes, I'm so sorry. I didn't mean to get you hurt. Honest."

"There, see? He's all remorseful and stuff."

"Personally, I think you're an idiot for not puttin' the screws to this punk. But, if that's how you're gonna play it..."

"It is," replied Joey, "officers you can let him go." The security guard released Keith, and he bolted for the exit.

"I'd at least have to punch him, at least once. Just on general principle," said Alex.

"I thought you were a hippie pacifist?"

"Yeah, well, for him, I'd make the exception."

251

"You kill me, Alex." The boys made their way back to the team.

Gene Dagar slowly made his way to Don after the awards.

"I guess you're happy."

"Why wouldn't I be? The boys did their job, and it all worked out in the end, for us anyway."

"About that. I'm so sorry, Don. When I told the boys we needed something, I really meant from within them. I certainly did not sanction what Keith did."

"But you didn't pull him off the floor, Gene. Doesn't matter, everything worked out, so no hard feelings."

"I guess it's time for me to fade into the sunset and retire."

"Are you kidding? I was looking forward to kicking your ass for the next ten years or so. Just adjust your attitude and approach. Enjoy the sport for a change."

"I don't know, Don, I only know what I know."

"Eugene, that's silly talk," said Mrs. Banister as she approached, "you know what's good for gymnastics, you just have an abrasive way of presenting it. I think my Johnny would be happy to see you not quit, but turn things around. Remember, what's good for gymnastics is good for you. Find that inner child and you can still have a positive impact on the boys coming up."

"I'll give it thought," Gene replied with a voice that sounded like his mind was already made.

"Well, Donnie," said Mrs. Banister, "it appears you have your work cut out for you. Almost time to get back in the gym and get ready for next year."

"Are you kidding? We have NTI's to prepare for first!"

"Of course, I am so happy to see excited about gymnastics again, Donnie."

"Thank you for making it possible."

"Oh, peshwa, you would've found a way. I'm just glad I could help."

"Coach Wheatley?" asked a gentleman approaching from the stands.

"That's me. How can I help?"

"My name is Mike Middleton, Athletic Director at Michigan Tech. I'd like to talk to you about our, soon to be, vacant head coaching position."

"I'm flattered, but I'm not cut out for college coaching, besides, I just got started with these boys. My priority is with them."

"I can respect that. In that case, may I have permission to talk to one of your athletes about a possible scholarship?"

"Sure, who?"

"Why, Joey Johnson, of course," he said as Joey and Alex rejoined the group.

"Joey, this man wants to talk to you about coming to Michigan Tech to do gymnastics."

"Wow! That's awesome! But, my mind is on NTI's. Can we talk later?"

"Sure. How's the knee?"

"OK. I'll be ready for NTI's. Trainer feels it's just a strain. A couple days off and I'll right as the mail."

"Great, well, we host a big gymnastics camp in July. Why don't you let me bring you in as a clinician, and we'll hammer it all out then?"

"Sounds good!" said Joey, "Just give Coach your contact info and I'll see you in July!"

"Great!" Joey and Mike shook hands, "I'll leave you to your celebration and I'll see you in July?"

"Awesome!" Joey replied.

Joey and the rest of the team exited the arena. Carmen carried Joeys bag, Alex carried the trophy. As they got on the bus and got settled, Joey stood and faced the group.

"Guys, I can't tell you how much this all means. You guys gave up a lot for this and I can't thank you enough."

253

"It was our pleasure," said Logan, "now, sit down and let's go home!"

Don stood, "Guys, I won't bother getting sappy, we still have work to do. But, I want you guys to take the next couple days off. We'll get together Thursday and start getting ready for NTI's!" The team cheered as the bus pulled away.

32

"Welcome back, guys," called Coach Wheatley as Joey and Carmen entered the gym after a, well deserved few days off, "How's the knee?" Joey was without crutches, but still favoring his left leg.

"It's fine. Doc says no hard impact this week, but that leaves a bunch I can still do."

"Well, there's still four weeks before NTI's, so there's plenty of time to get back."

"Yessir. These past few days have dragged on! I couldn't wait to get back in the gym."

"It was all I could do to keep him from breaking into the gym on Monday!" said Carmen.

Don laughed, "I'm glad to see you, Carmen. I hadn't had the chance to truly thank you for, well, everything you've done."

"Oh, sir, I didn't do that much."

"False modesty does not look good on you," chimed Joey, "if not for you, not only would we not be getting ready for NTI's..."

"You might still be a wanted drug dealer!" said Alex as he burst through the door, with Rodney close behind.

"Indeed," said Coach Wheatley, "and in recognition, I'd like to offer you a position."

"Position?" asked Carmen, "what kind of position?"

"Why, dance coach! Now that we've gone from a public rec center to a private club, we have to put a program together, and I need your skills to teach these boys about artistry. Plus, I'd like to see how you do with marketing the gym."

"I don't know what to say. Can I think about it?"

"Of course. We'll talk more later. Think about it."

Logan, Bobby and the twins burst through the doors.

"Did you hear?" asked Logan.

"Hear what?" replied Joey.

"Keith is done with gymnastics! The Federation has banned him for his conduct."

"Well, I sure hate that."

"Are you kidding?" said Alex, "he got what he deserved!"

"Yeah, but I'd like to think that he could redeem himself. I mean, maybe if he could go an extended period of time without being a total dick, he could, maybe, asked to be reinstated."

"Seriously, Joe?" asked Alex, "you still looking for the silver lining in Keith's dark cloud?"

"I'd like to think anyone could change."

Just then the doors burst open again, only this time it was three of Dagar's Edge's gymnasts; Senior Tom Schultz, Junior James White, and Sophomore Danny Dukes.

"Something I can do for you fellas?" asked Coach Wheatley.

"Um, yeah," said Tom, "we'd like to come train here."

"You guys just trying to compete at NTI's!" demanded Alex.

"Not at all," said James, "we talked it over. If you don't want to use us, we're good with that. But we want to come here."

"We realized something," added Danny, "we weren't having fun. Dagar was always about winning."

"Why now?" asked Joey.

"Scared, I guess," said Tom, "Coach Dagar is quite intimidating."

"Keith's nonsense at state was the last straw," added James, "before, there was no place else to go, unless you wanted to travel an hour each way. Plus, he did get guys to NTI's."

"But we totally get it if we can't start until after NTI's," said Tom.

Coach Wheatley scratched his salt and pepper head, "Well, I'd hate to be the one to make this call, so I'll leave it up to you fellas."

"Can I discuss this with the current line up?" asked Joey, "Fellas?" Joey gathered the rest of the team and moved to the other side of the gym to discuss their options. They huddled.

"So, what do you guys think?" asked Joey.

"I think they should've bailed a long time ago," said Alex, "I got no problems, but it's really up to the guys who stand the chance of not competing at NTI's."

"Dude," said Tommy, "if they can beat us out, that makes us better right?"

"Right," replied Joey, "adding them makes us stronger, for sure."

"I was a nervous wreck!" said Timmy, "I'll gladly watch those guys take my place."

"Yeah," added Tommy, "I think we're gonna go back to the warehouse. This was fun, but to tell the truth, I'm glad these guys are here. Makes it easier for us to back out."

"You guys have come so far!" said Joey, "I'd hate to lose you guys now."

"Seriously?" added Bobby, "you've got some real gymnasts to work with. It was a gas, but I think we're more relieved."

"Okay, is anyone opposed to bringing them in?" asked Joey. No one objected, "Alright, you guys tell them."

The team rejoined the threesome, extending their hands to congratulate the new Rams.

"You're gonna have a blast here, guys," said Logan.

"Then it's settled," said Coach Wheatley, "Welcome to TAG, boys!"

"GENTLEMEN!" called Joey from the stereo, his finger on the play button. Everyone turned their attention to him.

"IT'S TIME TO ROCK!!"

Fin

Printed and bound by PG in the USA